RETURN FIRE

RIMFIRE REVENGE

BUCKSKIN

Kit Dalton

LEISURE BOOKS NEW YORK CITY

A LEISURE BOOK®

September 1995

Published by

Dorchester Publishing Co., Inc.
276 Fifth Avenue
New York, NY 10001

Printed in the United States of America.

TWICE THE BULLETS! TWICE THE BEAUTIES!
TWO PISTOL-HOT ADULT WESTERNS
IN ONE BIG VOLUME! SAVE $$$!

RETURN FIRE

"That's why I'm here, to put a stop to all this. You tell me who probably killed Vanderstone, and I'll stop them from killing anyone else, including you."

A man in a tan jacket and no hat kicked open the front door and surged through it, a smoking six-gun in his hand. Morgan snapped off a shot and saw him take the bullet in his right shoulder. Then the man darted out through the door and into the street.

Morgan slammed after him. He'd check Eastin later. By the time Morgan got to the front of the store, the man was across the street heading for an alley. There were too many people to try for a shot. Morgan leaned against the side of the bank and watched. He knew for sure that behind one of the windows along the street, or through the peepholes in some of the tents, the man watched him. When Morgan left, the man would leave. How in the hell could he catch him?

RIMFIRE REVENGE

Morgan was coming closer to the buildings. He could see all plainly. Claresta had stopped firing from the barn. There were no lights on in the house or the other buildings. He figured that the two ranch hands were up and waiting with six-guns. He had to be careful not to get shot at by a friendly.

A shadow moved. He froze. The shadow was near the barn. Morgan waited. The shadow had blended with the side of the barn nearest him but he wasn't sure where barn shadow stopped and a possible man shadow started. It could be one of the hands.

Morgan heard a noise. A curious crackling sound. Then he heard a scream. It was a woman's scream—Claresta!

As he watched in horror, flames burst out the back door of the barn, where he had ridden out a few minutes before.

The barn was on fire and Claresta was trapped up there in the haymow!

Buckskin Double Editions:

SCATTERGUN/APACHE RIFLES
LARAMIE SHOWDOWN/DOUBLE ACTION
COLT CROSSING/POWDER CHARGE
SILVER CITY CARBINE/ CALIFORNIA CROSSFIRE
PISTOL GRIP/PEACEMAKER PASS
REMINGTON RIDGE/SHOTGUN STATION
WINCHESTER VALLEY/ GUNSMOKE GORGE
GUNPOINT/LEVER ACTION
RIFLE RIVER/GUNSTOCK
HANGFIRE HILL/CROSSFIRE COUNTRY
BOLT ACTION/TRIGGER GUARD

BUCKSKIN
RETURN FIRE

Chapter One

Lee Buckskin Morgan sensed someone behind him but ignored it. He was in Deadwood, South Dakota, and there were dozens of men on the muddy street. Before he could turn to look, someone slammed into him as a heavy object cracked against his skull.

Morgan saw only the flash of a face as he looked over his shoulder. He made out a black beard, beady dark eyes and an ugly grin before the Black Hills sky turned gray and Morgan smashed into the muddy Deadwood street.

The tall, bearded man pulled the unconscious man's hand from under his body and tied them together behind his back with a kerchief. When the attacker stood, he was joined by a second man, also six feet tall. Together they picked up Morgan and carried him to the nearby alley, then down 50 feet to a back door, and took him inside.

"Heavy son of a bitch," the black bearded man said.

"Too heavy. Bigger than we are. Why the boss want him?"

"I don't know and I don't ask. I live longer that way. I do my job and don't ask questions. You better learn that fast."

"Right, I just did."

They dropped the man in a room with no windows and one door and tied his feet together. When they went out they locked the door from the outside with a six-inch hasp and a heavy padlock.

Reality came back slowly to Morgan. He felt the headache, a booming, pounding, iron spoon in an iron kettle hammering away continually. Soon he realized his hands were tied. There was no light in the place and he had no idea where he was. Morgan rolled to his side, bent at the waist and sat up. His hands were bound with a piece of cloth behind him. He could feel the soft bands of the material.

Slowly he worked his hands around so he could touch the knots. Gradually they loosened and gave a little. As he kept at the knots, he wondered why he had been assaulted. Nobody knew he was in this gold rush town. Nobody knew he was coming except one small lady in Denver. She wouldn't tell anyone.

At least the assailant hadn't wanted him dead or he would be ready for the Deadwood undertaker by now. He had heard that Deadwood was a rough miners' camp of a town. Since the gold rush started in the Black Hills the year before, men had flooded into this area around the rivers and streams looking for gold.

Morgan knew that Deadwood, as any mining town,

was a magnet for the worst elements of society from all over the country. The miners came, but also the madams and their girls, gamblers, confidence men, claim jumpers, riffraff and criminals of every stripe, all looking to take away by foul means or fair any gold the miners could wrestle from the streams and sand bars and bends in the creeks.

But why would one of the residents want to clobber a just arrived stranger walking down the street?

Morgan worked on the cloth and at last stretched and tore it enough to slip the fabric over his right thumb, then he had the rest of his hand free and quickly untied his feet. He searched the room for a weapon. When he checked he found that his six-gun had been lifted from his gunbelt as well as the six-inch stiletto removed from his right boot.

He touched and identified a straight chair. It would work if he found nothing else. Along the far side of the room Morgan discovered a board, a two-by-four nailed to the floor. He kicked it loose. It was three-feet long. Yes, that would do nicely.

Now he felt along the wall where he saw light seeping in. The door. Morgan tried the knob. Locked. He settled in to wait.

It gave Morgan time to think it through. He could come up with no reason why he had been assaulted and captured. There were no sailing ships here that needed seamen. The shanghai experts were in San Francisco, Portland and Seattle.

Slave labor? Identification to use for setting up a ghost mining claim? He'd seen it happen. Was that the reason for his capture?

He heard noises in the hallway outside the door. Now he would get some questions answered. He moved to the knob side of the panel so it would open away from him and listened as someone worked on the lock. Then he heard metal scrape that could be a hasp coming free. A moment later, the knob turned and the door swung inward.

Morgan held the two-by-four over his head and powered it down sharply as he saw a man's arm holding a six-gun. The heavy stick crashed down smashing into the jailer's right arm and bringing a roar of pain. The revolver dropped to the floor but did not discharge. Before the man could move, Morgan brought his forearm around the man's throat cutting off his breath and the scream. He was the same man with the black beard.

"Now, what the hell is this all about?" Morgan whispered in the man's ear. "I'm going to let up on your throat. You get your breath and then you answer my questions or I'll kill you, you savvy?"

The head nodded.

Morgan relaxed his arm but kept the stranglehold in place.

"Oh, god! Hurts. You broke my arm."

"Lucky it wasn't your head. Now talk."

"I . . . I don't know why you're here. The man said to grab you without hurting you, so we did. Now he says he wants to talk to you."

"Good, that's what I want, too. Where's my six-gun?"

"In his office along with your wallet."

"Kneel down," Morgan said. The man with the black beard hesitated and Morgan kicked his legs and mashed him to the floor. Morgan spotted the fallen six-gun in the light from the door and picked it up. Now his eyes were accustomed to the light of the hall.

He motioned to the black beard. "Get up. Who do you work for?"

"Lash Kincaid."

"Who is he and what's his place here in Deadwood?"

"He owns three or four stores, saloons and whorehouses. He's the richest man in town. Around here he says shit, and most men drop their pants and squat."

"Why did he bushwhack me?"

"I don't know."

"How do we get to where you were going to take me?"

"Down the hall and up one flight of stairs."

"Will anyone see us along there?"

"Probably not."

Morgan motioned for the bearded man to move out.

"Take me there. You make any sign or say anything to anybody and you're one dead kidnapper, you understand me?"

"Then can I go to the doc with my broken arm?"

"You might have a broken head by then. Let's go."

They walked into the hall and down 20 feet to a turn, then up steps that had been outside once but enclosed when a new building was constructed beside it. At the top of the steps, the door was unlocked. The man with the black beard opened it and Morgan shoved him inside. Morgan stepped into a small room with one door.

"He's right in there," the bearded man whispered.

"He have any guards or gunmen around?"

"No."

"Does he wear a gun or keep one in the desk?"

"I don't know. The room's more like a living room but it has a desk."

"Don't knock, we'll go in fast and you drop to your knees just inside the door, understand?"

The bearded man nodded. Morgan checked the six-gun. It had five rounds and was on a loaded cylinder. He pulled back the hammer and motioned to the door. The man turned the knob and opened the door. Morgan pushed him so he slammed the door wide open against the wall. The bearded man stumbled ahead and went to his knees.

Morgan took in the room at a glance. Living room, small desk, big man sitting in an upholstered chair with his feet up. A woman stood beside him. She was young, paid for.

The man looked up with a frown, saw the gun and chuckled. Lash Kincaid was big, Morgan figured 300 pounds, maybe six feet. He had a fleshy face with eyes deep set, cheeks fat and red lined. Rolls of fat filled the area where his neck should be.

"Well, so the worm turns," Kincaid said. He looked away from Morgan at the woman. "Star, you may go."

"She stays!" Morgan said evenly. The woman looked up, lifted her brows and stepped back from the big man.

Kincaid shrugged. "So she stays."

"Do you greet everyone who comes to Deadwood by kidnapping them and throwing them in a locked room, Kincaid?"

"Not at all, not at all. I was telling Star here that you seem to be the wrong man." He moved his right hand toward his desk.

"Keep both hands on top of the desk, now!" Morgan barked.

"Yes, yes. I see I did make a mistake. For that I am truly sorry. I have your goods here, your wallet, papers, your cash. Yes, every dollar, and your weapons. That is a nice Colt, one of the new ones, isn't it?"

"Why did you savage me, Kincaid?"

"I told you. A mistake. I thought you were a man who owed me money. I saw you on the street and ordered my two men to bring you here."

"Not gently."

"I don't question tactics or methods. I pay for results."

Morgan fired a .44 round through an unlit lamp that sat on the small desk three feet from the man's hands. The bullet shattered the thin glass chimney scattering glass from desk to wall but didn't scatter the kerosene. The sound was like thunder in the closed room.

Star jumped and took a step backward. Kincaid hardly lifted an eyebrow.

"I see that you're a shooter. What more can I do? I said I made a mistake and that I'm sorry."

"Kincaid, I'm not a vindictive man. I could simply rob you of every dollar in the place. I could put four slugs into your brain. Or I could have you arrested and charged with kidnapping, and assault and battery. If this town has any law at all, I could keep you in jail for a year, maybe two.

"But as I say, I'm not vindictive. Pay me a hundred dollars and we'll call it square. With a warning. Keep your people away from me. I don't like the way you do business, and I honestly think I would enjoy killing you. Killing a blight on the face of humanity, like you, always lifts my spirits. Do we understand each other?"

For a moment, Morgan saw a flash of fear in the obese man's eyes. Then he chuckled. "I like your style, Lee Morgan. Yes, I like your style. I'm no piker. I'll pay you two hundred and consider myself chastised. I'm not a man who can't learn from his errors in judgment."

He looked at Morgan. "May I retrieve some funds

from my desk?"

Morgan took three steps closer so he could see all three of the people and the desk. He nodded. The big man opened a desk drawer which had a small safe concealed inside. He turned the combination lock, opened the safe and took out ten $20 bills and passed them to Morgan.

Then he pushed Morgan's papers, wallet, some pocket change, a small folding knife and a compass toward him over the polished surface.

"I believe that satisfies the arrangements between us."

Morgan folded the greenbacks and stuffed them into his pocket. He checked to be sure everything was there. All the time he had the six-gun up and covering the three of them.

When he was satisfied that all was in order, he eased down the cocked hammer on the borrowed weapon and pushed out the remaining rounds. Then he helped the man with the black beard to stand.

He gave the revolver to the man who had captured him. Morgan picked up his belongings from the desk and put them in his pockets. Then he holstered his Colt and slid the knife in place in his right boot.

He stepped up to where Kincaid sat. "On your feet," Morgan said evenly but with a ringing tone of command.

Kincaid stood with difficulty and held onto the back of the overstuffed chair with one hand.

When Kincaid had his balance, Morgan slashed out his big right fist, connecting with the side of Kincaid's mouth, smashing him against the chair and then to the floor.

"Yes, that's better, now, I feel reasonably

revenged," Morgan said. "Kincaid, Miss, it's time for me to move on. I don't expect to see or hear from you again, Mr. Kincaid."

"That would be my wish as well, Mr. Morgan," Kincaid said from where he sat on the floor.

Morgan started for the door and turned. "Miss, if you would show me to the street, I would appreciate it."

Kincaid nodded and she hurried to the door.

She said nothing as she led him along a short hall to another set of steps and down to a door. She was twitching her sleek bottom more than was required.

She turned and smiled. "If you would like—"

"Not a chance, sweetheart. Take care of yourself."

He stepped through the door and directly onto the street. There were no fancy boardwalks in Deadwood. The door he left was between a good sized saloon building and a second building beside it that housed a jewelry store and a liquor store. There was no sign on the door about where it led. Figured. It was probably locked from the inside. When he looked at it again, he realized there was no knob on the outside of the door.

He glanced down at his clothes and saw that he was muddy. He had been knocked down stomach first in the street back there. The mud was drying but not all would brush off. So he was dirty.

Morgan had been heading for a cafe when he was attacked. He saw it now, across the street. In town for two hours and already he had been kidnapped, hit on the head and threatened by Deadwood's leading citizen. Great.

He had arrived a few hours before after a jolting 40-mile stagecoach ride in a bare bones celerity wagon, dropped his gear at a tent style hotel and headed for food. Now he completed that interrupted trip.

Morgan looked around the mining camp. He knew Deadwood was barely a year old. Two dozen wood frame buildings were up. Most of the businesses were still in tents. The temporary canvas structures served for everything from saloons and gambling dens and bawdy houses to individual shelters and shops for mining supplies, shovels, hardware, clothes, general merchandise and food.

He saw a freight wagon train pull into town. Each large wagon was pulled by a string of four, six or eight oxen, depending on the size of the load. He had heard that the freight wagons came overland all the way from Pierre which was the closest port on the Missouri River. It was a 110-mile trip by wagon road. Everything used, sold, worked or wanted in Deadwood came into town on the wagons. The teamsters broke up the train and angled for various stores where the rigs would be unloaded.

The red-shirted teamsters cracked their bullwhips and swore at civilians with their own wagons, or horsemen, when they got in the way of the freighters. The drivers worked the heavy rigs up to the front of the stores in the muddy street and stopped.

Morgan saw now that the town had been built on a gully, at first called Deadwood Gulch, on the sides of the Deadwood Creek, a branch of the Belle Fourche River. Wooded inclines went up on each side of the stream.

Morgan looked at the swarms of men who walked the muddy street. Some looked like they were hell-bent on being entertained by gambling, drinking, whoring, or all three.

Many idled from saloon to saloon, nearly out of money, not willing to work or able to file on a placer gold mine claim. It was as if a wave of humanity had been dumped here with little desire or skills to do any work.

It was easy for Morgan to tell the successful miners. They swaggered from saloon to saloon with whores draped over them as they worked hard at being entertained.

Someone had estimated the population around Deadwood at nearly 25,000 people. Morgan hoped they never all came to town at once into the two-block-long muddy street of tents and raw-lumber buildings.

He let a red-shirted teamster drive his team of eight oxen with a huge wagon past him heading for the hardware store, and walked across the street toward the Andropolis Cafe. It was a large wall tent with center poles, a plank floor, a counter and six wooden tables with benches attached for customers. A partition had been built to separate the cooking area from the customers.

Ten men were eating at the tables. Morgan had lost track of time. He touched the sore place on his head and was thankful that his headache was gone.

As he entered the cafe, he saw a man talking to someone who looked like a cook. Morgan went to the counter, which had individual chairs, and sat down in the end one.

Almost at once a dark-haired young girl brought a glass of water and smiled at him.

"Good afternoon, sir. What would you like for your dinner today at the Andropolis Cafe, the best eatery in Deadwood!"

Chapter Two

Buckskin Morgan grinned at the pretty girl and sipped the water she had just brought him at the Andropolis Cafe. "What's on the menu today, young lady?"

"We're out of steak. Ain't had any steak now for three months since it got warm this summer. Can't bring it this far in a wagon, and we kilt off all the steers and bulls in the county. But we got fried chicken, or a chicken stew with country vegetables. We got chicken 'cause we raise our own out in back aways. Not too hard to raise chickens and you kill one and eat it up the same day.

"Then, too, we got all the flap jacks or bacon and eggs and fried potatoes that you can hold. What sounds best to you this evenin'?"

He ordered the fried chicken. "Are you one of the Andropolis clan?"

"Yes, sir! I'm Alexandria. Only child. My Pa wanted a son. He got me. Then Ma died 'long three, four years ago. Now we do with what we got. Let me fetch your fried chicken."

She hurried away and Morgan noticed the one he figured owned the restaurant still talking to a tall, thin man at the far end of the counter. It was the same pair that had been talking when he came in. The dark man had on a white apron and evidently had been cooking. He could be Andropolis himself.

Morgan picked up a folded and much read newspaper laying on the counter. It was the *Pierre Journal*, and dated two days ago. It was fresher news than he had read in some time.

The paper said there were more recriminations about General Custer and his now famous defeat at the Battle of the Little Big Horn. Ever since the July 25th slaughter, the army had been trying to figure out reasons why it happened and the politicians had been trying to place the blame.

A small story on the front page reported that Mark Twain, the traveling newspaper reporter, had just published a novel called *Tom Sawyer*. Morgan made a mental note to get a copy of it when he could.

Morgan looked critically at the other patrons in the eatery. It was early, only a little after four-thirty and the evening crowd wasn't there yet. He was determined not to let himself be surprised again, even when he knew it shouldn't happen. He had been lucky this time. Lucky to be alive.

As Morgan looked around, the tall, thin man who had been talking to the cook came toward him, watching him, trying to make eye contact with Morgan. When Morgan looked him in the eye, the man smiled and came on forward.

"Don't mean to intrude, but have you seen this boy? He's a little over twelve years old."

The man held out a tintype. The photographs reproduced on a metal plate and usually in shades of black or brown were clear and detailed. The small photographs were becoming more common now since the tintype camera and process was invented back in 1856.

The boy stood in a formal pose with his mother, Morgan surmised. He was sturdy looking with short-cut hair and wide set eyes.

"No sir, I'm afraid I haven't seen him."

"He's my son. Somebody kidnapped him in Rapid City a month ago and I heard he headed this way. There's so many people around here I'm having trouble."

"I'll certainly watch for him. Not many children in this place, thank god. What's your name?"

"Dale Johnson. I've got a small tent out on the edge of town."

"I'll watch for him. What's the boy's name?"

"Dale Junior."

"I'll keep a lookout for him."

"Much obliged." The man nodded and a look of resignation slid over his features again as he turned and walked toward the pair of men at the far table.

Morgan looked up as the girl brought his dinner: four big pieces of fried chicken, mashed potatoes and chicken gravy, peas and carrots, thick slices of white bread and a pint-sized cup for coffee.

"You want more you call out," Alexandria said. "We're gonna get busy here in a shake, but I'll be back to talk."

Morgan finished his dinner, paid the 75¢ fee and figured it was a bargain the way most gold rush camps charged.

He waved at Alexandria and walked down the dirt and mud street until he found the Lost Mining District office. It was made of new lumber and looked as if it had not been there for more than a few months.

Inside he found the district recorder, William Lardner, who said he handled death certificates. He checked but had no one reported as dead with the name of Harvey Vanderstone.

"Ever heard of the name?" Morgan asked. "The gent has vanished hereabouts and I'm trying to locate him, dead or alive."

"Name is not familiar to me, but you might check with the town marshal. He usual keeps a record of the people he arrests and throws in jail as drunks and such. His list is a lot longer than mine."

A stop at that small platform tent down the street proved to be no more productive. By that time, the sun was flirting with the western hills and Morgan had made a start on his assignment. So far Vanderstone was not legally dead and not on the town marshal's reports.

That much accomplished, Morgan went back to his "hotel" in a tent and found the cot he had claimed had a man sleeping on it. His gear had been tossed aside.

Morgan found a free cot, put his bag under it and stretched out on top fully clothed. As a precaution, he took out his .45 revolver and rested it on his chest firmly gripped in his good right hand. That should dissuade anyone from trying to get his bed, at least for tonight.

This twelve-bunk tent was one of ten strung down the street and roped together for support. It had been years since Morgan had slept in the same room with

11 other men.

He wasn't sure he would do much sleeping that night. Tomorrow he would find better accommodations, if he had to buy his own tent.

That night Morgan woke up three times when gunfire erupted on the street outside; once when a drunk tried to dislodge him from the cot; and a fifth time when the man in the next bunk had a screaming fit brought on by strong drink or a bad dream. Nobody seemed in a mood to ask the man which one.

As soon as it grew light, Morgan packed up his worldly goods in his carpetbag and headed out for breakfast. The Greek cafe was open. This time he saw a sign over the door that said: "We're open whenever you're hungry."

Already ten men sat at the tables eating. Alexandria came up to him at the counter and grinned.

"Hi there, I guess our food didn't kill you last night."

"Nope, I'm ready for those eggs and bacon and potatoes. Oh, is there a real hotel with a frame building in town?"

"Not yet. Cost too much to build. Best deal is to buy a small tent and pitch it somewhere under a tree."

"Might do that."

When she brought the big platter of eggs and shredded potatoes and eight slices of bacon, she set them down and watched him. "Look good?"

"Mouth watering. Looks good enough to eat, and I'm starved."

"It's the mountain air. You know we're less than five-hundred-feet from being a mile high in the sky?"

"I didn't know."

"Oh, you asked about a hotel? Pa says you can use

the cot in our storeroom. Our handy man usually sleeps there, but he went gold digging last week and never came back. Pa says two dollars a night."

"Rented!" Morgan said. He reached in his purse and handed her a $20 bill that had recently belonged to Lash Kincaid. "I'll take it for ten days."

Alexandria looked at the $20 bill, then grinned and pushed it down the front of her dress. She laughed. "At least that's one way to get you to notice me. I'm nineteen."

"Getting to be an old maid."

"I've had sixty-four proposals so far," she said grinning. "I think two or three of them were from men who were nearly sober."

"Wait for the right one. Can you show me where that cot is, I might want a daytime nap."

He paid for his breakfast, only 50¢, and she took him along the far wall of the tent to the back, out a flap, and around to the rear where another tent stood. It had a separate door, and the tent was fitted over a plank floor and three-foot-high wood sidewalls. It was half building, half tent.

"The outside door is always locked, but you can get in through the kitchen." He showed him. They stepped from the kitchen tent into the smaller floored storeroom and he saw at once it was a real storeroom. There were cases of tinned goods, sacks of potatoes, cartons of eggs, dozens of long lasting foods and some perishables.

At the far side sat a cot and two wooden boxes.

"Home, sweet home," she said. Then Alexandria reached up and kissed him on the lips. She lingered there a minute and then came away and watched him.

"Are you shocked?"

"No. Pleased."

He dropped his carpetbag, put his arms around her and kissed her, pushing his tongue into her open mouth and bringing a long soft sigh from her when he broke off the kiss.

"Now that was more like it," she said grinning. "We'll have to try that again sometimes. Right now I have to work."

She laughed softly and hurried away to the eatery where the customers were calling for their food. He watched the sway of her hips and grinned. She was slightly on the tall and lean side, with full breasts and a sweet face. He'd remember Alexandria.

Ten minutes later, Morgan was at the land office. There were six men in line ahead of him. It took a half hour for him to get up to the counter in the small wooden building.

"Yes, sir, I'd like to find out if Harvey Vanderstone ever filed a claim and if so, where it is."

The recorder lifted his brows, went to an alphabetical crossfile and came back with a card.

"Yes sir. He filed a claim, Clear Creek Four above. That's the fourth claim up from the junction of Clear Creek and South Fork. About five, six miles out of town to the south. There's a map on the wall right over there."

Morgan made a note on a small pad of paper he usually carried and consulted the map. It didn't look that hard. He'd been lead scout before. Up Deadwood Creek for two miles to South Fork, upstream on South Fork until he found Clear Creek, then another four miles. Simple.

Two hours later Morgan was lost. He found South

Fork but there were so many small tributaries running into the stream that he became confused.

There were miners on more than half of the claims along the streams. Some had pans and worked the gravel. Some had joined together and built sluice boxes, shoveling the sand and gravel into the six- to 30-foot-long, flat-bottomed boxes a foot wide and a foot high. They had cleats along the bottom.

The box was placed so a small board could be pulled which allowed the stream to flow through the box, dragging the sand and gravel down and out the far end. Hopefully, there would be heavier gold dust and nuggets left where they fell to the bottom and lodged along the half inch high cleats.

Now and then Morgan heard a shout of discovery. He asked every other miner where Clear Creek was and when three different ones gaved him the same directions, he went that way.

It was nearly noon when he came to a spot that actually had a hand painted sign that pointed up a three-foot wide stripe of water that was Clear Creek.

A short way up Clear Creek he found the same kind of sign that had been planted in the ground and said in foot high letters: "#4 Above." He had found it. There was no sluice box here, no tent. There had been work done along the far side of the water to set up some kind of a sluice box but only a few sticks remained.

He had heard that any abandoned claim lost any developments it had almost at once. Someone had probably carted off a box if one had been here. He stepped across the foot-deep creek and walked the claim. It was all staked out properly. He found where there had been a shelter of some kind, probably a small tent.

A fire ring remained in front of the spot. Brush and trees had been cleared around the area.

Where was Harvey Vanderstone?

He went upstream and found another miner. The man was in his forties. He wore the tops of long underwear and jeans that were so dirty and mud caked they would stand by themselves. The miner shot out a squirt of tobacco juice and glared at Morgan. "You don't got a claim up here, we don't want you messin' around here," the warning came.

Morgan grinned. "Yeah, I understand. I'm not a miner, no worry there. I'm trying to find Vanderstone. He has a claim Clear Creek Four Above, down the way there. His gear is gone. You know what happened to him?"

"Don't know the gent. He was gone when I came two weeks ago. Ain't seen nothing of him. I didn't steal his gear. It was cleaned out before I got here."

He bent, lifted a shovel of sand and gravel from the small creek and let it sift slowly into his sluice box where the water caught the material and washed it down the length of the six-foot device.

"Hit anything today?"

"Wouldn't say if I had. Vanderstone. He in trouble? You look like a lawman."

"Nope, not true. He's in no trouble far as I know. I'm a friend of his wife's in Denver. She hasn't heard from him and I said I'd try to find him."

The miner shoveled two more scoops of gravel into the sluice and watched the water do the work.

"Tough place, this Deadwood. Should have called it Deadman. I seen more corpses up here than ever did in my life. A man can get murdered and buried and nobody thinks to look for him for a month or two and then nothing can be found.

"Vanderstone there. Heard he was getting some color. But he must not have found much or somebody would have jumped his claim by now."

"That the way it works up here?"

"We got twenty-thousand miners in these hills. Who can police this place? How do you know I'm the man who claimed Clear Creek Nine Above here? You can't. Neither could I. Sorry, can't help you with Vanderstone. Heard tell he was a good man. He even took care of old man Marshall when he got sick on his South Fork Eighty-Two Above."

"That's downstream aways?"

"True, about half a mile below here. Eighty-Two is the only one with a cabin. Old man Marshall said he was gonna have a cabin before another winter came, so he built one."

"He still around, this Marshall?"

"Yep. Fit, mean, cantankerous, half rich, and working in a good claim. Don't forget his shotgun if'n you want to talk to him. He'd rather shoot a stranger than take the time to talk."

"Sounds like a wonderful person."

The miner snorted. "Hell, he's sixty years old. Nobody out here is wonderful at sixty. Spend half your time staying warm and the other half trying to figure out where you don't hurt."

"Thanks, I'll watch for him."

The miner looked into his sluice box and screeched a yell of jubilation.

"Molly Pitcher in a hand basket, would you look at

that!'' He glanced up at Morgan. ''Come here, young feller, and cast your eyeballs at this. Best one I've found yet!''

Morgan walked over to the sluice box and squatted on the bank to look into the man-made riffles. There lodged against one of the cleats was a rock about the size of a fifty-cent piece. It had rounded edges that looked as if they had been melted slightly and was a rich, heavy gold color.

''A nugget?'' Morgan asked.

''Damn right!'' the excited miner bellowed. He reached down and with a trembling hand picked up the nugget and lifted it out of the water. The sun glinted off the burnished gold. He hefted it. ''Six, maybe seven ounces. Maybe a hundred and fifty dollars worth! By damn!''

''Congratulations. You found that one, there must be more in that same bunch of gravel.''

The middle-aged miner's eyes sparkled. ''Right! You get on about your business. I got to work me some more nuggets!''

Chapter Three

Morgan found the claim that belonged to Old Man Marshall. It had a sign crudely lettered that said plainly enough, "No Trespassing." The cabin sat back from the creek 50 feet and from the looks of it was made of scrap lumber, a few sheets of tin, some branches, part of an old tent and an indifferent group of clapboards that almost met.

Morgan didn't see anyone so he fired a pistol round into the sky. At once a shotgun poked out a hole in the cabin.

"State your business or get blown to hell!" a voice that quavered here and there demanded.

Morgan grinned. "I'm looking for Harvey Vanderstone. Understand he saved your worthless old ass when you were sick."

"No such thing!"

The shotgun vanished. A door which was well hidden in the near side opened and a man hobbled out. He was stooped and hurting, his beard was untrimmed white. Most of his hair was gone except for a fringe around the back. He waved at Morgan.

"You might as well come on over and sit a spell. You're right about Van, I owe him but looks like he's dead and gone."

"Why you say that, Marshall?"

"Ain't seen him, have ye? He was a worker. Came and was about to get started with a rocker. Worked every day, daylight to dark. Singing, whistling. Then he went to town and never came back. Some varmint dry-gulched him and took his purse and that old horse."

"You think so?"

Marhsall eased down to a log and stared at Morgan. One of his eyes had misted over with a soft milky whiteness. "Damn right, I'm sure. Nobody leaves a claim like that. Van bought it with his last dollar and borrowed my pan first two days. He was getting good color, sometimes a dollar a pan." He shook his head. "Nobody just ups and leaves a dig like that without being dead."

"Who did it?"

"Take your pick. We got twenty-five thousand around here. A claim ain't 'worked' for so long, the man who filed on it loses it. Then somebody else can file. If'n more than one man files for it in the first twenty-four hours they hold a drawing, a raffle for it, by those who done filed. Hell, I might have killed him myself."

"But you didn't. Anybody in town who didn't like Vanderstone?"

"Everyone. Nobody likes a man with a good claim."

"I hear tell you're looking for a partner, Marshall."

"Hell no! Why I do that?"

"Because you can't see the gold dust in the pan. No crime to get hard of seeing."

"I can see the nuggets. Maybe I just wash for the nuggets."

"Maybe. I better be moving along. My name is Lee Morgan."

"So what?" Marshall looked up and a slow smile edged around his mouth and then twinkled his eyes.

"So the next time I stop by you won't be shooting off my head. If this Vanderstone is dead, I figure it's about time somebody worked his claim to keep it in his name. His wife, or widow, sent me up here to find him."

"He's gone, just don't know who did it. You find out. He was a good man."

Marshall turned and took a half step at a time back to the cabin. He was bent and hurting, but he turned at the door and waved. "Oh, he said one day he found a man in town he knew from somewhere else. Said the guy would be a real bonanza. Then he wouldn't have to dig gravel all day. Said the guy was gonna pay, I remember that. Well, you get the bastard who killed Van." The old man scowled, waved and slipped inside the cabin.

Morgan walked faster back toward town. He did four miles an hour, a mile every fifteen minutes and got to town in mid-afternoon.

He headed for the nearest bar that had a real wooden building, the Moneytree Saloon. It looked familiar. Then he remembered it was just down from the plain no-entry doorway where Star had shown him to the street after his confrontation with Lash Kincaid.

That Kincaid smelled rotten, but Morgan wasn't there as a disinfectant for the whole town. He just wanted to find Vanderstone or his killer.

The Moneytree Saloon was like the rest of them, primitive, a plank bar set on barrels, a few tables and chairs on a plank floor.

He ordered a beer, rinsed the trail dust out of his throat, then had another beer and sat down at a table near where a poker game was going.

"Come on, Hickok. You gonna bet or ain't you?" a player said.

Morgan looked up quickly. He and everyone else in the West knew about one Hickok, Wild Bill Hickok. Could this be the same man? He looked at the gambler and grinned.

The player wore a low-crowned, wide-brimmed hat and a frock coat. His long yellow hair hung down to his shoulders. He leaned back in his chair and hooked his thumbs in the red sash that circled his waist. He preened his full moustache and the twin tails of a goatee and looked up at the man who had asked if he was going to bet.

"Your five and raise you a hundred," Wild Bill Hickok said.

That's when Morgan knew the man was the famous wild man of the Western plains, Civil War scout and hero, army scout against the Indians. Later he quit the army and became a deputy marshal in Fort Riley, Kansas. Sometime after that, Morgan remembered, Hickok was sheriff in the rough little town of Hayes, Kansas, and then in Abilene.

A man moved his chair over near to Morgan, looked

at him a second then whispered. "Is that really the Wild Bill Hickok?"

"Seems to be," Morgan said softly.

The man shivered. "Damn! Heard him and his buddy, Charley Utter, got claims here and are working them. But it looks like he does mostly gambling."

"Not a good man to cross," Morgan said in a low voice.

The stranger nodded. "Hell, everybody knows that. Wild Bill can be damn dangerous anytime he fists his gun. I hear he likes a Navy Colt percussion six-gun. That weapon is so big and heavy I couldn't hit a stone wall with it."

Morgan nodded, absorbed now in the game. Wild Bill raised one more time, then was called and won the pot with three queens. One of the men swore. He had been bluffed out when he had a better hand.

"That's why they call it gambling, my friend," Wild Bill said. "I'll give you another chance. Your deal."

Morgan grinned and stood. Watching Wild Bill Hickok wouldn't help him find out what happened to Vanderstone. He walked into the sunshine. Even the air smelled pure and fresh up this high. He had always liked the mountains. Across the street he saw a familiar face: the man from Rapid City searching for his son.

Morgan walked across and talked to Dale Johnson.

"Nothing yet," the anguished father said. "I can't even find anyone who remembers seeing my son here in town. I'm sure he's here somewhere."

"You didn't know this man who took him? He wasn't a relative or anything like that?"

"Absolutely not. I have few relatives and we didn't know this killer and kidnapper."

Morgan nodded. Johnson looked worse today. He had a week's growth of whiskers, not a beard, just hadn't shaved. He was about 5' 8'' with brown hair and wore work clothes and an old hat. A kerchief around his neck was soiled and much used. When Morgan looked at his eyes, Johnson's were gray and now cloudy and sad.

''I'll keep a watch out. I'm into the mining areas now and then. Think he was taken by a miner?''

''I . . . I just don't know. I tried everyone I thought might want a young boy to do hard work, but I haven't found a thing.''

''I'll watch.''

Johnson nodded and walked away slowly without purpose, talking to everyone he met who would stop.

Morgan stepped into the street where he dodged a collection of horse droppings and crossed to the mining district headquarters. It was a small building made of donated lumber and a bit misshapen but serviceable. A sign over the door read: Lost Mining District of Deadwood.

Inside he found William Lardner, the recorder. The line to talk to him was gone now. The recorder, dressed in white shirt, vest and tie with his shirt sleeves raised and held in place with blue garters, looked up.

''Wondering about a claim that isn't worked,'' Morgan said. ''How long does it lie idle before it can be reclaimed?''

''Most places sixty days. But this district voted on ninety days, so that's what it is. You referring to any particular claim?''

''Oh, no, sir, just in general. I thank you.''

Morgan went out and pondered it. He would have to do some work on the claim, or refile on it as a representative of the widow to keep the claim in the widow's name. He had a few days on that.

Across the street a new building caught his attention. It had been finished only a few weeks before and the raw lumber had not yet been painted. A sign over the door said it was the *Black Hills Pioneer*. Set up a town or a mining camp of almost any size and a newspaper was bound to sprout up quickly.

He walked past it on the way to the small town marshal's office. It was a platform tent, a wooden floor and three-foot sides with a tent set up on top of the framework as roof and sides. Inside he found the local lawman he had talked with before.

Marshal Kirk Quentin was five feet ten inches and lean. He nodded when Morgan walked in. "Find him?" Quentin asked.

"Not so you could notice. Friend of his up by his claim says that somebody killed Harvey Vanderstone. You have any unidentified bodies lately?"

"Nope."

"Hell, I was hoping. How does one man police twenty-five thousand miners, whores, gamblers and merchants?"

"Mostly I don't. I can do just so much. But you show me who killed that man and I'll surely have them up before the miners' committee on a murder charge inside of a week."

"Wish I could. It's a cold trail. You said Miners' Committee. Then this isn't a legal town, it's all under the Lost Mining District rule?"

"Yes sir. South Dakota only been a U.S. Territory for five or six years. We got to have sixty thousand people and have all the counties organized before we can be a state. Don't reckon that's gonna happen right soon. So we're under the old miners' committee system. Works good. All legal. We hung a man two weeks ago. Our laws can't go against any of the Territorial or Federal laws. Outside of that, we're free to make our own laws and punishments."

"I've heard tell." Morgan creased the crown of his hat and looked around the small office. It felt right, honest, but Morgan just didn't feel that this lawman would get much done.

"Thanks, Marshal. I'll be getting back to tracking down this killer. Afraid I've got a cold trail to follow." Morgan walked outside and kicked at the dirt in the street where one section had dried out.

Cold trail? Hell, he didn't have any trail at all to follow. What he should do was just go back to Denver and tell the lady she was a widow. But he couldn't get a death certificate here until he produced a body, or a witness to the kill, or a grave site. He had about as much chance of that as a one-armed miner shoveling high yield gravel into a rocker.

A woman came out of a doorway and crossed the street. There weren't that many women in Deadwood yet and the ladies always caused a stir even if they weren't ladies. This one was Star, the paid-for whore of Kincaid. He spotted her at once by the long blonde hair that came to her waist. She looked his way as she came toward him, then walked by slowly not looking directly at him.

"I need to talk to you," she said softly so just he could hear. "Five minutes from now in the gunsmith's shop."

She stared straight ahead as she said it half in whispers, half out loud. He looked at her, then when she passed, he headed down the street away from her direction. Thirty feet ahead he saw the town's only gunsmith store.

At least the shop was of wooden-frame construction and had a house-type window in front. He scraped the mud off his boots and walked inside. It was a typical gun store of the West. It had a few new guns for sale, a rack on the wall with a dozen used guns probably on consignment. There was a shelf with boxes of rifle and pistol ammunition and a workbench littered with weapons in all states of repair.

Morgan picked up a box of .45 rounds for his Colt and waited while the owner talked to another customer. The gunsmith was small and slender, with strong eyeglasses and thinning red hair. He smiled at Morgan.

Morgan loved fine weapons and this man must too. Morgan didn't need any misfires in his line of work.

When he had paid for the items the owner motioned to him and he went through the curtain over the door into the rear.

"Straight ahead down the hall to the first door. Somebody to see you."

Morgan wondered at the secrecy. Star must not want anyone to know she was talking to him. With Kincaid paying for her body, he didn't blame her. Kincaid was not a man to share anything, especially his woman.

Morgan opened the door and saw Star inside. It was a small bedroom and she sat on the bed combing her hair.

She smiled. Star was young and vigorous, pretty in a slightly unfinished way. In another two or three years her face would mature into real beauty. He saw brown eyes glance up at him and she waved him to the bed beside her.

"Thanks for coming, I appreciate it."

He was surprised by the softness, the quality of her voice.

"As you may have figured out, Lash would be unhappy with both of us if he knew I was talking to you. Josh, the old gunsmith, is a special friend. I knew him in Ohio and was surprised to see him here. He doesn't judge me. He knew my parents." She looked up at Morgan.

Morgan had seen the frightened eyes of a fawn once when a hunter had just shot its mother. Now he saw those same frightened eyes, asking for help but not knowing how.

"Mr. Morgan, you're helping some woman in Denver. She's probably paying you to find her husband. But I was hoping . . . I mean, I don't have any money, not much. I could get some. He really owes me a lot. Oh, dear." She cried softly and he waited.

She dried her tears and looked at him. "I'm doing this badly. This is my room. Josh fixed it up for me as a favor to my parents, he said."

Star looked away. "I want to get away from here and go to Chicago, but I can't as long as Kincaid wants me to stay. If I try to take the stage, he'll pull me off. He has a man watch it every time it leaves the station. I don't want to buy a horse and ride all that way to Rapid City alone. I . . . Oh, *damn*! I shouldn't have done this. I'm sorry. Please leave now. Please."

He stood, and for some reason felt like a schoolboy. He even turned his hat in his hand.

"Star, I've been known to help people without getting paid for it. If you want to contact me again, leave a message for me in a sealed envelope at the Andropolis

Cafe." He turned and walked back down the hall and into the gunshop.

He checked out a new rifle the man had, a Spencer repeating rifle that fired eight shots without reloading. He'd used one before and liked it. You just had to push down the trigger lever under the weapon to bring in a new round to chamber from a long tube through the stock. They were hard to beat in a close-up fight but they were simply not very good at long range. Outside he thought for a moment about the girl, then shook his head. He had troubles enough without adding hers to his list.

Chapter Four

Lee Buckskin Morgan left the gunsmith shop and headed down the street. It was time he went to the general store. The man who ran it evidently had become friends with Vanderstone when he was in town.

Martha Vanderstone said the merchant should be the last resort. Morgan should go to him if he had come up against an absolutely blank wall. That was the position he was in right now. No leads, no body, no suspects, no trail . . . not a damned thing.

The general store was a frame building. He'd heard that the man who put it up brought in six big freight wagon loads of lumber stacked high, and that it cost him more than $2,000. The man's name who ran it was Ray Eastin. Morgan went in, checked over revolvers and, when the last customer left, approached the merchant.

Eastin was a middle-sized man, large of girth from good food, with a moustache and big-sized eyeglasses that perched on the end of his nose. He had almost no hair, looked to be about 40-years old, and wore a white shirt and necktie with yellow garters holding up his long white shirt sleeves.

"Yes sir. How may I help you?"

"I'm here to find Harvey Vanderstone. Could we talk in private?"

Eastin's eyes widened. He nodded. Sweat popped out on his head. For a moment Morgan thought the man was going to faint. He took a short step backward and caught his balance. Then he nodded and swallowed hard.

"Yes, sir. Right this way. I wondered when someone might be looking for him. Lord knows I can't do anything about it."

They went into the storeroom in back of a thin partition walling it off from the front of the store.

Eastin's face was flushed now and he was breathing rapidly.

"Are you all right, Mr. Eastin?"

"I will be. You were quite a shock. I expected it, but I just didn't know who or when."

"Martha Vanderstone sent me. She had no word from her husband in three months."

"Yes, I know. He hid during the day for two months, worked his claim at night as best he could. Not easy. I'm afraid he didn't get much done."

"What happened to him?"

They finally caught him, I guess. He stopped coming in. He used to come to the back door for supplies just after dark."

"Who caught him, Mr. Eastin?"

"I can't say. I mean I shouldn't. By now they must know you're looking for him. I knew after the first day. Not a lot of people here in town, usually. If I knew you were hunting for Vanderstone, then they will, too."

"That's why I'm here, to put a stop to all this. You tell me who probably killed Vanderstone, and I'll stop them from killing anyone else, including you."

"I'll . . . I'll have to think about that. Now, I'd appreciate it if you would go out the back door."

"The back door into the alley?"

"Yes, sir. Then they won't see you come out. Maybe they didn't notice you coming in."

"You're terribly frightened, aren't you, Mr. Eastin?"

"Oh, damn, I sure am. Terrified is the word. I know what those men can do. Leave now, please."

"What if you and I go to the Marshal. You can tell him and me, and then we put it up on a bulletin outside the message tree and on the bulletin boards around town. They can't kill everyone."

"I don't care, they'd start with me. If I'm dead I wouldn't care who else they killed. I'm sorry. Out the back door."

Morgan left, not sure that he should. He had walked down the alley a half dozen steps when he heard a scream from inside the general store, then three shots. Morgan spun around and raced back into the store.

A man in a tan jacket and no hat kicked open the front door and surged through it, a smoking six-gun in his hand. Morgan snapped off a shot at the man and saw him take the bullet in his right shoulder. Then he darted out through the door and into the street.

Morgan slammed after him. He'd check Eastin later. By the time Morgan got to the front of the store, the man was across the street heading for an alley. There were too many people to try for a shot.

Lee Morgan waved his gun, cocked it for another shot and tore into the street dodging wagons and horses as he barged across and into the alley. A figure with the same tan jacket ran 50 yards down. Morgan blasted two more shots at him. The man kept running.

He jolted around the building at the end of the alley and vanished. By the time Morgan got to the same corner he had to go around slowly in case the man was waiting for him.

He wasn't there. On this side street there were three whorehouses, a barrel saloon, a small liquor store and the side of the bank. The man with the light tan jacket was nowhere to be found.

Morgan walked the block twice, looked in at the liquor store, then one of the bawdy houses. Even if Morgan questioned the women in one of them, the women there wouldn't tell if the man Morgan chased was there. Their code of silence.

He leaned against the side of the bank and watched the street. He knew for sure that behind one of the windows along the street or through the peep holes in some of the tents, a man watched him. When Morgan left, the man would leave. How in hell could he catch him?''

Then Morgan remembered the gunshot. He was almost certain that the man had a bullet wound. If the bullet didn't go right on through, somebody would have to dig it out. Morgan grinned and jogged back to the general store.

Town Marshal Quentin was there and a dozen more men stood around the back counter gawking at something.

Morgan took one look at the stilled, bloody form on the floor and bellowed. "Get out of here! All of you except the Marshal. What's the matter with you people? Give the dead a little dignity here. Move it! Out, right now!"

He drew his six-gun and the men began backing up, then walking toward the door. When the last one went out, Morgan locked the front door and went back where the lawman squatted beside the victim.

"Ray Eastin?" Morgan asked.

The lawman turned over the body and Morgan saw that it was the chunky merchant. He had taken a round through his left eye and one in his chest. He must have died instantly.

"I heard the shots, Marshal, then chased a man out the front door. I'd been talking with Eastin only a few seconds before. He knew about Vanderstone but wouldn't tell me who killed the man. Now he'll never tell anyone. He said they'd kill him. I just wish he could tell us who they were."

"Then it wasn't you?" Quentin asked. "People said they saw you come in here and then run out."

"Did they tell you I shot the man in a tan jacket and no hat in the shoulder as he ran out the front door, then chased him across the street and lost him in some pussy palace back on First Street?"

"Damn! They didn't say that. Looks like we've got another unsolved one."

"You mean that's all you're going to do to try to find out who killed him?"

"I'm no damn detective. I mostly take care of drunks."

"The city fathers can feel safe tonight in your

protective hands. Take care of the body, lawman. You should be good at that by now."

Morgan turned and walked away. He dug into his pocket and took out the box of .45 rounds he had just bought and reloaded three rounds he'd fired. It wasn't so hard to do as you walked along once you got the hang of it.

By the time he came to the Andropolis Cafe, his weapon was reloaded, the hammer was safely resting on the empty chamber, and he pushed open the screened door and walked into the eatery.

"Where have you been?" Alexandria asked. She hurried up to him, touched his shoulder and led him to the end chair by the counter.

"You just sit. I have a special supper for you. No, you don't get to choose. Just sit and be ready for a feast."

He sat and worried over the latest development. He should have pressured the frightened little man into telling all he knew. A good chance lost. Now all he had was a man with a slug in his shoulder. He'd think of something.

The dinner came a few minutes later. It was a steak, eight inches wide and six long, an inch thick and cooked medium rare. There were three side dishes of vegetables and big slabs of homemade bread and two kinds of jam and more coffee than he could drink. He cut into the steak and grinned as he chewed it.

There was little chewing needed it was so tender.

"Venison steak," he said softly.

Alexandria grinned. "I bet my Pa you'd know what it was. Half the men don't know what it is. We got a venison brought in by a hunter. So we got to use it up today. We have steak and venison roast and venison stew and ground venison. It will be all cooked and eaten before morning. You're lucky you got here early. Once the word gets out we'll have all our tables full."

By the time Morgan had his meal eaten there were no more places to sit down in the small cafe, and men were lined up outside waiting their turn. It was a great change of pace from chicken and canned ham.

He finished his supper and stood so someone else could rush in to grab his chair. Alexandria wouldn't let him pay for the meal. She took him back through the kitchen to the storeroom and kissed him warmly.

She rubbed her breasts against him and grinned. "I'm just getting you warmed up. We close in two hours. You have a small nap and rest up. I don't want to let you out of my sight all night. I've got a bottle of wine I've been saving." She grinned at him, took his hand and pushed it hard against her breasts, then smiled and hurried away.

Morgan dropped on the cot and tried to think through the situation he'd gotten himself into. Hunting for a man who by all signs must be dead. How to prove who killed him? How to get a death certificate without a body? How to do the job without his being responsible for any more killings? He tried to sort it out, but came back to the killer in the store and how he must be tied in with Vanderstone and the mining claim. It had to center around those factors now.

The first thing he had to do was protect the claim for Martha Vanderstone. He'd go to the mining district recorder in the morning. In the afternoon he'd find the man who killed the store owner. Sounded simple. Morgan knew it wouldn't be.

Before he realized it, he drifted off to sleep. When he woke up it was dark out and a lamp glowed beside him. He heard a movement and turned to see a face hovering over him. The face and the body smelled faintly of sachet. A friendly face.

"Didn't mean to wake you up," Alexandria whispered. "I was going to try to undress you in your sleep."

She eased down to the cot and lay on top of him, her mouth covering his, her lips parted and willing. Morgan's arms came around her and he felt a growing need. It had been two months since he'd loved a woman.

Then he felt the heat of her body steaming through her clothes. Her mouth devoured him, nibbling at his nose, his eyes, his ears, his lips.

"You taste so delicious!" she said. Her breasts pushed hard against him and he moaned in anticipation.

"Are you always so sexy, so anxious to get fucked?"

She giggled at the word. Then she nodded. "Just the last six months or so. A young boy about sixteen seduced me in the woods one Sunday afternoon, and ever since then I've known what I've been missing. I just love to be loved."

"You know what could happen?"

"Sure, I could get pregnant. I have it all worked out. When I do get pregnant, I'll pick out the man I like best and say he's the father. He'll either marry me or my Pa will blow his head off with a shotgun. Simple."

She kissed him again and the heat built. Morgan couldn't stand it any longer. He got one of his hands free and pushed it between them until he could work it under her blouse. She had nothing else on underneath the blouse and his fingers closed around her bare breast.

Alexandria sighed and her eyes shone in the faint light.

She sat up. "Want to see my tits? Men like to look

at them. I'll never know why. Guess it's like I love to look at a man's good parts, too."

She peeled out of the blouse and he stared at her breasts. They were much larger than he had expected, perfect globes hanging from her chest, pink tipped with pulsating nipples now enlarged and hot red. Her areolas were wide and also a dark shade of pink against her soft white skin.

"Beautiful," Morgan said. "Most wonderful part of a woman, so delightful and rounded and a marvel of construction, and at the same time with a dual purpose."

He bent and kissed her breasts and she yelped and dropped to the cot. Her hips pumped upward as she thundered into a climax that shook her like a tiger kitten in its mother's mouth. She humped and moaned and let out a piercing screech of pleasure, then pulled him down and kissed him as the final tremors powered through her.

She brushed tears from her eyes and grinned at him. "I don't usually go so wild so soon, but your kissing my tits just set me off today. See, I'm one ahead of you already."

"I'll never catch up."

Morgan reached for her skirt, lifted her hips and pulled it down. She was a big girl, maybe five feet six inches, lanky, lean, but with large breasts. She was probably no more than 17 despite her claim of being 19. She had dark hair cut short, and a classic face with large dark eyes, high cheekbones and a generous nose. Her chin was slightly strong and wide for her face, but it didn't detract.

She helped him pull down the skirt and three petticoats and then lay there suddenly shy in her white cotton bloomers.

He hovered over her where she lay on her back. "Are you sure, Alex, sure you want to do this?"

"Damn right! Try and stop me!" She pushed and pulled and tugged the bloomers off and threw them on the floor, then slowly spread her thighs and lifted her knees.

"Try and stop me," Morgan said softly.

She sat up and undressed him. Each time she stripped off an item of his clothes she kissed it away. Soon she played with the dark hair on his chest. She shivered as she pulled his pants and his short underwear down. Then with a quick motion she tugged them below his crotch and Morgan's penis rose hard and ready.

"Oh, my Aunt Sally's maidenhead! Just look at that gorgeous prick! I want him inside me right now!"

She stripped his pants off, lay on her back and pulled Morgan over her. A moment later she had him positioned and pulled down on his buttocks so he slid into her waiting slot like a knife into a scabbard.

"Oh glory!" she shouted.

Morgan chuckled.

"You just don't know how good it feels," Alexandria crooned. "You just don't know! It's like a big orchestra playing, and music and dancing and wonderment and all the good things in life suddenly plopped down all together, and it's all mine, and it feels just glorious!"

She pulled his face down and kissed him. When she let go she hugged him to her chest and locked her hands behind his back.

"I ain't never gonna let you go, man thing. You got to just stay right there and pump up and down now and then so I know you're still alive. Oh, glory, what a beautiful, marvelous, wonderful, terrific feeling!"

"I think you like it," Morgan said.

She humped up at him and her inside muscles gripped him until Morgan let out a yelp.

"I'm surprised you can do that inside. Lots of women can't. But I'm warning you . . ."

"Yeah, I know, it makes you pop in a rush. We don't want that, do we?" She wiggled under him and he thrust in all the way and came out. Twice more he drove in hard, then he settled down on top of her.

"Oh, yes! I like it when you lay on me that way. Makes me feel like I'm really getting fucked." She grinned up at him. "Yeah, I like to talk dirty when I'm fucking. Just seems natural. Your old cock is doing a job on me, I can tell you that. Love it."

"Alexandria, how many times have you made love?"

"Really? You think I keep track? Lots and lots of times."

"More than five or six times?"

"Well, no, but . . ."

He kissed her. "You ever been on top?"

"Oh, glory no. This boy said that was unnatural."

Morgan laughed. There was no room to roll over on the narrow cot. He suddenly came out of her and she wailed.

He stood. "Get up, I've got something new for you."

She frowned but stood all naked and lanky with a flat tummy and those bouncing, swaying breasts.

Morgan lay on the cot, spread his legs and motioned. "Come on down and see me. Almost like you're sitting down on my whanger here."

A moment later she lowered herself onto him and squealed in delight.

"That feels wild, crazy . . . wonderful."

He got her to lean forward and soon she was riding him like a bucking bronco. She had another orgasm almost at once and trilled and wailed and moaned all through it.

"Glory! I'm two ahead of you."

But not for long. The action got him moving and soon he was pumping up against her and showering his juices deeply into her as he exploded again and again before pulling her down on top of him so they both could rest.

Later they sat on the side of the cot and sipped the wine she had brought. They didn't have any glasses so they drank from the bottle.

"What about your father?" he asked.

"He don't care. He knows I'm fucking around. He says when I get pregnant we'll decide what to do. Papa was a real cock hound when he was a kid from what he suggested."

"Sexy people run in your family line," Morgan said.

He settled down watching her, touching her. It would be a full night. The wine wouldn't be gone for hours. He might even give out before then. But that wouldn't be before at least five times, maybe six. Morgan sighed. This was one hell of a sexy little Greek lady, and he would have his fill of her before morning.

Chapter Five

When Morgan woke up in the bunk in the store room, Alexandria was gone. He remembered looking at his watch once about four-thirty. They must have gone to sleep right after that. Now it was barely six. He had forgotten that cooks and restaurant owners have to get up early in the morning for the breakfast trade.

He dressed, and went out for breakfast about seven. Alexandria gave him a big smile, then rushed away to take orders. They were busy this morning. She stopped at his place at the counter and squeezed his hand.

''Just so tremendous last night,'' she whispered, then she was gone.

He paid for breakfast, insisting, and walked over to the Lost Mining District office just as it opened. William Lardner looked up and nodded. There was only one man ahead of Morgan at the counter. When Morgan's turn came, he was ready with the letter from Martha Vanderstone.

"This is a notarized letter of authorization for you to transfer the claim of Harvey Vanderstone, Four Above on Clear Creek, into the name of his wife, Martha Vanderstone. I think you'll find it legal and in order. There's an almost certain probability that Mr. Vanderstone is deceased. Rather than let the claim fall into forfeit, she is requesting the transfer so that I, Lee Morgan, as her agent, can start working the claim."

The recorder studied the document for some time, then looked up. It was written on the stationery of a Denver attorney.

"Looks all proper. I'll make the necessary transfers and the lady now owns the claim. I will put an addendum on the letter that in case Mr. Vanderstone returns, the claim will revert to ownership in his name."

"Perfectly proper. Thank you."

Morgan had just left the recorder's office when he felt someone behind him. He spun around and dropped to one knee as he pulled his six-gun.

A man fired a revolver from ten feet away trying to adjust his aim as Morgan dropped. The lead slug sizzled through his left arm gouging out half an inch of tissue and continued on its way. Morgan fired almost at the same instant the other man did and his round hit the man in the left leg. The attacker turned and ran.

The man wearing a black hat and a gray shirt darted down the now dusty street, dodging early morning wagons and pedestrians. Morgan didn't have a shot at him through the traffic as he charged after the bushwhacker.

The man turned down the first side street and seemed headed for one of the tent bordellos, but Morgan cut him off and he hid behind a wagon in the street.

Morgan pounded to the side of a frame building for protection and shouted at the man.

"You tried and missed. You're a free man as far as I'm concerned. All you have to do to walk away free and clear is to tell me who hired you. Otherwise, I'm going to kill you."

A revolver round tore into the wood a foot away from where Morgan crouched.

"Have to catch me first," the man shouted.

A team and wagon came past then and Morgan darted out to the street and used the rig as cover as he moved up the street where he could see around the attacker's wagon protection. Before he could get there, Morgan saw the man in the black hat counter his move by dashing between two tents and toward the timbered hillside just behind them. He vanished in the trees by the time Morgan got past the tents.

Suddenly Morgan was in no man's land. He had no protection or cover from the tents, no chance to see his enemy, and 20 yards of open space to the nearest tree in the woods for cover and concealment.

He charged, changed directions twice and dove into the woods just as two shots parted the air with a faint whisper three feet over his head.

Now the game began. Morgan remained silent in the heavy pine forest waiting and listening. Soon he knew his quarry would move. He did, running through the woods evidently near the clearing alongside the town, moving generally down a slope.

Morgan ran with him, paused to listen, and ran again. Then all was quiet. Morgan moved up slowly toward the spot where he had heard the last sounds. The pines were thick here with some aspen mixed in and a few willows. He worked through a heavy growth and then came to a place where he could see 15 or 20 feet through the pines.

The brush and aspen were gone here. Directly ahead he saw the brush move. His search followed down the moving brush tops to the base where he could see the black hat the man wore. A ruse? He waited. The hat moved and under it he saw a frightened face.

Morgan found a rock on the ground near him and pitched it over the man's hiding spot so it would crash into the brush beyond him. When it hit, the man jolted backwards, scrambling on all fours and watching ahead of him at the spot from where the sound came.

He backed into plain sight, from behind. Morgan aimed his six-gun at the man. He was about 40 feet away across a nearly clear path.

"Move and you're dead!" Morgan bellowed.

The man jumped from surprise, then Morgan heard him swearing. He turned his head. "Bastard, how did you do that?"

"Never mind. You walk away free and clear. Just tell me who hired you to bushwhack me. Who wants me dead?"

"You're Morgan. Lee Buckskin Morgan. I heard of you. You know I can't say who hired me. Code of the West. You know I got to move, too."

As he said it he surged to the side and rolled. Morgan fired, thumbed back the hammer and fired again. The second round bored a small hole through the bushwhacker's chest and cut up his heart muscles so it couldn't perform. He gasped, tried to lift his six-gun and screamed as he died.

Morgan lay there and swore to himself. He'd lost

another chance to find out who was behind all of this. No time to reason with the man. No way to talk to him now. Morgan stood and walked into town, turned on Main Street and found the saloon he wanted.

It was the Hiring Hall Saloon. That wasn't its name, but every day miners who didn't have a claim and wanted to work by the day gathered there. Men who needed workers came by, made their picks, and they went to work.

By now most of the men needing workers had been there and gone. Morgan looked over the bunch. He found about 20 left. He motioned them together.

"Is there a Preacher's kid here? Anybody have a preacher for his father?"

One man held up his hand. Morgan eyed him a minute. He looked about 25, strong, alert.

"Over here. I need three more men. I want one man who can build a rocker."

He went down the line picking them out. He took the rocker man first, then the other two. He told them to get something to take with them for a noon meal. He suggested they take gloves and a jacket and told them to meet him on the corner in 20 minutes.

The general store was open again, Eastin's wife and 19-year-old son were running it. Morgan bought four shovels, two gold pans, new corner stakes and a small leather pouch to hold the gold dust if they found any.

"Tweezers, a stick pin?" the youth asked.

Morgan nodded. "Both," he said.

He picked up his four men and they walked out the six miles to the dig. He wasn't exactly sure what to do once they got there. He walked beside the man who said he could build a rocker and talked. He explained what they would be doing, working the claim to keep it active.

"Gonna need some material to build a rocker," the older man said who was named Earl. "I can get them tomorrow. Cost maybe two or three dollars."

"Sounds good. First I want you to look over the claim and make suggestions. I'm also needing a foreman, so if it works out, you might be the man."

"Meaning you won't be on the claim all the time?" Earl asked.

"Meaning I'll need a man I can trust with gold dust. Are you the man?"

"Never stole a nickel in my life, never going to."

Morgan nodded.

At the claim, Morgan checked the corner stakes. He wrote the Vanderstone name on them and set them in beside the old ones, then got the men working. He had two of them dig a three-foot-wide hole ten feet from the stream. "Want to see how far down the bedrock is here," Morgan told them.

The preacher's kid was named James. He had worked several digs. He and Earl walked the 300-feet of stream with Morgan and decided they should set up their rocker at a different place than Vanderstone had started to work. They put it higher on the dig where they would have some "float" so gold they accidentally washed out could settle out in the stream bed again.

They dug out a spot where a 12 foot sluice box could be set and then went to work digging a new "gopher" hole nearby to check the bedrock.

Morgan knew the ritual on a placer mining operation. The gold in the surrounding hills here must be in quartz. Over the past 200,000 years or so, the weather and wind and rain and snow had broken the gold free as the mountains eroded and the flake gold and gold dust was washed down the mountains until it came to the sides of the little stream. There the force of the water slowed and the gold flakes and dust filtered downt to the bottom of the stream and into the surrounding overburden that gradually built up of the erosion sand, gravel, dirt and decayed vegetable matter.

Generally there would be "free" gold dust and flakes and a nugget here and there from bedrock all the way up to the surface of the overburden. Not just the gravel in the stream was worth panning and washing. The whole 300-feet-wide stretch of soil and sand and rocks from cap rock to cap rock, or from one side of the little stream's valley to the other, undoubtedly held free gold as well. Was it enough to wash all of that soil and gravel?

All the miners had to do was dig it out, wash the free gold out of it and get rich.

But Morgan knew getting rich wasn't that easy. Some places they might find only 20¢ worth of gold in a washed pan of gravel and dirt and silt. Some places there might be a dollar or even more in a pan of ore, and in many places no gold at all.

Gold was 19 times heavier than water, Morgan remembered that. So the gold would drop out of the water soon, and then filter down through the porous sand and gravel as well. The old placer miners knew that the silt and soil and sand just above the bedrock had the richest lode of free gold in most any claim.

Morgan heard a shout from downstream and went to where the first two men were digging in the bedrock.

"We hit it already," one of the diggers said.

He stood in the three-foot-wide hole that was only three feet deep. Morgan stared into the hole. In many places the bedrock could be ten to fifteen-feet down. They had hit a lucky stretch.

"Dig me out a pan full and let's see what we have," Morgan said.

He handed the man one of the gold pans. The pan was typical, about 18 inches across and four inches deep tapering to a flat bottom six or eight inches across. It was made of mild steel so it would rust slowly and provide a better rough surface to catch the gold. Many of these particles of gold were so small that they couldn't be seen with the human eye.

Morgan took the shovel full of gravel from the bottom of the hole to the creek and bent down. He submerged the pan in the water as he gently stirred the mixture. This washed the dirt and silt from the gravel.

He brought the pan to the surface and threw away the larger pebbles and rocks that were of no value. But first he rinsed the pebbles to be sure he rinsed off any clinging gold dust.

Then he alternately dipped and raised the edge of the pan beneath the water, as he gently swirled the remaining sand. By working carefully he allowed the sand to slop over the edge of the pan. This was the worthless sand.

Morgan worked carefully here because now was when any small nuggets might be found. In this pan there were none. He kept working until all of the useless sand had washed out of the pan.

What was left in the pan now was black iron, cassiterite, which was tin ore, tiny red garnets, and any gold present. All of these were heavy enough to remain in the pan during the washing process.

Morgan gave the pan a strong circular swirling motion that spread the remaining material in the pan in an arc across its bottom. This usually came out a rough half-moon. At the farthest part of that half-moon, carried the farthest by its weight, would be the gold, if any.

The five men stared at the half moon of material in the pan.

Earl gave a whoop of delight.

"Look at there, and there and there!" he crowed pointing at the end of the crescent. "See those flakes! Not just dust but some real flakes. Where's the leather pouch?"

Morgan handed it to him along with the tweezers and the hat pin and Earl carefully lifted the larger flakes out of the pan and dropped them into the small leather pouch with a leather thong drawstring. When the larger flakes were gone he used his damp finger to pick up the gold dust. He held up his finger and they saw the golden smear on it. He wiped his finger off inside the leather bag. Four times he came up with more gold, then motioned for Morgan to swirl the pan once more.

They found two more flakes and three more fingers of gold. Earl settled back and played with the tiny red garnets.

"What you boys estimate that pan was worth?" Morgan asked.

Two of them shook their heads. Earl looked at James, the Preacher's kid.

"Twenty cents?" James asked.

"Closer to fifty cents, I'd say. Let's do about ten more pans and see what we wind up with."

Morgan nodded and Earl and James took the two pans

and the other men dug into the hole at the bedrock and scraped up the best sand and gravel they could find.

After the third pan, Earl turned his pan over to one of the other men. He motioned to Morgan.

"Not going to have enough water power from this sized stream to work a sluice box, unless we build ourselves a small dam. We can do it right there where that small pool already is. We move rocks from the upstream side and string them across right about, here. Then we use sticks and mud and fill in the chinks. We only need our dam to be about a foot high and twelve, fifteen feet long in an arc."

Morgan approved and they went back to the panning. Earl picked out the gold when it showed. One pan had almost none. The next pan had two small nuggets about the size of the lead at the tip of a pencil.

"Damn good sign," Earl said. "I've seen five or six claims around here and this is the best one so far. Just three feet from bedrock is a real advantage."

By five o'clock they called it a day. Morgan looked in the small gold dust leather bag and Earl took a look himself. Gold dust flaked off the sides where fingers had been rubbed clean of gold.

"Never get it one hundred percent pure," Earl said. "Always some iron dust in there as well. Most places figure sixteen dollars fifty cents an ounce. At that rate, I'd say we got about an ounce today."

"You men almost earned your wages," Morgan said.

He paid them the four dollars a day he had promised them and told them he wanted them full time. They should bring out their bedrolls and cooking gear and food enough for a week. He'd have a horse and a pack horse in the morning at six A.M. on the same street corner.

He gave Earl an extra $5 to buy what he needed to build a rocker. "We'll bring out that material tomorrow as well. Any questions? Anybody not want to come full time?"

One man said he was about ready to head back to Missouri and start farming. Morgan said he should leave. He'd pick up a new man in the morning.

They hid the shovels and the pans under some brush 50 yards from the stream. On the way back Morgan didn't see Old Man Marshall. He was going to go up and check on him but decided he'd do it the next day.

Morgan was caught up in the gold mining. He admitted it. He'd never worked a claim like this before. It was exciting, like the next pan full might produce a hundred-dollar nugget.

He got in late and went to sleep in the storeroom. Alexandria didn't come see him. The next morning he had breakfast at five-thirty, picked up the horses, and took his four men to the claim. He got them started and put Earl in charge. He left the gold dust bag with him and Earl swore he would be honest in his count.

Morgan rode the horse back and trailed the pack horse. He turned them in at the livery and then went to see the Marshal. He might have some idea by now about who killed Eastin.

Chapter Six

Morgan came into the Marshal's office slightly before ten that same morning and talked with the young man with the quick smile, long sideburns and leather vest, but not much in the way of lawman's skills.

"Beats me, Morgan, who it is who killed the store man. I ain't turned up anything. Just what you told me about the guy with no hat and a tan jacket. Oh, some woman said she thought the first guy out of the store had light colored hair. About all I know."

Morgan growled at him and left. He would check out the only other chance. He was sure he hit the killer in the shoulder with a .44 round. If it didn't go right through. . . . That's when Morgan remembered the hit he had taken in the left arm. It wasn't as bad as he thought it might be. He'd tied it up with a neckerchief, but he would get the doctor to look at it just to be sure.

At the same time he'd ask the sawbones if he'd dug out a slug from anybody's shoulder lately.

The doctor's name was Rodarte, Dr. George Rodarte. He looked at Morgan's arm and snorted. "You call this a gunshot? I've seen deeper wounds when a dance hall girl scratches her fingernails down some grabass's face."

"So put something on it and charge me a dollar. I'm paying cash money."

"Not a lot of that around. It's a deal." The medic spread some kind of salve on the three-inch groove and then bandaged it. "Good as new."

Morgan tossed him a silver dollar.

"You dig a bullet out of anybody lately?"

"Average about two a day."

"Yesterday, happen to take one out of a shoulder?"

The doctor looked up quickly. "Yeah, how'd you know?"

"I had the pleasure of planting the lead there. Any idea who the gent was?"

"Why you asking? You a lawman?"

"Nope, there isn't one in town. I'm an interested party who got shot at and returned fire. It's an old habit of mine as I try to stay alive. Do you know the gent?"

"Indeed I do. But medical ethics—"

"He's the man who killed Ray Eastin, the general store merchant."

The doctor stared at him. "You know that for certain?"

"I was talking to Eastin one minute, he shooed me out the back door, I heard the shots and charged back in there and shot this blond haired guy tearing out the front door. So who is he?"

"Yeah, that sounds about like Odell. His full name is Nance Odell and he's a gunman about town. Works for whoever pays him. Mostly he drinks and gambles."

"What's his favorite saloon?"

"The Moneytree. He's usually there."

"Any idea who might have hired him, Doc?"

"Not the slightest. Don't tell anybody I pointed out the gent, or this town will be without a doctor, again."

"Wouldn't think of it. This is a lot bigger problem than just that one killing. You'll be hearing about it."

Morgan walked out, had dinner at the Andropolis Cafe, and talked with Alexandria.

"Where have you been?" she asked.

He told her about the claim.

"You going to get rich?"

"Not without a lot of work. Anyway, I told you, I don't own the claim. That woman in Denver owns it."

"She'd never know."

"She might not, but I would. I never steal from my friends."

"Glad I'm your friend. You going to be here tonight?"

He leaned closer and whispered. "You seem hell-bent on getting pregnant in a hurry. I'm just as potent as hell."

"No, I'm not trying, I just want to have a fine time before I do. I'll stop by after closing." She squeezed his hand and brushed her breasts against him as she slipped past and went into the kitchen.

Morgan walked from the cafe directly to the Moneytree Saloon. He'd been there before. He got a beer from the barkeep and looked over the poker games. In the second one he found a towheaded young man with a shoulder covered by a loose jacket. He didn't move the shoulder unless he had to. Could be it was bandaged.

Morgan watched the third poker game but mostly kept looking at the blond man. He was about the right size. The man picked up his cards and fanned them out, but his left hand did little of the work. Usually it lay in his lap. He brought it up to play but plainly he had problems with his shoulder.

After watching another game Morgan went over and stood beside an empty chair across from the blond.

"Want some new money in the game?" he asked, clinking three $20 gold pieces together.

The other two men looked up and nodded. The third, the blond man, shrugged. Morgan sat down and pushed his change on the table. They were playing a dollar a pot and a dollar limit.

On the first game he lost only two dollars, dropping out after the first draw. On the second he lost eight, giving up on a pair of aces in five card draw. Three kings won the pot.

Morgan watched the man he decided must be Odell. He was a good bluffer. Knew how to sweat another player. On the third hand Morgan drew three jacks, threw away two and drew a pair of deuces.

He bet casually, kept in all the men for two rounds, then two dropped out and he bet against Odell. The man looked at Morgan, who stared back at him. Odell folded his cards.

"Let's see your openers," Odell said.

Morgan smiled. "I didn't open." He folded his cards and pulled in the pot. He was $30 ahead, but he had learned a lot about Odell.

An hour later, Morgan was a $10 loser when the game

broke up. He went to the bar for a beer and then tailed Odell as he left the saloon and worked his way down the main street, up a block, and went into a small boarding house under some trees. At least Morgan had found the contract killer. Now what the hell did he do?

Easy. He would watch Odell until he reported in to his boss, probably after dark. Morgan found a shield of brush on the slope of the hill and sat behind it as he waited. Odell couldn't see him even if he tried. There had been nothing to indicate he might have recognized Morgan. Morgan wore different clothes today.

Boots, he must remember to get rubber boots if he was going to work the claim any more. His feet were still wet from yesterday when he had waded around in that little creek.

Morgan dozed, but kept watch. Nothing moved around the house. It was nearly six o'clock when Odell came out and headed downtown. He went into Delmonico's Cafe and evidently had supper. Delmonico's was half platform and half tent on the top. It was a step above the Andropolis Cafe, but Morgan wondered if the food was any better.

He didn't have supper, instead he sat across the street beside a tent and waited Odell out. When Odell came out nearly an hour later, he headed straight for the Moneytree saloon. Morgan walked in the bistro a minute or two later, bought a beer and sat down at a back table.

Odell wasn't anywhere in sight. Morgan sat there watching the place, trying to figure out where Odell had vanished. He could have gone to the outhouse, but if so he would be back in a few minutes. He didn't show up. There must be a back room or a door that opened into an adjoining building. Either way, Morgan figured he was finished for the night.

Odell would get suspicious if he found Morgan in the Moneytree again so soon after their poker game. He finished the beer, watched a poker game a minute, then drifted out the front door.

What'n hell? He was stymied. One thing he couldn't do was to overplay his hand. He had a suspect who could lead to the man behind the whole damn thing. It had to tie in with Vanderstone's killing as well. Now he had to wait it out and see.

Morgan walked across the street in the soft, high country darkness. Why did the air feel so different up here at almost 5,000 feet? He didn't know. All in his mind, probably.

He sat on his butt for the next few hours as he hunkered up against a building in the alley and watched the front door of the Moneytree saloon. After two hours he gave up and headed back toward the Andropolis Cafe.

He was almost there when a shadow moved in the alley ahead and he darted flat against the store. He heard a high, soft laugh.

"Sorry I scared you, Morgan. It's Star. I need to talk to you."

He moved ahead cautiously toward the alley, his revolver in his fist ready to create quick death. He soon saw it was Star and she was alone. Morgan pushed the iron back into leather and smiled at the pretty girl.

"You need to talk?"

"Yes, at the gunsmith's. Do you have time?"

"Always time to talk to a pretty girl."

They went down the alley, across to the next street, into another alley and stopped at a small back door. She used a key and they went inside.

It was dark until she found a match, scratched it and lit a lamp. She knew where it had been left. Without a word she led the way down the same hall he had been in before and into the room she said was hers.

Star set down the lamp and lit another, then motioned for him to sit in a wooden chair she put near the door.

"I have some things to show you."

Star lit a third lamp making the room almost as bright as day. From a closet closed off with a quilt, she brought out several framed pictures and set them in front of the bed and against the wall.

"Is this an art show?" Morgan asked.

"It certainly is. A one woman show. I painted these."

Morgan looked at Star and then at the pictures. One showed a miner holding a gold pan. He was knee deep in water and in the process of sloshing the useless sand over the edge of the pan. The background had been painted in with bold, accurate strokes and the whole scene came alive.

The expression on the old miner's face was one of caution and hope, but the eventual despair could be seen creeping into it.

Morgan looked at her with surprise.

"Star, you actually painted these? That placer miner is wonderful."

"You really like it?"

"I could sell it in Denver for fifty dollars, with no problem."

She shivered. A tear crept out of one eye and she hugged herself. "I don't know if I'm dreaming this or if you're just being kind."

"You're not dreaming, and I'm being honest."

He looked at the others. A miner at a sluice box, a man shivering in the cold near a fire with the stream and a gold rocker in back. The next one was of a woman in a crib, smoking a cigarette, one breast revealed through her robe, her hair tousled, her legs spread wide with her crotch barely covered by the robe. She showed abject despair.

"I call the woman Sally. She worked in a crib here for almost a year, then one night she slit her wrists and died before anyone found her. Sally was my best friend."

"It shows the anger, frustration, hopelessness."

"I painted Sally two weeks before she died. She never saw the painting."

"You do your painting here or in Kincaid's place?"

"Oh, here. He doesn't know I even own a brush. I have to paint on wood and cardboard, whatever I can find. The general store owner got me some canvas once from Chicago, and he ordered my oil paints from the same place. My canvas is all gone."

Morgan examined the paintings more closely. They were good. She had a feel for the human form. She had an artist's eye. She looked at people and places and remembered them.

"I told you the other time we were here that I wanted to leave. Now you see why. I want to go to Chicago and study painting with the best teacher in town. Maybe even New York. That's why I must get out of Deadwood, Mr. Morgan, and you're the only man in town who can get me free of Lash Kincaid."

Chapter Seven

"Lash Kincaid is not my favorite person in Deadwood," Lee Buckskin Morgan said as he looked at ten more paintings that Star brought out. "Just because he's holding you here against your will gives me even more delight in helping you get away. I'm amazed at how well you're doing with your art work. Most of it is commercially saleable right now. With some formal training you'll be well on your way to fame and fortune in the art world. It's my duty to get you out of here."

Star ran up and threw her arms around him and kissed him on the cheek. Tears ran down from her eyes as she cried silently. "I . . . I . . . I don't know how to thank you. I had hoped that you might be a friend." She let go of him and began to put the paintings away.

"Leave the one out of Sally, it is powerful, moving. Such a tragedy in the making."

She left it there and when the others were put away, she walked up to him slowly.

"Mr. Morgan, I won't be offended if you refuse, but there is something I'd like to do. Just for you, as a small thank you. You know that I'm Kincaid's paid woman. You know that I was a whore before that, and I guess I still am. But I would really like to show you how good I can be in bed."

She glanced up at him quickly. She saw no disapproval in his eyes and so she went on. "This is my private place. No man has ever been here before. If it would be all right with you. . . ."

She let it trail off and Morgan stood there watching her. She was a tiny thing, maybe five feet two and not over 100 pounds soaking wet. Her long blonde hair was gorgeous, flowing in a white mane all the way to her waist. Her eyes were soft brown and she had a trim little figure.

"Star, it would be my pleasure and privilege to make love with such a talented artist." He reached in and kissed her on the lips. Her eyes went wide.

"Most men don't kiss whores," she said softly.

"Star, from this moment on, if you ever call yourself that again, I'll be most unhappy with you. You're an artist, you're going to Chicago and New York, and maybe even Paris to learn some of the finer points of your creative art. I'm right in the middle of something here, trying to find a man, but when I'm through with that, we'll both confront Kincaid if necessary, and you'll be on your way to the big city."

Tears rushed out of her eyes. She reached up and hugged him with all her strength. Star pressed her face against his chest and sobbed until he thought she was going to shake apart. When she at last tapered off the sobbing, she looked at him again and her face was radiant, shining, remarkably beautiful.

He kissed her lips softly, so gently she hardly felt the touch. Her eyes went wide as she pulled back from his lips. "Ohhhhhhh," she sighed. "Mr. Morgan, you've just made me so wonderfully happy that I don't know if it's another of my daydreams. Tell me again."

Her face was a painting in itself. Traces of tears still tracked her tender young cheeks, her soft brown eyes were so expectant and eager that they reached out to him.

"You're leaving Deadwood as soon as I can arrange it, and going to Chicago and New York to study art."

He bent and kissed her cheek and she cried softly again. She moved him to the bed and they sat down. Then she lay back, pulling him with her.

"Just hold me tight for a minute so I'll know it is true, absolutely true."

He held her until the surprise and wonder and awe left her face. When her old smile came back he grinned.

"Now, the first shock is off, you're convinced. Your big job is not to let on to Kincaid that anything is different. He simply must not know until we're ready to get you out of here."

"I can do that. We used to call it acting. I can act better than any of them. He'll never suspect. He's been worried about business lately anyway and hardly has any time for me."

"Good."

"Now, Lee Morgan, would it be all right. . . ." She caught one of his hands and brought it to her breasts. "I don't have the biggest breasts you've ever played with, but so far I've had no complaints about them."

"Star, you don't have to."

She smiled. "I know, that's what makes it so exciting for me. For the first time I want to truly make love, and I want to do it with you. Not have sex, not get fucked, not get banged or poked. I want to *make love* with a man I really like."

"Slow and easy," Morgan said. He kissed her lips and she pushed back.

"Really?"

Morgan grinned and kissed her lips again, then pulled her down in the crook of his arm and held her.

"Where did you grow up?" he asked as he moved his hand over one breast and began gently to caress it.

"Huh? Oh, yes, grow up. Mostly in Ohio. My dad was a farmer for a while; then we moved to town and he became a carpenter. He was pretty good. Then Ma died and my dad's new wife sort of eased me out of the house."

"How old were you?"

"Sixteen. She got me a job in a restaurant, but I didn't last long. Then a guy came along who said he'd guarantee me sixty dollars a week. I got suspicious and asked him doing what. He told me. I said what the hell, why not. I was still a virgin at the time. I didn't stay that way long."

"Then you came to Deadwood?"

"After a year or so. No, two years. I was in Chicago for a while, then I came west. Been here over a year."

"But you won't be here much longer."

He continued to caress her breast. She purred.

"Now that is what I call nice. Gives a girl a chance to get used to the idea. No matter how much she wants it in her brain, she's got to get her body ready. I learned that from hard experience.

"What about you, Lee Morgan? Where you from?"

He kissed her lips gently again and moved his hand to her other breast.

"I grew up in Idaho, with mostly my dad and our cook. My Ma took off when I was four so I don't remember much about her. Grew up on the Spade Bit Ranch, out of Boise. We raised horses. My Dad did, that is. Then when he got killed, I took over and tried to do it. I'm not as good at it as he was. Lost the ranch twice. Don't know now if I own it again or not. The sheriff out there wants the Spade Bit real bad."

"So why don't you go back?"

"You've heard of a wanted poster?"

"Oh, sure, I see them all the time." She stopped and frowned. "You're on a wanted poster?"

"Dead or alive. The paper is no good. That same sheriff put it out to keep me away from my ranch. Then another one down in Arizona came after a fair gunfight. Guy who got in the way of my bullet was the district attorney's brother. So much for justice. He overruled the Sheriff of Tombstone and put out the wanted. Lots of men will try most anything to get a two thousand dollar reward."

"How long ago?"

"Best part of five, six years on the Arizona. About the same time on the other one in Boise. I'm waiting for that sheriff to die or get booted out of office."

She sat up and took off her blouse. Morgan bent and kissed her breasts.

Star purred softly. "Now that is nice, warm and soft and all cozy feeling. Do that again."

He kissed her breasts again and she leaned over to kiss him. It was a long one and she touched his lips with her tongue, then drew back.

They didn't talk much then. She wiggled out of her skirt and bloomers, then sat up and undressed him slowly.

"I like to undress a man, slow and easy. Most men like that. You like it, Morgan?"

"Oh, yes. A pixie like you with all that talent in your fingers and your artistic eye. Somehow I have a feeling I'll wind up in one of your pictures down the road aways."

"You sure will. I have a good memory for faces, and line." She laughed softly. "That's why I want to get you undressed so I can see you all naked. Would it be all right if I sketched you, afterwards?"

"Sure."

She pulled down his pants and his short underwear and laughed softly. "Oh, yes, the best part. He's ready and raring to go." She bent and kissed his erection and then rolled over on top of him.

"You really think I can support myself by selling my pictures?"

"Absolutely. It might take a little while to get started. They have art galleries where they hang your picture. They get a percentage of the sale price, so you always tack on enough to cover their fee. Say the picture is worth a hundred dollars. You tell them to sell it for a hundred and fifty and they get the fifty."

"I understand." She kissed him. "Now, let's not talk for a while."

She moved her hand down and began stroking him slowly, then played with his up-tight scrotum. She rolled away and sat on his stomach, dropping one breast and then the other into his mouth. He munched and licked her hand-sized orbs until she shivered.

"Yes, yes!" she said softly.

Star caught his hand and moved it slowly down her belly, over her mound and to her crotch. He caressed her gently, working down one soft white thigh and up the other, then trailed across the soft wet lips and rubbed her mound until she stirred.

He touched her outer lips and she sighed. Gently he worked them around and around, then tried to touch her small node, but she shook her head.

"No, not that. It's turned off somehow. It just doesn't work anymore." She humped her hips at him hard. "Now, darling Morgan, come in now, please!"

He moved over her and entered gently. She was ready for him and he eased forward until they were locked together as deep as he could penetrate.

"Yes, yes," she said softly.

He felt her inner muscles playing with him, and he worked gently stroking in and out and then waiting as she toyed with him.

Before he knew it was coming, his surge blasted and his hips pounded and drove and battered at her a dozen times before he could stop. When he had recovered from his mini-death he lifted up from where he had crushed her into the mattress.

"Star, how did you do that? I wasn't even getting started and suddenly I'm exploding."

"My little secret. Hush now and rest."

She put her arms around him pinning their bodies together.

It was 15 minutes before she let go. They came apart and sat beside each other on the bed.

"You really think I can sell in a big town like Chicago?"

"Chicago is a bunch of small villages. With your

talent, you can sell your paintings anywhere. Believe me. I've been in a lot of art stores. If I like your work, others will as well."

They talked about art and what she would do, where she would go. Morgan knew one art dealer in Chicago and he said he would give her his name and address and write him a letter that she was coming.

She leaned back so she could focus on him and frowned. "How come I was so lucky to find you?"

"It wasn't luck. I'm really a fallen angel banished back to earth and I must do a thousand good turns to a thousand deserving humans so I can repay my transgressions and regain my eternal state in heaven."

She watched him a minute, then giggled. "You are not. No angel can make love as well as you do. It was glorious."

"But you never did climax," he said.

"Right. I haven't had a real orgasm for two years. I used to have to fake it with the men in the house. Now I don't have to with Kincaid. He hardly knows I'm there anyway. He just pounds off and rolls away and gets up.

"Don't talk about him."

"It bothers you?"

"Yes."

"He's my meal ticket, has been for almost a year. I . . . I do what he wants me to and he keeps me."

"Not for long. Just as soon as I get this other mess straightened out."

"I want to sketch you." She went to the closet and brought out a big pad of rough paper and some lengths of charcoal.

"What should I do?"

"Just sit there. Lace your fingers together behind your

head the way you did before. That's it. Hold it a minute. That's it, now just relax."

She worked on the tablet, frowned, made some more strokes, then turned the page. "Now lie down on the bed."

For the next five minutes she had him pose in various positions, some natural, some that seemed odd. Then she told him to relax and frown slightly at her. She asked him to hold that pose for two minutes, then three.

"My frown is getting tired," he said.

She laughed. "Just a minute more."

When she was done she showed him the sketch. When he looked at it in the good light, he was surprised how much of him she had captured on paper. It was a dramatic likeness, stronger, angrier, but it was a face that would attract attention.

"I want to do an oil of you when I have time. I'll combine some of the sketches with the frown. You have a remarkable frown."

"Thanks, and you are a remarkably talented artist. Couldn't you just hide here for the rest of the time?"

"How long, a few hours?"

"I'm not sure. It could be a couple of more days."

"No, I'll go back. I told him I was going out for supper and then to see one of the tent drama shows. I'm covered."

"Let's both get covered. I usually like my portrait artist to be wearing at least a few clothes."

"Was I that bad?"

"You were that wonderful. That was making love. Doesn't happen very often for me, either."

They dressed and then sat and talked. At last she took a deep breath. "Let me put these sketches away and then I better get back to Kincaid's place. He can get touchy."

"I don't blame him."

"Oh, not about me. It's about power. He has this urge to control everyone and everything he can touch. It's a disease with him."

She put the last sketches behind the curtain, blew out two lamps and took the other one and they went down the hallway and out the alley door. Morgan walked her to the alley where Kincaid's back door was and he left her there when she insisted. He waited until he saw her unlock a door several buildings down and vanish inside.

Poker. What he needed was a rugged, mean game of poker. He walked to the Moneytree Saloon, bought three beers and sat down at a game with an empty chair.

Morgan played poker for three hours, and it was slightly after midnight when he cashed in, found out he was $15 ahead and bought a round of beers for the five still in the game.

Morgan took his time walking back to the cafe. He checked out each alley before he crossed it. He went around the two corners wide so no one could surprise him. Then he slid into the cafe with a key Alexandria had given him and was pleased not to find her waiting for him.

Tomorrow had to be more productive than today. He had to find out who hired the blond man Odell. It was the only lead he had.

Chapter Eight

Morgan awoke early the next morning, and saw by his watch that it was nearly six A.M. He wanted to talk with the men who hired miners at the Hiring Saloon. He got there just as three men came to get workers.

Morgan talked to each of them. None had ever heard of a man named Vanderstone on the Four Above on Clear Creek. Morgan waited and two more claim owners arrived. The second one scowled a minute thinking.

"Yeah, I do remember him, up on Clear Creek. I'm below him aways. I figured he had a pretty good claim. He bought it just before I decided to take it.

"The man was in his thirties, had a gold nugget on a gold chain around his neck and talked to me about hiring some men. He wanted to know how it worked.

"Vanderstone, yeah. I came into town with him one

Friday night. He said he had business in the Moneytree Saloon. Seemed strange to me 'cause Van wasn't a drinking man. Never touched a drop. Hard worker. He seemed really happy that night. Said something about more than one way to get rich in Deadwood."

The miner shook his head. "Van wasn't a gambling man either. I had to get some supplies before the store closed so I let him go. Last time I ever saw him. Heard he vanished after that. Sorry, that's all I can tell you. I better get moving. I got some quarter-a-pan gravel I got to get worked before the snow comes."

The miner took his three men and trudged down Main in the opposite direction.

Morgan thought it through. From what this miner said, and what Old Man Marshall had told him, it was sounding like Vanderstone was going to try to blackmail somebody. Who? Why? And did it all happen at the Moneytree Saloon? None of it made much sense.

He sat in a chair leaned up against the dry goods store and pondered it. The only thing that tied together was the Moneytree Saloon. It kept cropping up. Vanderstone vanished after going in there. He could have come out, but Morgan had no witnesses that said he did. Then the man who killed Vanderstone's friend, the general store owner, seemed to be a regular customer and maybe more at the Moneytree Saloon.

It was a start but not enough. Maybe some honest work would spark his brain into action. He bought a pair of rubber boots, rented a horse and rode out to the claim.

All four men were still working. Earl waved when he saw Morgan coming and met him before he got off his horse. Earl held up the small leather pouch.

"We been doing just dandy," Earl said. "Hit a hot

streak for a while and found some real nuggets. I got the cradle built and set up like you told me. About to get her into action. Hell, we got gopher holes all over the place. The bedrock is still only a little more than three-feet."

Morgan looked inside the leather bag. There was enough gold in the bottom so he could see it. He figured there were two or three spoons full now and saw a few tiny nuggets, one big as a raisin. He closed the bag and put it in his pocket. He'd brought two more with him and gave a new one to the foreman.

"The rocker, good idea. Let's get it working."

Morgan had never even seen a gold rocker. It was a strange-looking contraption made from a wooden box that had the bottom bored full of holes. This was called the riddle. It was mounted over a sloping trough about the size of a baby's cradle and had rockers under it so the whole device could be rocked back and forth and sideways.

Earl put a shovel full of bedrock gravel in the riddle and began rocking it as Morgan poured buckets of water over the gravel. This washed the fine sand, gravel and silt through the holes into the trough.

When the fines had washed from the riddle, it was lifted out and the useless rocks and pebbles discarded. More water was added and the slurry of sand, water and hopefully some gold, flowed down the trough and over a number of transverse riffles. It was behind these that the heavier gold, iron sand, garnets and cassiterite would settle.

The lighter mud, silt and sand flowed out the end of the trough and back into Clear Creek. The trough had been set down at the water level so a small gate at the end of the trough could be opened an inch or two to get enough water to wash out the fines, yet not enough to carry the gold back into the stream.

"I can work about ten times the gravel this way that a man can with a pan alone. Course we still have to gather up the good stuff behind them riffles and work it in a pan to get the gold splayed around in that half circle. But that goes quick."

Morgan shoveled another batch of gold-bearing sand and gravel into the rocker and they repeated the process. As he worked his mind was mulling over the problem of finding Vanderstone's killer.

There had to be a man in town who set this all in motion. Who was it? The sheriff? Hardly. The barkeep at the Moneytree Saloon? Maybe the man who owned the Moneytree drinking establishment? Yes, he would find out who that might be. He watched another shovel of sand and gravel go through the rocker, then Earl stopped and worked his pan on the promising material behind the riffles.

After six quick pans they found enough gold to be productive, and several flakes, but no nuggets. It was getting warm this day in August. He wasn't sure what the date was, he'd find out when he went back to town. Morgan took off his shirt and kept working the rocker with Earl.

He rode back into town about five, had supper at the Andropolis Cafe and had to fend off Alexandria's questions. They were so busy at the eatery that he managed to pay his bill and slip out. On the street, he asked three people who owned the Moneytree Saloon, but none of them knew.

He walked down to the newspaper and the newsman was just closing up. Morgan asked the editor publisher.

"Owner? Not the foggiest idea. Ted is the barkeep,

farthest I ever got in there. No real way to check ownership since there isn't a county clerk or recorder to file with, and only mining claims get filed with the Mining District recorder. I'll have to ask about that. How do we know we really own the property we have our businesses on?''

Morgan waved at him and turned the other way. He'd never thought about legal ownership of the town itself. Were all of these businesses just squatting on federal lands? Probably. He shrugged. If the gold ran out this town would consist of six men and a dog within two years. Nobody would care who owned the wasting away ghost-town buildings.

But now it was different. The owner of that saloon could be the man behind the killings.

Morgan walked back down to the saddle shop across from the Moneytree Saloon and sat in a chair placed outside. The enticing smells of the leather shop drifted out the door and Morgan almost went in. Instead he sat there and stared at the saloon.

On one side it was nestled up to a tent that housed a small canvas topped hotel that had six of the shelters extending back to the alley. On the other side was Benoit Jewelers. A sign in the window said that the proprietor specialized in handmade gold jewelry of almost any kind.

It was a small shop, with a second story not used by the jeweler, by the looks of things. Next to it was a good-sized establishment with a sign that said it was the Deadwood Liquor and Spirits store.

Not much help. He looked back at the jewelry store. Maybe he should get some earrings made out of genuine Black Hills gold. Maybe. Something stirred in his memory, then it came full blown.

That first day when he came to the street after being clubbed on the head and talking with Kincaid, he had come out an unmarked door near a saloon.

In the gathering dark he couldn't be sure. Now he stood and walked across the street and looked at the door between the jewelry store and the saloon. It was the same one. It had no identification on it and it had no knob or any other way to open it from the street side.

So, Kincaid was directly beside the Moneytree Saloon. Kincaid might have something to do with this whole vanishing act and murder. Morgan scowled. The huge man would be a good target for blackmail. He was sure that Kincaid had plenty that he didn't want talked about.

The blond killer, Odell, could have gone from the Moneytree Saloon through a back room and upstairs to Kincaid's office. Sure, and the moon could be made of green cheese.

Morgan was feeling the challenge of the puzzle building up in his mind and soon he would be screaming. He could use a beer to relax him a little. That would help.

He walked into the Moneytree Saloon, nodded at the barkeep who almost seemed to recognize him and took a bottle of beer to a back table. He put his back to the wall and worked slowly on the beer.

His mind felt like mush. Nothing seemed to make sense. All he had were straws. He looked up as a hush fell over the 25 men in the saloon. About half of them played cards, more stood at the bar and some probably too poor to play themselves watched the card games.

Morgan saw what caused the hush. It was Wild Bill Hickok. He wore the same black frock coat and the black pants. Wild Bill stood there just inside the saloon, hooked his thumbs in his belt and rolled his head from side to side, glaring at everyone in the place. Morgan thought that he looked like a mad old bull trying to decide who he wanted to take apart just for the sport of it.

Wild Bill shrugged, went to the bar for two bottles of beer and sat at the table. Another man came in just behind Hickok and sat at the table across from him. The second man broke out a deck of cards and dealt a hand.

A minute later the barkeep came up and talked with Wild Bill for a moment. He shrugged and when the barkeep signalled two more men came over and sat in on the poker game.

Morgan had heard a lot about Wild Bill Hickok over the years. He had lived through some of the toughest, roughest times of the wild West. He had stood out there offering any fast gun the chance to come into town and beat him to the draw. Unlike most of the tough gunfighters of the day, Wild Bill had come through such confrontations still alive.

That was when Morgan remembered something. He'd read an item that Wild Bill told a reporter once. It was to the effect that any gunfighter had to protect his back at all times. "You don't sit down in the middle of a room unless you know who's behind you and who can get there," Wild Bill had said.

Morgan scratched his jaw and wondered about it. That must have been in the old days. Wild Bill was just another claim owner here, not out to gun down half the town. Still it didn't seem right, Wild Bill Hickok sitting there in the middle of a saloon with ten or 15 men behind him, and most of them wearing guns.

Wild Bill said he always sat with his back to the wall

whenever he sat down or got his back aimed at a safe place when he faced off against somebody.

Morgan finished his beer, and the conversation in the saloon came back up to normal level. The gunfighter's poker game seemed to be going well, but Wild Bill never took off his hat. He was from cowboy country and cowhands always wore their hats inside as a kind of a mark of distinction.

The man in Deadwood behind the killings still eluded Morgan's best figuring. It could be the sheriff covering up everything and taking a cut of all the cheating in the saloons. Maybe Vanderstone found out the Marshal was taking payoff money from the saloon owners so they didn't get in trouble. Maybe.

Maybe Wild Bill would miss the next time he was called out in a gunfight. Maybe, but not likely.

Morgan lifted his second beer and found himself looking at a man who moved slowly across the room. In another six paces the dark haired man with a moustache would be directly behind Wild Bill. Morgan lifted an eyebrow. Half a dozen people had crossed behind the wild one. But this man seemed different.

He wasn't a tall man, he had a revolver on his thigh as most men in the place did. He took two more steps, then drew his six-gun and before Morgan could more than start to draw his own weapon, the small man's revolver went off with the muzzle not more than an inch from the back of Wild Bill Hickok's head.

The gambler-gunfighter's body slammed forward until his head thunked on the table, splattering the paper money, coins and cards that lay there. All three of the other players were showered with bone fragments and blood and froth of brain cells.

The man who had fired the shot turned and sprinted

out of the saloon. Half a dozen men stormed out behind him, caught him and subdued him without another shot being fired.

Morgan went over to the table where Wild Bill lay. He touched the artery in the side of his neck. There was no sign of a heartbeat. With a big caliber bullet like that through the head, it could only result in instant death.

The saloon was a bedlam of excited men yelling and talking. Nobody else touched the body. The man who was Wild Bill's friend, Charley Utter, sat there staring at his dead friend as if he couldn't believe it. Wild Bill's hand fell face up . . . aces and eights, a dead man's hand.

It took the marshal five minutes to arrive. He looked at the body, took down some statements and stared at the killer who had been dragged back to the saloon.

"What's your name," Marshal Quentin asked.

"McCall, Jack McCall."

"Did you shoot Wild Bill Hickok here?"

"Hell, no."

The men in the saloon gasped. The Marshal took McCall away. At the door he turned. "Notice is given, this man McCall will have a fair trial tomorrow starting at ten A.M. in this saloon, it being the biggest open-spaced building in town. Any witnesses here should come tomorrow so you can testify."

Morgan watched while the undertaker draped Wild Bill's remains in a wheelbarrow and rolled him away to the morgue.

During the past few days Morgan had heard rumors that the Mining Committee might hire Wild Bill and his friend as the new marshal in town to clean out the graft and corruption.

Somebody must have encouraged McCall to do the job. If he did it so blatantly, he must be sure that he wouldn't hang. That would mean someone with a lot of power in town. Who?

Morgan didn't go back to his table. He'd seen enough for one night. The rest of the beer would be flat by now anyway.

Suddenly he wanted to talk to Star. He knew he couldn't, but it was an urge that surprised him. She was a whore. But she was also a talented artist. He had to get her out of there and to Chicago as soon as he could. She had too much talent to remain buried here.

He slanted across the street and down past the general store to the Andropolis Cafe. It was just closing.

Alexandria came running to him.

"Is it true? Did somebody murder Wild Bill Hickok?"

Morgan nodded.

"Were you there? Tell me about it."

He told her about the killing, but only after the cafe closed. Alexandria cried, then kissed his cheek and told him she just couldn't get into his bed tonight. She was too upset.

Morgan patted her shoulder, went to the storeroom and had a good night's sleep.

Chapter Nine

While Morgan settled down to sleep, Lash Kincaid was just getting to work in earnest. He sat in his softly lighted room over the near side of the Moneytree Saloon and watched the gamblers below. He viewed them through a series of small slots along the top of the saloon wall. They provided Kincaid and his other two watchers with a perfect place to see poker hands, to catch other men cheating on cards, and generally to regulate the activity below.

Tonight had been an exception. That fool Jack McCall had gone against all of his instructions and killed Wild Bill Hickok in the worst possible place and time, and with 30 witnesses. The man was an idiot, but he must be protected and he must not be convicted. The man would bellow out everything he knew through his broken nose if he were facing the gallows.

Dammit! why did he pick a stupid loser like McCall for a delicate job like killing Hickok?

Kincaid pointed to two men who sat near the back of his office. "You two. Get down there and slide into that four man poker game and the one with five men. I've got one player in each game. I want you to bid up the hands the way you usually do. If you have a good hand, drop out, you kow the tricks. Just don't make it so damn obvious. Now move."

Kincaid talked next to his manager who worked the Golden Nugget Saloon. The man had on a gambler's vest and suit and string tie. He came in when called.

"Henderson, you know what you're supposed to be doing. We want to get paid in gold dust, at sixteen dollars an ounce, and you have your barman weigh it right out of the poke. You can spill some and make sure the girls don't get away with too much with wet fingers into the poke. You can get an ounce and a quarter every time if your people work at it.

"You haven't been producing enough there, Henderson. The miners work hard for a week, when they come to town they want entertainment, girls, and liquor and games of chance. Give it to them, and be sure every man leaves with an empty pouch where his gold used to be. Now get out of here."

When the last man left, Kincaid threw a paperweight at another door and yelled. "Star, get your pretty little ass in here. We've got business to talk."

Star came in. She wore a modest dress this time and her hair was in a big braid down the side of her head.

"Don't like that damn braid, told you that."

"It's easier to keep clean this way."

"What did you find out from that Morgan guy? I told

you to go talk to him. Took long enough. You fuck him, too?''

''You don't have to worry about Morgan. He doesn't know a thing. He's harmless. This widow asked him to find her husband, but he can't and he's about ready to leave town. Don't think it is worth the trouble to try for him any more.''

''He doesn't suspect what happened to Vanderstone, then?''

''Suspect? No. He doesn't have any idea. He thinks somebody probably killed him to get his claim. He's even working the claim now to take money to that guy's widow. He's a real dumbbell. Harmless as a kitten.''

''Then how come he's killed two of the men I sent out to kill him?''

''Just luck, I'd say. He's getting scared too. My guess he'll be gone in a few days.''

''Good.'' Kincaid struggled to lift his bulk to the chair and smiled at the girl. ''You do fine work, Star. I'm gonna get you them new dresses I promised you, three red ones. Damn, but you look good in red. Come here.''

She walked toward him. He pulled her up to him and his hands grabbed both her breasts.

''Mighty fine. Tits don't have to be huge to be good. I always say that. I should give you a good poke right now. A mouth poke, but I don't have time. Got my men coming in from the other three saloons. Sometimes I think I'm working too hard.'' He fondled her breasts a little more, then pulled his hand up her leg and rubbed her crotch.

''You run along now, I've got to work. Don't worry about Morgan. He won't bother us any more. I've got plans for him.''

Star watched him a minute, shrugged and went out the door trying not to sway her bottom the way she used to do to attract the cowboys in the saloons.

Five minutes later Kincaid had adjusted his 300-pound body on the specially reinforced couch and stared sullenly at a man who stood in front of him.

"I really hate to do this, LeFevre. You've been a good worker for me, but I can't allow this to happen."

The man was shaking. He had dropped his hat and stood there, sweat beading his forehead. His glance went to the door, but he knew there was someone outside. He saw the man inside with one hand near his six-gun. There wasn't a chance in hell for him to pull his hide out and get away.

"You stole from me, LeFevre. Stole gold. I know it's tempting, but it's *my* damn gold. I found that bag with twenty ounces of gold in your room. That's over four hundred dollars, LeFevre. That's a hundred day's wages wading in the creek panning for gold or digging gravel on a claim. You know I can't let this happen and go unpunished. Twenty, maybe twenty-five of my people know about it. What do you suggest that I do, LeFevre?"

"You got back the gold. Fire me and send me out of town on the stage."

"I could do that. But you wouldn't remember it long. Hold up your left hand, LeFevre."

The man did. Kincaid nodded. The man who had been standing at the door walked over to LeFevre, grabbed his arm and pulled him to the edge of Kincaid's heavy oak desk. The big guard forced LeFevre's hand down on the desk. Then he doubled back all but the man's little finger and left it extended on the heavy desk top.

"Noooooooooooooooooo!" LeFevre bellowed.

Before he could jerk his hand away, Kincaid swung down sharply with an eight-inch fighting knife. The heavy weapon cut through flesh and bone and sank a quarter of an inch into the desk.

LeFevre looked at his severed finger and fainted.

Kincaid snorted. "Damn thief will never forget what happens when you steal from Lash Kincaid. Bandage his finger and get him out of here."

He looked at the severed finger on the front of his desk. Tomorrow he would put it in the sun to dry and then add it to his collection. This would be the fourth.

He just had the blood washed off his desk when Big Betty came in. She was his kind of woman, bulging and generous wearing tight clothes to make her bulk look even greater and easier to see. She came through the door and straight to him. She popped one huge breast out of her dress and lowered it gently to his mouth. Kincaid's mouth opened automatically.

"Yeah, that's how I like to talk to the boss. Get his mouth busy as all fuck so he doesn't interrupt me. Lash, I need three more girls. One got pregnant, one sneaked out and ran away on the stage dressed like a boy, and the other one I sent to Rapid City to get married.

He spit out her breast and glowered. "Told you we don't let none of them go. Damnit!"

"Look, when I signed on with you, I said if one of my girls gets a chance to get married, I help her. I don't want them all winding up sagging and poked out and alone like some people I know. I don't compromise on this one. You want to suck my sugar tit, you let me have this one favor."

He got both his hands on her bare breasts and sighed. "Oh, hell, all right. I'll put in an order for three more girls from Chicago. How about a China girl and a black?

Lend a little variety."

"Hell no, they don't carry their share. You want some slant-eyed pussy, you buy one yourself and give me back Star. She's the best fucker I've ever had."

"Maybe, in a few months. Any other problems?"

"Yeah. I want you to hire a guard, some muscle who can use a gun and a knife for when one of the customers goes crazy. One of my girls got beat up last night. I want somebody six-four and two hundred and fifty pounds who can fight."

Kincaid chuckled. "Just the right size for you, Big Betty. If I get one, I don't want you fucking him to death. Twice a week he gets his poon free. After that he pays the way anybody else does."

"Agreed. Find me one today. He can live in one of the back rooms. I want him on call twenty-four hours a day."

"Except when he's punching out your pussy."

Betty laughed. "You ain't done me a poke lately. You got time right now?" She lifted her heavy skirts to her knees, then up her heavy legs until he could see her silk bloomers.

"Woman, get your legs out of here. I got work to do."

She giggled. "Almost had you there. If I hadn't worn my bloomers it would have worked."

He slapped her on the bottom and she laughed again as she waddled out the door.

Kincaid settled down to his serious work. He called to the man outside the door who opened it and looked in.

"Bascomb here yet?"

"Yes sir."

"Send him in."

Bascomb was a slender man with a dark brown

business suit, white shirt with starched collar and a string tie. His hair was slicked back and he wore half-spectacles perched on his nose.

He walked in, sat down across the desk and opened a briefcase.

"Difficult," Bascomb said without any preliminaries. He stared at Kincaid. "Damn difficult. There were twenty-six witnesses to the shooting. Of course, some had their backs to the scene. Others were playing cards. Still, there must have been eight or ten who saw the whole thing."

"So get to the jury. There's always three or four who will take fifty dollars to vote for acquittal. In this Miner's District it takes a unanimous vote of the jury to convict. You'll be defending Jack McCall. I want you to get it done quickly, tomorrow if possible. Then we'll get McCall out of town."

"You could have a lynch mob break McCall out of jail and hang him. That way he wouldn't have a public forum. In an hour it would be over."

"No, no mob rule," Kincaid said sharply. "Legal and proper. Just pick a jury with enough men on it you can bribe. That's the defense. Make it short and quick. Now get out of there and line up your jury."

Bascomb sniffed. "Mr. Kincaid, I didn't go through two years of reading for the law under Judge Bromfield. . . ." He stopped. "What the hell," he muttered, closed his briefcase and marched out of the office.

Kincaid looked at the guard. "Where is Streib?"

"Still in the holding room," the big guard said.

"Let's go down there."

The guard helped Kincaid stand. He shuffled as he walked to the door, his bulk going through with little room to spare. They went down steps toward the back. When they got to the ground floor they stepped toward the rear and the guard unlocked a room with no windows.

The guard held up a lamp so he could see in the cell-like room.

"Streib, on your feet," the guard growled.

A man with a suit and a fancy vest stood up. He was haggard, unshaven and evidently had been in his clothes for more than a day.

Kincaid waddled into the room and leaned against the wall. He stared at the prisoner for a minute.

"Streib, I'm disappointed in you. I trusted you. For almost a year you ran the Golden Slipper. What happened?"

"A woman, and I started gambling. My fault. I'll make it up to you. I will!" Streib's cheeks were hollow, his voice rasped. He was pleading and begging and he didn't care.

"Bit late for that now. Half the town knows you cheated me. Can't let that happen. Now and then an example has to be made."

"No! I'll do anything. Just name it, Mr. Kincaid. I'll work for nothing. I'll swamp out the place, wash gold out of the bar cloth, anything."

"One thing you can do for me, Streib."

The man looked up, gaunt, pleading eyes with a hopeful gleam.

"Just name it, Mr. Kincaid. You just name it."

The big fighting knife drove forward, the point biting into flesh, slashing between ribs, slicing through Streib's heart. His surprised eyes looked up in anguish.

"You can die for me, Streib. Die nice and quick and quiet and be found out on the edge of town."

Streib made a wild, inhuman sound in his throat, then his arms fell to his side, his head dropped to one side and he slid slowly to the floor.

Kincaid pulled the big knife out, saw the gush of blood and then heard the death rattle as Larry Streib died. His head slowly rolled to the center and sightless eyes stared straight at Kincaid.

"Clean up this room and get rid of the trash," Kincaid said. He bent and wiped the blade off on Streib's jacket. "One thing I won't tolerate is a cheat and a thief, especially a smart one who gets away with it for so long. You cost me over five thouasnd dollars, Streib. That I don't put up with from nobody."

Kincaid turned and began his slow shuffle back to his bedroom on the ground floor. He was tired. It had been a long day. Now he could sleep until noon and then have a man-sized breakfast and dinner combined. As he moved away he was thinking exactly what he would have his private cook fix for him.

Chapter Ten

Morgan rose early, skipped breakfast and from his hiding spot watched the boarding house where Nance Odell lived. Two men left about seven A.M., then another shortly after that. Nance didn't come out until nearly eight, and he walked directly to the gunsmith and spent a half hour inside talking with the man, evidently getting some work done on a revolver.

When Odell left there, he stopped by at the general store, then walked across the street to the Moneytree Saloon and went inside. Most of the saloons didn't open until ten A.M., but this one evidently did. Maybe some of the regular poker players liked to get an early start.

Morgan watched the place until ten, then went in and settled into a poker game. It was a quarter-limit game so he couldn't lose much. Soon he had checked the rest of the saloon and the blond head of Odell was not anywhere in the big room. That's when he remembered there would be a trial there that morning. The marshal and his prisoner and the mining committee who would stand as judges were late in arriving.

They came about eleven and the trial got underway. Odell had still not shown up. The saloon began to fill up with spectators. The tables were stacked to one side, a jury box set up with 12 chairs, and the prisoner brought in. Three of the Mining District elected directors would act as judges.

Morgan had seen enough rough justice. There were at least a dozen eye witnesses. There was no possible way that Jack McCall wouldn't be convicted of murder and probably hung at dawn tomorrow.

Lee Morgan walked out of the saloon and went to the Deadwood General Store. He bought a half a sackfull of dry food for the claim, threw in some loaves of fresh bread and some fresh vegetables that came in on the wagon trains, and two fresh dressed chickens. Then he carried the sack to the stables. After renting the same horse he had used before, he rode out to Claim Four Above Clear Creek. The work progressed. He unloaded the sack of food and the men cheered.

Earl motioned Morgan aside and spoke quietly. "Had some vistors yesterday. Two gents on horses, both well armed. Both good sized and tough looking. They said they represented the Miner's Protective Association. It only cost $10 a day to join and them that didn't join had no protection from claim jumpers, common criminals and killers."

Morgan grinned. "A protection racket. They're trying to gouge the claim owners for that much? Some of these claims don't pan out that much a day."

"I didn't argue with the gents. Just said I was a hired

hand, they'd have to check back and find you."

"Thanks. Maybe they'll come today and I can 'reason' with them with my forty-five. How is the work going?"

Earl showed him. They had tried some new gopher holes farther up the bank and at another place where it looked like the stream bed had once been located.

"I swear, the first two pans out of that hole must have had a quarter of an ounce of gold each. Found a nugget twice as big as the other one, and about half flakes and lots of dust. We're working mostly now on that section and going to try to follow that old stream bed. The only trouble is the overburden there is almost five feet. We're thinking of tunneling along the old stream bed."

"Sounds good. You're making yourself some money here, Earl. Do you think we should put in a sluice box?"

"Probably. Only thing that would be eating up the profits. Take another man at least to run the box right. We'd need a long box here, say thirty feet. That means we have to move the pay ore to the top of the box to get it washed all the way down. We'd need two more men and two wheelbarrows. They're as hard to find around here as egg-sized gold nuggets."

"But couldn't we work a lot more gravel and sand quicker that way?"

"Yep. But put an inexperienced man on the gate at the head of the box and he could let in too much water and wash all the gold behind the riffles right back into the creek."

"Think on it, we'll decide next couple of days. Now, let me get to work and earn my keep. What do you want me to do, dig a gopher hole, tunnel or work with you on the cradle?"

They worked with the cradle the rest of the morning, and put the chickens cooking in a pot over a slow fire. At noon they ate sandwiches of cheese and pickles and the five of them devoured the boiled chicken like it was chocolate candy.

Slightly after one that afternoon, Morgan saw two men riding toward the claim. They called over and they approached.

Morgan quietly asked Earl if they were the same two. Earl said they were. They were as Earl had described. One was tall with a gray hat and a big Navy Colt showing out of leather on his right thigh. The other one held back a little and to the side, evidently as protection.

"You Morgan?" the first man asked.

"Depends who's asking. You a sheriff with a warrant or a wanted on some Morgan?"

The man laughed. "Not a chance. I'm Lester and my friend and I work for the Miner's Protection Association."

"Heard about that." Morgan moved slightly and his right hand dropped to his side near the butt of his revolver. "From what I hear that's nothing more than an illegal conspiracy that thrives upon the timidity of the claim owners."

The man on the horse scowled. "Mister, I'm not quite sure what you just said. But it didn't sound friendly. All you have to do is pay us ten dollars a day and we make sure that nobody bothers your claim."

"You post a full time guard right here on my claim?"

"Well no, we ride a circuit and keep things under control."

"In a pig's ass you do. Can you understand that? All you do is scare hard-working miners into paying you money. You're nothing but a pair of rattlesnakes looking for someone to strike. Get off my claim before I run you off."

The second man started to draw. Morgan's hand darted upward, lifting the butt of the Colt .45 revolver. At the same time his thumb caught the hammer drawing it back to full cock and when the tip of the barrel cleared leather the weapon moved forward, came up and fired.

The second man screamed in pain as the slug drilled into his gun hand shoulder and spun him off the horse, his six-gun flying from his hand.

Morgan's thumb pulled back the hammer cocking it for another round and the muzzle zeroed in on the first man who had started to reach for his big Navy Colt.

Morgan grinned. "Go ahead. I really wish you'd try it. Give me all the excuse I need to shoot you dead right here. Course, then we'd have to drag you away from the stream and dig you under. Wouldn't want your ugly carcass fouling up the stream any."

The tall man on the horse kept his hands well away from his weapon.

"Then I guess you're refusing to sign up for our service?"

"You're a lot smarter than most people say. Lift that Navy out of your holster and drop it on the ground. Now!"

The man frowned, checked the revolver covering him and shrugged. He looked at his partner dazed and sitting on the ground holding his bleeding shoulder. The first man dropped the weapon.

"Now get off your horse and bring your friend up here. Want to make sure he doesn't bleed to death on the way back to town. Take off your shirt and rip it into bandages and wrap up his shoulder. Do it now, sheep shit, before I get unhappy.''

It took the taller man five minutes to cut his shirt into strips and bandage his friend's shoulder.

Morgan watched it all with a grin. ''Now since you're in the habit of robbing the claim owners, we'll reverse the procedure. Strip the saddles off those nags and drop them right here. Do it now because I don't have a lot of patience left with the pair of you.''

''I can't ride bareback,'' the taller one said.

''Easy, walk back to town,'' Morgan brayed.

The saddles came off. The tall one made a move to take something out of his saddlebags but Morgan put a round into the dirt beside his foot and he left it alone.

''Now, both of you shuck out of your clothes. I want you two buck-assed naked in two minutes. Boots and everything. Get it done.''

''Won't do it,'' the already wounded man said.

''Don't matter to me. Then I kill you where you stand. I haven't had the pleasure of killing a rotten bastard like you in two or three days.''

Morgan lifted his revolver and aimed at the man's head. At once the wounded man stripped off his shirt and continued until he was naked.

''Better, much better. Now you gentlemen may leave at your leisure. I'd suggest you move out before I get into one of my unsettled, crazy moods again. Ride or walk, I don't care. You have five seconds to get out of range.''

Both men grabbed the reins of their horses and rushed downstream, running with them until they were 50 yards away. Then the men tried to mount the animals. They couldn't. One found a fallen tree, stepped on it and got up.

Morgan watched them move out of sight, then looked through the saddlebags. He found $30 in cash, three small bags of gold dust and a list of claims whose owners evidently had paid their "dues" today.

"They'll be back, mad as thunder," Earl said.

"Maybe, maybe not. You gents have weapons. Use one man as a lookout, and sleep in the brush after dark. They'll have a lot more trouble to worry about than coming back out here. I'm going to tail them and see who they report to. That pair couldn't come up with an illegal protection racket like this one on their own."

Morgan peeled off pay money for the four men from the cash he'd taken from the strong-arm men.

"That pays us up to today. Earl, you still have your ten percent coming. Keep up the good work."

Morgan took the two saddles and dropped them off in the brush three claims down, then rode until he spotted the two naked men on horseback ahead of him. They were riding slow, and as he watched one screeched in pain and slid off the horse. He walked beside the animal as he kept moving toward town.

Morgan grinned. Riding a horse bareback while naked was no fun, but it was just what this pair deserved. He made sure he stayed out of sight, but the two travelers, now both walking, had no interest in looking behind them. Morgan guessed they were probably trying to figure out how to get some clothes so they could sneak into town.

As it turned out, the two bareback riders found a tent near the edge of town that had a clothesline out. Some miner had just washed his pants and shirts and the naked men quickly stole two pair of pants and two shirts, dressed and rode on into Deadwood.

Morgan followed them. They headed into the alley that went behind the Moneytree Saloon, tied their horses and vanished into a back door. Morgan counted buildings and tents, and rode into the alley and out through a vacant lot next to the tent hotel that was next to the Moneytree Saloon. The two "association men" had disappeared into the Moneytree Saloon's rear entrance.

It seemed to fit the pattern of the saloon that cropped up in half the clues and pointers that he had found. But they were all just clues and not conclusions. He still needed a name.

Star!

She might be more of a help than she knew. She had been there that first day when he confronted Kincaid. She had led him to the street door directly beside the saloon. Kincaid said he couldn't let her go because she "knew too much about him." What did she know? How could he get in contact with her?

He had seen her on the street only once since he had been in town. Once she had contacted him after dark. Maybe he could send her a note. How? If he sent it to her, Kincaid would read it first. Which meant he would have to word it in a way the fat man would not understand.

Morgan went to the general store, bought a pad of paper and three envelopes, and stood at the counter trying to compose the note. He could apologize for the surly way he had treated her in Kincaid's office. That might do it. Kincaid could read nothing into that. But neither would Star. There had to be something in it about art, or painting.

Yes, that might do it. He could say she was pretty as a picture when he had seen her. He'd like to meet her again, perhaps take her to dinner. He could tell her he had met an artist in town who said he'd like to paint a portrait of her in oil, but he didn't know how to meet her.

Yes, that would do it. She would figure out that he wanted to get in contact with her. She would locate him as she had before.

He wrote the message. Morgan read it, changed some parts and wrote a fresh copy. This time he was satisfied with it. He folded it, put it in one of the envelopes and sealed it tightly. Then he wrote her name on the outside, and put it "in care of Lash Kincaid" and hired a small boy for a nickel to run the envelope over to the Moneytree barkeep.

If anyone could get the note to Kincaid, the barkeep must know a way. Slowly it seeped through to him. The bearded man who captured him that first day said Kincaid owned a number of stores and saloons. His office seemed to be directly beside the Moneytree Saloon. It would seem likely that Kincaid owned that saloon. Then did all the tie-in with that saloon mean that Kincaid was the man behind the Vanderstone disappearance and Ray Eastin's murder, and the hiring of Nance Odell and the two "association" protection people?

It was possible.

Almost anything was possible. He had to find out if it were true. Morgan went out of the store and stretched in the early August afternoon. It was August 3, 1876, the day after Wild Bill Hickok was gunned down by cowardly Jack McCall in the Moneytree Saloon in

Deadwood. Morgan figured the day would be a small footnote to history, at least to those who followed the lives and deaths of the famous gunfighters of the American West. But on the other hand, in a hundred years none of those brave and cowardly men might be remembered at all.

He walked the street, watching out for Odell and the pair of naked desperados he had infuriated. He didn't walk the same route twice, and was about to give up and sit in a chair in front of the hardware when a soft, woman's voice called to him as he passed the dry goods store. Star stood just inside and motioned to him.

Morgan turned and entered the store. She smiled, pulled the sunbonnet down over most of her face and whispered that he should follow her. Star went through the store, into the back room and then into the alley.

They walked quickly down the alley to the right, past the general store and to the gun shop where she had her studio. She used a key on the alley door and then they were in her art world.

"I couldn't believe you sent that note," she said. "You must have known that Kincaid would read it first." She smiled. "I did enjoy your references to art. I figured it might be important."

"What did Kincaid say?"

"He laughed, called you a lovesick puppy. Said you just wanted a chance to get my bloomers off. Oh, I forgot. I'm going to be a lady. I can't talk that way anymore."

"But he gave you the note anyway."

"Yes. I told him you were a strange person, and that he didn't need to be worried. Now, what is this all about?"

"I'm not sure. I get all of these clues about Vanderstone's disappearance and it seems to center on the Moneytree Saloon. Do you know who owns it?"

"Of course I know, why didn't you ask me before."

Chapter Eleven

Morgan laughed softly as he watched the pretty blonde girl. ''I didn't ask before because I wasn't sure I needed to know who owned the Moneytree Saloon.''

''Oh,'' Star said. ''Kincaid owns the Moneytree, his office is just to the side of it and he has viewing slots to look down in the place below. He can see everything that goes on down there.''

''Kincaid. That would answer some questions. Do you know if Kincaid had Vanderstone killed?''

''I heard them talking about doing it. The man was coming to see Kincaid one evening and Kincaid told two men to take him down the back stairs and get rid of him. I didn't actually see them do it. Vanderstone was supposed to wind up in a filled-in gopher hole on some mining claim.''

''Did one of the killers have a black beard?''

"No, the two evidently were supposed to leave town the next day heading for Denver."

"Well, that takes care of that. The only problem is I can't prove it."

"Proof isn't all that important in this town. Did you know that Jack McCall got acquitted of killing Wild Bill Hickok?"

"No. Not a chance."

"He did. They had the trial this morning. The jury was deadlocked and finally voted for acquittal."

"Somebody bought off the jury."

"Probably, but that's hard to prove as well." Star watched him. "So what are you going to do now?"

"Not sure. I guess my job is done for the widow. I found out what happened. But I hate to leave with work to be done yet. Kincaid has to pay for the killings. He's been behind more than one, I bet."

"Getting him charged with murder wouldn't do much good in this town the way the court works," Star said.

"The man buys whatever he wants. He made one mistake, he can't buy me." Morgan reached down and kissed her cheek. "Thanks for coming, you helped me a lot. I'll get this little problem taken care of with Kincaid, then I'll get you out of here and on your way to Chicago. Hang on for a few more days."

"Don't worry, I will. I can now. I better get back before he misses me." She stretched up and kissed his lips gently, smiled at him and went to the door. He walked her through the dark streets to the alley behind the Moneytree drinking establishment. She unlocked a door and slipped inside.

Morgan walked a side street back to the cafe. He was trying to work out a plan to get Kincaid. The best way would be to cut down his gunmen. The blond killer would be first. He could nail him when he left the boarding house in the morning. It was one idea. He'd have more.

The cafe was still open. He hadn't eaten since that noon at the dig. Inside, Alexandria grabbed him and sat him down at a table and brought him the special dinner of the day. Fried chicken. They weren't very busy and she sat with him eating a piece of her own homemade apple pie.

"You've been busy lately, Morgan."

"Yes, the claim and my other business."

"You never did tell me all about it."

"Too complicated."

"We've got all night. We're about ready to close up. Yep, it's time. I'll close the flap on the front. Then we have a half hour of cleanup. You want to help?"

He did.

Twenty minutes later Morgan and Alexandria were in the storeroom with the door flap tied shut and locked. Alexandria pulled off her blouse and tossed aside her chemise and shook her shoulders so her big breasts rocked and rolled and jiggled. She grinned at him.

"Tonight I want to get fucked until I'm exhausted!"

Morgan reached for her breasts. He didn't know how such a slender girl could produce such big ones. At that moment he didn't care.

They stretched out on the cot and tore off clothes. She pulled his face down to one of her breasts and he chewed on it.

"Oh, yes, now that does feel fine." She laughed softly. "Morgan I've got news for you. I think I'm pregnant."

He came off her breast. ''Congratulations, but it wasn't me. I just got here a few days ago.''

''Don't matter, I'm picking you as my husband.''

''Does matter. Pick the one who made you pregnant.''

''How can I tell?''

''That many?''

She shrugged. ''A girl's got to have fun while she can, before she gets big and fat with six kids. My pa says you're the one and he's got a shotgun.''

''Doesn't matter, I've got a six-gun and it shoots quicker than a shotgun. You want a husband or a dead father?''

''Don't tease me.''

''I'm not.'' He pulled her cotton bloomers off and she squealed in delight.

''Be rough with me. I kind of like it when you get a little tough and make me do things. Tonight I'll do anything that won't hurt me.''

Morgan caught her face in his hands and kissed her lips with a hot demanding open mouth, then he left her lips and pulled her head down to his crotch.

''Eat me,'' he said, his voice husky with anticipation. She nodded and went down, letting his erection slip into her wet mouth, tonguing him at first, then taking in more and more of him. Slowly she began to bob up and down on him. It excited him more than he wanted to say.

Her motion caught him by surprise and soon his hips responded moving only a few inches each way as he thrust into her willing mouth deeper and deeper until she made a noise and came off him a little.

She murmured at him and he moved again, the excitement of her sucking him off building and building.

Almost before he knew it the flood gates released and the juices were driving down the tubes. He pumped at her harder and then again and again and again as he exploded, jetting his jism into her throat.

She swallowed automatically, then when he slowed she sucked on him, milking him of every drop of his cream, licking the last as she came away from him. Then she kissed him and he could taste his own cum on her salty lips.

He eased down on the cot. She nibbled at his man breasts and then went to work with her hands. Soon he felt a stirring in his loins and then he was coming to life again.

A moment later he was fully erect and ready.

"Damn, you have talented hands," he said.

She giggled and pushed him on his back and spread her bottom over his crotch. Holding his erection straight up, she lowered herself, found the right spot and then slid down his pole as it lanced upward into her open slot.

"Oh, glory! That feels so good. A man just never can know how good it feels. Just wonderful, like I want to stay here all night with you sliding up my little cunt. It's the best. Women who say they don't like to fuck are just fooling themselves. They've got to let go and relax and have some fun."

She squeezed him then with her inside muscles, and he responded. Slowly she began to lift and drop on him, then she leaned forward over him and began rocking forward and back. It was like she was riding a bronco on the range. She kept up the rocking motion and bent forward dropping a big breast into his mouth.

"Chew on me, honey, chew my nipples right off!"

She increased the tempo and she moaned with each thrust. He responded by pumping his hips upward with each thrust and soon they set up a rhythm that powered them along faster and faster.

"Oh, God, I'm going to explode!" she wailed. Her face got red and her chest flowered crimson and her hips bucked as the first tremors of the orgasm rattled through her. Then she was panting and wailing and pumping at him so hard he couldn't keep up as the climax tore through her again and again, shaking her long, lean body like a leaf in autumn, sending shock waves through him and turning her into a trembling, gasping bundle of motion.

The last of the tremors powered past her and she pushed back her legs and dropped hard on top of him, her breasts crushing against his chest, her chin nestling just below his shoulder.

"God, I'm gonna die!" she breathed. Then she panted, sucking in enough breath to replenish her fatigued system.

She lifted her head and blew on his face until he opened his eyes. "Hey, sexy man. I'm gonna remember this night a long time. After I'm married with three or four brats running around screeching at me, I'll think of tonight and I'll smile. Gonna do it all tonight. All three holes." She fell back and continued her recovery.

They sat up ten minutes later and stared at each other in the dim light of the kerosene lamp.

"You recovered yet?" she asked.

"Enough. You have any ideas?"

Alexandria grinned. He moved his hands over her body. She was a sturdy girl, a little lanky at five-six, with big bones but nicely formed and with those incedible tits. Her dark hair was now moist and framed her face. Her dark eyes smiled at him.

"Ideas, yeah, I have some ideas." She got up on the cot on her hands and knees. "Top hole. I never had it in my little asshole. You take the cherry off my ass and poke me good."

He watched her. "You sure?"

"Fucking sure. Now do it."

He needed little encouragement. In the heat of battle he'd been this way a time or two before, but not often. Entry was slow and then he was in and she groaned a moment, then wailed in rapture.

"Glory, now that is low-down, dirty fucking! I've never felt anything like that before. Easy, easy, you feel like you're about ready to explode already."

She moved gently and he added a little motion. He quickly climaxed, dumping his load deep up the wrong tube. She lowered down to the cot and held him inside as he came down on her back.

"Nice," she said. "Unusual, but nice. Not an every-time fuck, but good to know about. You sure got off in a hurry."

Morgan didn't respond. All he could do was smile and rest.

They sneaked out to the kitchen for a snack about midnight, then came together twice more before morning. When he woke up, she was gone. Cooks always get up early.

Morgan turned over and had another nap. It was almost seven before he awoke. He got up and shaved in the cold water and then dressed. Now that had been a night, a real three-way affair. He grinned and slapped some bay rum and witch hazel shaving lotion on his face, then went in for breakfast.

Alexandria was radiant. She brought him her choice

for his breakfast: three eggs sunnyside up, a big pile of grated potatoes fried to a soft brown, three half-inch high hot cakes and hot syrup, six slices of bacon and three rounds of pork sausage, besides toast, jam and coffee.

"You want anything else," she said.

He grinned and whispered. "Yeah, but we can't eat it here."

She laughed. "Last night was the best fucking session I've ever had, even my very first," she said in a whisper. Then touched his shoulder and went to take orders from six men who filled the rest of the counter.

She wouldn't let him pay for breakfast. He told her he'd see her soon and went out to watch for Nance Odell. This was the morning he'd settle up with the man for killing Ray Eastin and for sending a shotgunner after Lee Morgan. The law clearly couldn't function in this town, so somebody had to be judge, jury and executioner. He kind of liked the idea, especially if it led to getting Kincaid in his sights.

He walked down Main Street heading for Odell's boardinghouse when he heard a click behind him as a gun hammer cocked. Morgan's instant reaction was to dive to the left behind a horse trough just before a shotgun blasted behind him.

Birdshot stung his calves and ankles but not enough to stop him. He pulled out his six-gun as he drove and now edged it over the top of the heavy plank water trough. Then he fired a slug at the man who carried a shotgun and rushed toward the general store's front door. The round hit the bushwhacker's right arm, jolting the weapon from his hand.

Morgan came up running and grabbed the man before he could recover and get away. He twisted the killer's left arm behind his back and marched him on through the general store and out the back door, then down the alley and past a few tents and buildings into the pine woods.

Morgan hadn't said a word yet, and neither had the bushwhacker.

Once they were out of sight of the buildings, Morgan slammed his six-gun down across the gunman's head, smashing him to the ground.

"Why?" Morgan asked.

The man shook his head to clear it, and stared up at Morgan. "Why? For fifty dollars, that's why."

"Murder comes damn cheap in this town. You wasted a round and didn't get paid. Who hired you?"

The man looked away without answering. Morgan's gun butt slapped the man's bleeding right arm where the bullet hit.

A scream of pain snarled through the pine woods. The gunman curled up on the ground and bellowed in pain.

Morgan kicked him in the side. "Hell, get used to pain, killer. We ain't halfway even yet. You wanted me dead, so now I want you dead. It just depends how hard it'll be on you and how much pain you suffer."

Dark eyes turned and stared at Morgan. "You can't just kill me in cold blood."

"Like you tried to do to me? Shoot me in the back with a goddamn shotgun?"

The dark eyes looked away.

"Who hired you?"

"Know I can't tell you. You're a gunman who's been hired. You know I can't say."

"Take it to the grave if you want to. I got a good idea, anyway. But I do enjoy a little old-fashioned torture. You ever see the way the Comanche's torture a white man? It's an art with them. Damn, but they are good at it.

"I think I'll spread eagle you on the ground faceup in the sun, then I'll cut off your eyelids. Yeah, they'll bleed some, but before long you won't even notice that pain. After about half an hour you'll be sun blind. I could let you up then and use you for target practice, but you'd just run into trees and fall down and it wouldn't be no good sport at all."

"Hey, what if . . . what if I told you?"

"Never can tell. You tried to kill me. Gets a death penalty where I come from. But you might get lucky. Oh, I don't turn anybody over to the local marshal. Jury system don't work here in Deadwood. Somebody buys off the jury."

Morgan nudged the man's leg with his boot. "Who hired you, backshooting bastard?"

"Oh, damn, he'll kill me sure as hell."

"He might not. I get my hands on him he won't travel far. Who was it?"

"If I tell you, you'll promise not to kill me?"

Morgan tapped the bullet hole in the man's right arm with his six-gun barrel bringing a scream of pain.

"You're not the one setting the conditions here. Who hired you?"

"Oh, god. It was Odell, Whitey Odell."

"Nance Odell?"

"Yeah, but don't call him that, he hates that name." The man looked up at Morgan, his eyes pleading for his life. Morgan squatted down beside him.

"Sit up."

The man did.

"Let me look at that arm." Morgan took the man's

arm, held the elbow on top in one hand and his wrist in the other and brought the arm down hard across his knee. Both arm bones broke with a crack and a white spear showed through the bloody flesh. The bushwhacker fainted into the mulch of the pine forest floor.

Morgan snorted, let him fall back. He'd live, come to and get to the doctor. Right now Morgan was going to find Odell and put an end to this kind of threat.

Chapter Twelve

By the time Morgan walked back to Main Street it was only a little after eight A.M. Odell probably wasn't even up yet. Morgan stopped and looked at the buckshot marks on his legs. Only one of them had broken the skin. Most had been deflected by his heavy jeans.

He walked down so he could see the frame house where Odell took room and board and waited behind three small pine trees. It wasn't a long rest for him. Odell came out just past nine and headed downtown. Morgan came to his feet at once and angled to cut him off before he got to Main Street.

Odell didn't notice Morgan until the two were less than 40-feet apart. Odell stopped, his hand moving low near his gun. Morgan had been carrying his hand low from the start of his walk.

"Just had a short conversation with your shotgunner,

Odell. He's all broken up about trying to kill me on your orders."

The man threw back his head and laughed. "He tell you that?" But at the same time Odell's hand snaked up to his six-gun. Morgan moved a hair-trigger of a second faster and his six-gun went off before Odell's did. Morgan's bullet caught the gunman in the right thigh and spun him around. His shot went wild.

Odell didn't fall down. He snapped a shot at Morgan over his shoulder and ran for the timber 30 yards away. The pine woods had been cut to build log houses the first year and now had been logged higher off the slope for the whipsaw that painstakingly sawed out one-by-ten boards to make the sluice boxes.

Morgan's second shot fell short as the man was out of range. Morgan chased him. It was an uneven chase from the start. Odell was not a woodsman, he proved that at the first by continually running through the brush and pine woods giving away his position. Morgan moved cautiously, pausing every 20 feet to listen. Odell was running scared, generally heading south toward town. Morgan came out of the woods and ran along the cleared section above houses and the backs of stores. He could move twice as fast in the open as Odell could through the brush. Morgan came up to an outhouse well behind a frame residence and paused behind it.

For a moment he could hear someone running through the brush, then the sound stopped. Morgan looked around the outhouse. Odell stood there facing the brush, panting, his weapon still in his hand.

Morgan came around the small building and lifted his six-gun to cover Odell who was 50 feet away, just in fair range.

"Drop it, killer, or die," Morgan snarled.

Odell turned slowly, started to lift his hands, then pivoted away, and fired as he turned.

Morgan snapped a shot as the man turned, thumbed back the hammer, and the second the man stopped, Morgan fired. The round hit Odell in the shoulder and drove him back. He dropped his weapon and reached for it, but Morgan put another round an inch from the weapon.

"Don't try it," Morgan snapped. He ran forward, pushed Odell toward the woods and picked up the six-gun and shoved it into his belt.

"Move, bastard," Morgan growled. "Into the woods. We're going to play some games and you're it."

"Morgan, I got nothing against you. We even played poker the other night."

"Sure, just after you killed Ray Eastin. Now move or take a slug right here. Your choice."

Odell watched Morgan a minute, lifted his brows and walked toward the woods. He limped badly on the leg where he had been shot.

"Nothing personal, Morgan, just a job to do, right? You're a hired gun. I even heard about you a place or two south of here and in Montana."

Morgan said nothing and poked the muzzle of his Colt .45 revolver in Odell's back.

"Hey, we're both professionals. We do what we get paid to do. Who is paying you to pay back for this Eastin guy?"

"The devil himself is paying me, so shut up."

They walked into the woods until the slope came up too steep and Morgan ordered Odell to sit down.

"What we doing out here?" Odell asked.

"Don't want to scare the women and children with

your screams and your blood. The violence could scar some kid for years."

"Hey, it's business with me. You were an assignment."

"Same with me, Odell. You killed Ray Eastin before I could talk him into telling me what Vanderstone told him. So you became part of my business. Did Eastin say anything about that before you murdered him?"

"Hell no. I wouldn't tell you if I knew. You gonna let me tie up these two bullet holes you put in me? I should get to see the doctor."

Morgan shot Odell in the right knee. The heavy .45 slug shattered Odell's knee cap, burrowed deeper and tore up the knee joint as well as slicing through tendons and cartilage and bringing a long wailing scream of agony from the small killer.

Odell fought against passing out. He steadied himself and looked at his knee. "Bastard! I'll always have a limp now. Fucking bastard!"

"Who hired you to kill me, Odell?"

"Go fuck your horse!"

"Stallions don't like it. Who hired you, Odell. You might as well tell me. You've still got another knee, two ankles, two elbows and two shoulders. I'll have to reload, but what the hell, rounds don't cost that much."

Odell stared at him. Surges of pain twisted his face as he tried to keep from crying out. He moved his leg and screamed until his face turned red.

"Bastard! You should have been easy. How could he miss with a shotgun?"

"He was sloppy. He had to cock the shotgun after I got in range. I heard him and dove away. Right now he's looking for the doctor because he has a compound fractured arm and two bullet holes. You have three. Trying to get an even dozen?"

"Don't know who hired me. Some guy in a saloon."

"No good, Odell. No professional works that way. It's always face to face. You went into the Moneytree Saloon and then up to Lash Kincaid's office and he hired you, right?"

Odell's head snapped up. "How the hell did you. . . ." He stopped. "Don't know what you're talking about. I play poker in the Moneytree."

Morgan grinned and took the stiletto from his boot. He wasn't really a knife man, but sometimes it had its uses. He bent down in front of Odell and drew a thin blood line with the knife across Odell's forehead. Blood formed in the one-eighth inch groove and ran down toward the killer's eyes.

"Let's reason out this matter, Odell. As long as you don't tell me, I go on shooting and carving on your body until it refuses to stay alive. You can't win. Your only choices are to lose or not to win. Pick one and live longer."

"Crazy bastard! When I do a kill I do it clean and quick. None of this torture."

"You think this is torture? Wait until I string you up to a tree by your feet and let your head come down to a small fire built directly under your skull. I'll lower you and raise you by a rope so you'll get the right amount of heat. I saw a guy the Comanche did it to. First his hair burned off, then his ears turned crisp and his eyelashes and brows went. Long before the man died the blood in his brain heated up and when it boiled I guess he died. Blood ran out his ears and nose and mouth. Before they were done, the pressure built up in his skull and it exploded like a melon dropped on a big rock."

Odell shivered.

"Think about it, Odell. I might not be neat but I do get results. Let me find a tree that's big enough and has a limb that goes far enough out that will hold you."

"Morgan, stop it. What kind of assurances will you give me that if I tell you who hired me I can ride out of town with no more wounds?"

"What kind of assurances did you give Eastin? Absolutely none. You die slow if you don't tell me. You tell me and it increases your chances of living for a while."

Morgan felt a growing surge, a feeling he didn't get very often, but one of extreme gratification, a high-spirited emotional lift that came more often when he was dealing with a man like Odell. The man could not live. Morgan had automatically resolved that question before he started the hunt. Now the way of his death became more important.

Morgan lifted his colt and shot Odell in the shoulder, up high where the bullet would churn through the joint itself and inflict more pain. The force of the close shot slammed Odell backwards to the ground. He screamed for two minutes before his voice gave out.

"Bastard! Sadistic bastard!" Odell wheezed at Morgan. The big man sat down on the ground near Odell and took out the stiletto, sharpened it on a small whetstone from a snap case on his cartridge belt, and tested it. Sharp.

He moved the blade toward Odell's cheek.

Suddenly Odell quieted. He blinked the tears out of his eyes and tried hard to control his voice. When he spoke it was nearly in his normal range, but a little whispery.

"All right. The man who hired me was Lash Kincaid."

"Now wasn't that easy? Odell, you could have said that a half hour ago and saved yourself a lot of pain."

Odell looked away. "Now what?"

"What do you expect? Has anyone ever tried to kill you?"

"Guy in Wyoming once."

"What happened to him when you caught him?"

"I killed him."

"Figures."

Odell looked away then, watching the green trees, the grass, the woods he had never come to appreciate.

Morgan's .45 blasted one more round. It hit Odell in the side of the head and slanted upward, churned into his central brain cells and exploded out the top of his head taking a six-inch chunk of skull and brain with it.

Odell slammed backwards and stared at the patch of blue sky overhead with unseeing eyes.

Morgan took two long, deep breaths, and felt the jolting emotional surge slam through him again. He didn't know if he should love or hate the feeling. Now and then it came. Usually he feared it, afraid it was turning him into a maniac who loved to kill.

He stood and walked away. He went through the woods around the town, crossed the trails when no one saw him, and came into Deadwood from the other side of the settlement.

Morgan ambled into the first saloon he came to. This one was almost as large as the Moneytree. It had more tables, and six girls who walked around selling drinks and letting the men pat their fannies.

He paid two dollars for a bottle of whiskey and a glass

and took it to a table where he could sit with his back to the wall. Never again would he sit in the middle of a room. The memory of Wild Bill Hickok slamming forward onto the table from the point-blank ambush would never be forgotten.

He sipped the whiskey, then downed half a glass and tried to understand himself. He was coming down from the high, emotional surge. Sometimes whiskey helped. A girl sat down beside him. She was in her late twenties, plain, flat chested and fading.

"Want to bring the bottle upstairs and let me play with your balls?" she asked.

Morgan drank all but a half-inch of the whiskey in his glass, then poured the rest down her blouse. She didn't even jump, just scowled.

"I guess that's a no, shithead." She left.

Nobody else bothered him. He drank for half an hour, lowered the level in the bottle nearly halfway, and he still didn't feel a bit drunk.

He thought for a moment of the expression on Odell's face as he lay there in the grass with half his head blown off. Not surprise, not resignation, something in between. He deliberately faded the picture from his mind. It was gone. He'd never see it again.

What he had to do now was nail Kincaid. He had guards, Morgan was sure. When somebody found Odell, Kincaid would have twice as many guards. Morgan had to get past them and have a one-on-one with the King of Deadwood. How? He'd figure it out. He picked up the bottle and walked outside. It was not quite noon. He felt sleepy.

Morgan took the bottle and walked up the opposite slope from where Odell slumbered, and found some shade under a trio of good-sized pine trees. He stretched out on the mulch of a thousand years of pine needles and leaves and took a pull on the bottle. It didn't even taste good.

He had to get to Kincaid. How? Morgan yawned. He trembled for a moment, then shivered. After a long sigh, Morgan knew that the emotional surge was past. Now he was tired, extremely tired. He pushed the cork in the bottle of whiskey, set it carefully beside him, and closed his eyes. Yes, he needed a rest. A moment later he fell asleep.

A ground squirrel ran toward him, stopped when he saw the frightening human and sat up on his hind feet for a better view. The human wasn't moving. The squirrel wasn't taking any chances. It turned around and ran the other way, leaving the human thing alone in his slumbers.

Chapter Thirteen

Morgan jolted awake. A shaft of sun bored through the needles of the tall pines and grew hot on his cheek. A small squirrel chattered its defiance of the huge man thing as Morgan sat up and looked around.

He felt fine. The tiredness was gone. The surge of emotion of the killing was past and tempered. When he checked the sun, Morgan decided it was about two in the afternoon. He'd had a two-hour sleep.

Now for the rest of his problem. Kincaid.

He had to move carefully. If the man could hire half a dozen killers, he must control a lot of other people in this town as well. Perhaps a number of otherwise good men who had come under his financial domination. With his money he could buy anything—almost anything.

The Mining District court. How could it have been

rigged so quickly? The jury had been bought. By Kincaid? Why would he want to do that? Then Morgan remembered the rumor that the town might hire Wild Bill Hickok to clean out the riff-raff. Kincaid wouldn't like that. It could have been the fat man who engineered Hickok's killing and the subsequent defilement of the jury system.

Careful was the watchword now for Morgan. He'd be extra cautious where he slept. The woods would be his best bet for the next few nights. It was warm during the day, and the nights were not too chilly yet, even at nearly a mile in the sky.

He started walking back toward town. Morgan had gone halfway when he realized that he wasn't drunk, and didn't have any effect at all from a third of a bottle of whiskey. His anger must simply have burned up the alcohol. He shrugged and continued on to the livery, past Delmonico's toward the center of town. On the Corner of Main and Dakota Streets he saw a familiar face.

Dale Johnson didn't even look up as Morgan stopped in front of him. The man seemed worn out and used up.

"Mr. Johnson."

He lifted his head slowly and blinked. Morgan was surprised by the haggard appearance of the man. His eyes were surrounded by dark circles, his face pinched. He had made no attempt to wash, shave or comb his straggling hair. His clothes were ragged and dirty.

"Oh, yes, hello."

"You probably don't remember me. How is the search going for little Dale?"

"Search? Impossible. They say there's over twenty-thousand people here. I can't look at every one. Thinking about giving up."

"Don't you want to find him?"

"Well, sure, but. . . ." He looked off into the distance and his eyes closed a moment. "Not any chance now."

"Have you had any word at all?"

"Sure. Two men said they saw little Dale. He was with some miners, but the men couldn't remember where or who the men were. I've been to most of the mines up and down the creeks. No luck. One man said some unscrupulous mine owners used young boys sometimes to tunnel in mines because they could get through a smaller hole. Christ! To think that Dale Junior may be worming his way through the ground like a gopher!"

"Tunneling? That would mostly be hard rock deep mines," Morgan said as he tried to think it through. Something nagged at him. "Oh, yeah. Somebody told me that where the overburden is thick over the bedrock, some men do tunneling to bring out the bedrock gravel without having to dig out all the overburden."

Dale Johnson looked up and there was a flash of interest. Then it died and he lowered his head. "I already seen one or two of them. They didn't use my boy."

Morgan had a thought. If Kincaid had any mines, any with a thick overburden, he was the kind of man to find a boy and use him to tunnel.

He touched Johnson's shoulder. "You been eating right, Johnson? You hungry right now? Why don't we go down to the cafe and get a good meal. You'll feel better then. After that I have an idea."

They went to the Andropolis Cafe and Johnson at first said he didn't want anything. Morgan had been in that condition a time or two himself. Johnson was probably out of money and hadn't eaten much the last few days.

He wouldn't be hungry. The smell of food might even make him sick. But he had to eat.

Morgan ordered a breakfast for him, eggs, bacon, fried potatoes, four big thick hotcakes and sausage and six slices of toast. He drank three cups of coffee. When the meal was over, Johnson pushed the hair back out of his eyes. He looked at his hands.

"Suppose before we do anything else I could go down to the creek and wash up a bit? I got dirty somewhere."

A half hour later Morgan walked into the Lost Mining District office with Johnson.

"Mr. Lardner, we've got a problem. Need to know if Lash Kincaid owns any mining claims. I would figure these mining claims are public records?"

"Correct. You can look through but you won't find his name. I checked two or three times. Got me to thinking." Lardner preened a short moustache. "I did some checking and I can give you the numbers of six claims that suddenly changed hands, and the only man in town with enough money to buy them is Kincaid."

Lardner grinned. "I kind of figure that he's not a bosom buddy of yours."

"Not hardly."

Five minutes later the two men left the Lost Mining District office with the numbers of four claims and their approximate locations.

Morgan rented two horses and saddles and they got to the first two mines before three o'clock. One was up a creek close to Deadwood. The overburden was only four feet and they weren't doing any tunneling.

"Looking for a tunnel job," Morgan said rolling a cigarette and offering one to the miner on the site. "Got me a twelve-foot overburden and I want to tunnel, but need to see one in action to see if I could do it."

The miner had been helpful. He told Morgan where another claim was that had a nearly 20-foot overburden.

"I think the same gent owns that one as does this one. They got to tunnel up there. Keep right to the bedrock and bring out that high producing gravel." He gave them directions.

A half hour later they came to a claim that was shown as 24 Above on Willow Creek. Four men worked a sluice box in the stream, and a fifth came out of a tent holding a shotgun. He didn't point it at them but it was in a position to be turned quickly.

"Yeah? What the hell you want?" the shotgun toter called.

Morgan told him about his mythical overburden claim. "So I wanted to see a good tunnel operation and try to figure if I could do it that way myself. You tunnel here?"

"Some," the shotgun man said.

"Mind if I take a look? Do you put in bracing? How big is the tunnel? You keep it floored out right on bedrock, I'd guess. How high is your bedrock gravel here worth working in the sluice box?"

The shotgun man scowled. "Sure as hell got a lot of questions."

A man came up from a gopher hole up the slope about 20-yards. He carried two five-gallon buckets evidently filled with gravel. He went directly to the sluice and set them beside the intake boards.

"I can tell you all you need to know," the shotgun man said. "See them two buckets? Come from about fourteen feet down. We got a tunnel, but it's more a cavern now. Damn near twenty feet square, but the gravel is only good about a foot and a half deep. So we don't build our cave no four feet high."

"Must be hard working down there."

"Sometimes. Now, if'n you're satisfied, be obliged if you'd turn around and get off my claim."

Morgan hesitated and grinned. "Yeah, I understand, but I'd really like to go down your gopher hole and look at the tunnel."

"By damn, no. How many times I got to tell you!" The shotgun man threw back his head and looked at the sky. "Jesus but you are. . . ." he started to say, but when he looked back down, he was staring into the muzzle of Morgan's six-gun.

"Lay the scattergun down careful and then you drop belly down ten feet away on the ground," Morgan said.

The other men were going about their work on the sluice. None of them wore guns.

"Call your men over here," Morgan ordered.

The man on the ground did so, and rather than be angry, the four men above ground grinned when they saw their boss flat on his belly.

Morgan looked at the four. "You men worked here long?"

"About a month," one said.

The others nodded.

"Who you got underground?"

"Little Joe and Wilbur," another man said.

"Call them up here," Morgan demanded.

"Won't come unless Pete there does the calling," the youngest of the four miners said. "Pete warned them about that."

Morgan searched Pete carefully, then ordered him to stand up.

"Bad ass, you're going to go over to the hole and call up the workers below. You do it now, or you get a pistol alongside your head. Is that clear?"

"You're a dead man, bastard," the man called Pete snarled. His face was white with anger and his hands opened and closed into fists. "Whoever you are, you're not about to see another sunrise."

"Prove it."

Pete charged Morgan who calmly lifted his six-gun and shot Pete in the shoulder. The force of the round spun Pete backwards and dropped him to his knees bleating in pain.

"Damn!" one of the miners said.

"Now, Pete, so over to the hole and call up those people."

This time Pete sat down holding his shoulder and refused to say a word.

"Go over and take a look," Morgan told Johnson.

One of the other miners went with him and showed him the hole. Johnson called but got no results.

"Go down and get them," Morgan called. "I'll keep the top side under control." Morgan punctuated the message by firing a round between Pete's legs as the man started to crawl away.

"Stay!" Morgan snapped. "Good dog, Pete. You stay right there like you're on a leash."

Johnson went to the hole and climbed down. They had put a ladder against one side. The gopher hole was four feet across and went down the 14 feet they had talked about.

Johnson vanished and a short time later Morgan heard a screech of delight from the hole.

Pete glared at Morgan. "Bastard, you're dead, you just don't know it yet."

Morgan picked up the shotgun, checked the rounds in the twin barrels. "Double ought buck," Morgan said. "I'm more than willing to see if I can cut you in half with one round instead of two and I will if you keep yammering. Shut up!''

When Morgan looked back at the hole, he saw Johnson surge up the ladder and jump to the top. His face was one glowing smile. A moment later a boy about 12 scrambled up the ladder. He grabbed Johnson around the neck and wouldn't let go. Johnson carried him over to Morgan.

''It's him! It's Dale Junior! How did you know? I've been looking for a week!''

Johnson whispered to his son, pulled his hands apart and set him on his feet.

Dale Junior stared at Pete again and then nodded.

''You're sure, son? We wouldn't want to make a mistake about this.

''He's the one, Pa. He's the one who came to our house in Rapid City and . . . and hurt you and Ma.''

The two of them walked closer to Pete who sat on the ground holding his wounded shoulder.

''I want you to be absolutely positive. You wasn't just scared and now this man *looks like* the one in Rapid City?''

''No, Pa. It's him. He has one gold tooth in front, and he likes to use a knife, and he's as mean as a she bear. It's him all right, Pete Vandercovering. I won't never forget what he looks like.''

''You go back over there, boy, and watch what happens. Usual I tell you to tell the truth and be kind to folks, right?''

Dale Junior nodded.

''I tell you to mind what older folks tell you and to be respectful, and to do good for people. But sometimes bad men come along who don't believe the way we do.

That's the time when the good people have to do bad things, to even up things."

Dale Junior frowned slightly trying to remember it all. He bobbed his head.

"Dale Junior, is that man, Pete Vandercovering, the man who killed your ma in Rapid City?"

"Yes, sir, Pa. He sure is. Pete Vandercovering killed my Ma."

"He's lying!" Pete thundered. "He's just a kid."

"Then he attacked me and left me for dead?" the older Johnson asked.

"Yes, Pa, Pete done that, too."

"Then he kidnapped you and brought you here and made you a mole in the ground in them tunnels?"

"Yes, sir, Pa. I was a mole and a gopher 'cause Pete made me do it or he wouldn't give me any food."

"How much he pay you for your work?"

"Nothing, Pa. Not one cent."

Then it happened so quickly that Morgan wasn't ready. Before another word came, Dale Johnson drew his .44 and fired three times. All three rounds thundered into Pete Vandercovering. One caught him in the chest where he sat and slammed him backward. It drilled through the side of his heart and nearly killed the man.

The second round hit Pete's supine form under the chin and drove upward through his mouth and into his brain, chopping up and shredding his brain cells and nerve paths and blood vessels, killing him instantly.

The third round caught the side of his face, tore half of it off and then the lead slug slanted off into the brush.

"My god!" one of the miners said.

"About Goddamned time," another one said. "I never did like that bastard. He tried to tell us Dale there was his nephew."

"Where does he keep his gold dust?" Johnson asked. "He owes this boy for his labor."

One of the miners showed where Pete had hidden it in the tent under his bedroll. It was a good sized leather poke half filled with gold.

Morgan hefted it. "I'd say about two pounds," Morgan guessed.

"Not enough for what he did to our family," Johnson said.

"He's a hired hand for Kincaid," Morgan said.

"Any more gold dust here?" Johnson asked.

The men shook their heads. "Not that we know of," one of the miners said. "He took it into town every week."

Johnson shrugged. "Guess it'll have to do. Six hundred dollars or so. Not much for a wife and a slave son and all my gun shots and hurts." He sighed looking at the Pete's dead body. "Hell, guess it'll have to do."

Johnson reloaded his six-gun, pushed it back into leather and reached for his son. "Come on, Dale Junior. Time we got back home and put things right again. I've missed a whole bunch of days of putting flowers on your mother's grave."

Morgan handed him the sack of gold.

"Stage leaves in the morning," Johnson said. "We'll be on it." He held out his hand to Morgan. "God bless you, sir. Never would have found Dale Junior without your help."

Morgan took the hand and shook it firmly. "That's what we're here on this green earth for, Mr. Johnson, to lend a helping hand."

They turned back toward town, father and son on one

horse talking quietly. Morgan thought about what he had to do. He still had to get to Kincaid before Kincaid got to him. Just how to accomplish that little task was not at all clear.

Chapter Fourteen

It was dark when the two Johnsons and Morgan rode into town. They turned in their horses at the livery and waved goodbye.

Morgan had a quick supper at the Andropolis Cafe. Alexandria said hello to him, brought him supper and vanished. Morgan was just as happy. He still hadn't come up with any ideas how to settle with Kincaid. He knew the man would have guns out looking for him.

He thought of sleeping in the woods, decided it was the best idea and wandered outside, snaked between tents and hit the yellow pine forest before anyone saw him. He cut a bed of ponderosa pine limbs, then some more thick, green ones for a blanket and lay down. It had been years since he'd been on a pine bough bed. Morgan dropped off to sleep almost at once.

He awoke just at dawn. Some foreign sound roused

him. He didn't move as he came back to consciousness. Only his eyes rotated as he stared around at what he could see. Three feet from him a white-tailed doe nibbled on late shoots of grass. At her side wobbled a small fawn that couldn't be over two or three days old.

It seemed too late in the year for a fawn, but Morgan didn't question it. He lay there concealed by the pine boughs and absolutely motionless as he watched the scene. The doe's ears came up. Her nose quivered. She had heard him breathing. Morgan held his breath and the animal's nose took over as she sniffed. She took a step backward. Her fawn came ahead a tottering step. The doe bleated softly and reached forward with her nose and turned the small fawn around to nudge him away from the strange smell.

She wandered away, nibbling here and there, looking back, sniffing again. Morgan had to let his breath out and breathe again after thirty seconds, but it had been an interesting confrontation.

For a moment he was glad it hadn't been a she bear with a cub. He wasn't sure if the Black Hills had bears. When the doe and her charge had wandered out of sight, Morgan sat up and stretched. Nothing like a pine-scented bed to freshen the whole day.

Morgan had decided what he would do. He had to finalize his arrangements with Earl at the claim. He got a pad of paper and a pen from the general store, bought a five-man tent and some cooking gear, a gunny sack full of potatoes, dry beans, flour, sugar, a dozen eggs and some long lasting food stuff and bundled it all on board his horse.

By eight o'clock he was at the Clear Creek claim Four Above and found the miners hard at work. He called them in and they selected a spot to quickly put up the tent. It even had a floor for it. They put the food inside and vowed they would build a table out of split logs in their spare time.

He sent the other four men back to work and talked with Earl. "We need to finalize and get our agreement in writing. Is it all right the way we talked that first day?"

"Ten percent? Right. And it'll be an honest accounting. My mamma didn't raise no cheaters."

Morgan wrote out an agreement, and Earl admitted that he didn't read none too good, but he signed the paper after Morgan read it to him.

"Be it known to all men. On this sixth day of August, in the year 1876, I, Lee Morgan, acting as agent for Martha Vanderstone of Denver, Colorado, do agree to hire one Earl Handshoe as foreman and general manager of mining claim Clear Creek Four Above, in the Lost Mining District, Deadwood, South Dakota.

"Handshoe is to be paid ten percent of the gold dust mined from said claim. He will deposit gold dust and any nuggets found in the Deadwood bank each Saturday afternoon. An accounting will be sent to the owner of the claim, said Martha Vanderstone, monthly.

"Handshoe is authorized to withdraw ten percent of all monies deposited as his fair share. He is also to be allowed to draw on the funds as is just and reasonable to operate the claim and to pay the four hired workers at four dollars per day.

"All accounting will be kept by Handshoe and sent to Mrs. Vanderstone monthly.

"Agreed to and signed this day, *Earl Handshoe.* Witnessed and agreed to for Martha Vanderstone, *Lee Morgan.*"

Morgan said, "Now we're all legal and proper. I'll

leave you a hundred dollars to use for wages and supplies. You withdraw what else you need from the account. I'll arrange that at the bank tomorrow."

Earl wiped a sleeve across his eyes and turned away a moment. He gave a long sigh.

"Don't rightly know how I got this lucky, Mr. Morgan. But by damn, I'll not let you down. Oh, I never did see anything more of them two that was trying to sign up miners for their protection association."

"I think the two found some other type of employment," Morgan said, and both men laughed.

"Now, let me get a shovel and do some honest work for a change. Where do you want me to work, in a gopher hole or on the rocker?"

"The guys are getting ahead of me with the good bedrock ore. I could use a hand on the rocker."

For the rest of the morning, Morgan worked the rocker, bouncing the gravel around in the box. Throwing out the heavier pebbles and rocks. Washing it down with buckets of water. Then helping to lift the "heavy sands" from the riffles and spin out the gold dust.

After a half dozen pans on the first series of riffles he got better and better at it. He never emptied the pan, just added a little water each time with more of the new heavy sand and swirled out the gold. Twice he found small nuggets.

"Been finding a few," Earl said. "Seems there must have been a real gully washer come through here from time to time, so the larger chunks of gold didn't get so pulverized before they got down this far. Wish we could find a good-sized nugget."

Morgan knew that placer mining is hard, gruelling, repetitive work. By noon Morgan's shoulders ached and he had blisters on his hands. He suggested that Earl buy himself a horse to get to and from town quicker, and that he get some gloves for the men.

About midday, one of the men quit working and went to the small camp and fixed a noon meal. Today it was beans and bacon and fresh biscuits the cook made up from a starter. Coffee, of course, finished the meal.

After that, Morgan and Earl talked again. Morgan had brought out a dozen of the small gold pokes when he came from the store. Now he took the one Earl had been adding to. It had five or six ounces of gold. They were averaging about four ounces of gold a day, Earl said.

"If we can double that, then everyone will make some money," Earl said. "We'll work the best deposits first, then search around for more. By the time we get the best gravel done, we can still get probably two ounces a day from the overburden."

"How long will you work out the claim?"

"Can't possibly get it all done before the freeze comes. Which means we'll have to lay over until spring. I'll let the men go and hire new ones next thaw. I'll get a job in town doing something. I'm a fair carpenter on the side."

Morgan shook hands with Earl and rode for Deadwood. He had to see the banker before he closed.

The banker's name was Spencer Paulson. Morgan showed him the contract with Earl Handshoe.

"Earl will be making regular deposits with you, Mr. Paulson. I'm here to open an account with the first three bags of gold from the claim. Maybe two hundred dollars worth all together. I plan on putting more seed money in the account before I leave town."

"Yes, that would be good. When Mr. Handshoe comes in I'll have him sign some papers to open the account properly. Then too, I'd like one of my people to make a copy of your agreement, without the signatures, of course, just for our records."

It took 20 minutes for all the formalities, then Morgan left the bank.

He went to see Alexandria. It was during the slow time of the day and they should have some time to talk. The dark eyed girl smiled and waved when she saw him come in. She darted into the kitchen and came back with two pieces of cherry pie. She sat down at the counter with him and provided him with pie and a fork.

"Have I got great news for you, Lee Morgan," she said, her dark eyes sparkling, her short hair flouncing around her head.

"I could use some. What is it?"

She lowered her voice. "I found out today that I definitely am pregnant. I feel a lot different already. I'm not all wild to get . . . to have a man as I was. And, best of all, I've picked out a man I really like and who is crazy to marry me. I met him six months ago and liked him then, and two nights ago he came in for some pie and I talked with him and the next night we had a formal meeting. Later, I got into bed with him and it was fantastic. We lasted almost until morning.

"He said right then we had to get married since I might get pregnant. Didn't tell him, of course, and you damn well better not." She laughed softly. "So looks like everyone is happy. Now all we have to worry about is a baby that's two months early, but hell, it happens all the time. Won't be no trouble, not by that time."

"Who is this lucky young man who is getting to play

with those two beautiful, big, bouncing breasts of yours?"

"You might have seen him. He's the son of the woman who owns the general store. His father got killed a few days ago. His name's Wally Eastin, and he's nineteen, and has the biggest—" She stopped and laughed. "Not as big as yours, of course."

They laughed and finished eating their pie.

"I'm really happy for you, Alexandria. You'll make a wonderful mother, and a fine wife. You just keep your little bottom covered up and your knees together, except for Wally, of course."

"Oh, no bother there. I'm not all that wild for it anymore. Having a baby helps quiet a girl down, I guess. At least it seems to be starting that way for me."

He kissed her cheek and she leaned forward and rubbed one breast against his chest.

"Little something to remember me by," Alexandria said. Morgan chuckled and headed out the door.

Now he had to figure out some way to get in touch with Star. He walked down the street, watching every doorway and each alley. Kincaid must have missed Whitey Odell by now and would be gunning for Morgan.

He made it to the gunsmith's shop with no trouble. Josh might have some idea how to get Star to come to her room. Morgan went in, looked over the new Colts, then after a customer left, he asked Josh about Star.

The gunsmith grinned. "Must be your lucky day, young man. She's back there now working on a painting. She wouldn't let me look at it. Probably one of them naked girls."

Morgan thanked him, made sure no one saw him from the street and slipped through the back room curtain and went down the hall to Star's room. He knocked.

A moment later she opened the door and her face blossomed with a smile.

"Hello, nice man. I was just thinking about you."

She was a delight to see again. So fresh and young and ambitious. He stepped inside the room and she closed the door. It smelled of oil paint and turpentine. She held two pieces of charcoal in her hand and waved him forward.

"Take a look at this."

A two-foot-long piece of canvas had been stretched on a frame and sat on her easel. On it was the start of a sketch of a man on a couch. The man was nude.

"Guess who?" Star said.

"I like the costuming," Morgan said and grinned. "Don't let me stop you working. But we need to talk. I want you to tell me everything you know about Lash Kincaid. Where he came from, if he had any trouble before, what he does here, all his rackets and stores and everything."

"Take too long, Lee. I'll just tell you the important parts. He's from Pierre originally. Grew up there, I guess, and never knew his parents. He was a roustabout in a saloon, came up rough and tough. I heard he got run out of Pierre for cheating at cards and trying to start his own gambling house against the town's big boss."

"No law chasing him?"

"Not that I know of. He landed in Rapid City for a month just as the gold strike began over there, but was run out for I don't know what and has been here ever since. Almost a year now. He bragged to me one day that he stole everything he owns. That was what got him run out of Pierre, he said."

"He brag about anything else?"

"Everything. Kincaid is all bluster and scream but he needs to have somebody to talk to, to brag to, to get approval from. That was me."

She turned, holding the charcoal in her right hand and watched him a moment. Morgan realized what a pretty girl she was, with her long blonde hair now loose and flowing around her shoulders. She smiled and Morgan smiled back at her.

"Pretty as a picture," he said. "You should paint yourself."

"Thank you, we all need approval. Oh, Kincaid was wild this morning. His favorite gunhand, Whitey, didn't come back yesterday and he was crazy mean. He said he relied on the man. He's afraid Whitey got killed. Then too, this morning there was a guard at the alley door when I went out. There's never been one there before. I saw four new men all with guns. He introduced me to them so they would know I belonged there. The place looks like an armed camp. He's mad and I think he's afraid as well. Only way I got out was to tell him I had to do some shopping."

"Maybe you won't have to go back."

She looked up quickly. "You mean it? You saying it could be over today?" She ran to him and hugged him and kissed his lips. Then she hugged him again. "You don't know how happy that makes me right now."

"I've been working out some plans to get to Kincaid, but so far nothing fits. I have decided that Kincaid is going to pay for your schooling in Chicago. Does he keep any money on hand? I know he owns the bank."

"He still keeps quite a bit in his office. Maybe five thousand dollars in paper money and gold coins. He's afraid most of the time of something, and having money around gives him a good feeling."

"He keeps it in a safe?"

"Yes, has one built into a wall behind a picture."

"I tried to figure out how we could get him charged with something by the miner's committee. But he'd just bribe the jury again and would be free. I'm going to have to handle the matter myself: judge, jury and executioner." He looked up at her. "Does that bother you?"

"No. He certainly deserves it. I don't know how many men he's killed or ordered killed. I just don't want to watch."

"You won't. Is there a stairway from the Moneytree Saloon up to his quarters?"

"Sure, but he's got a guard there now, too. Oh, something else. One day he told me he was trying to figure out how long Deadwood would be roaring. He said he'll pull out the minute it starts to go downhill. Like if half the miners picked up and went to a new strike.

"He told me just before that happens he'll clean out the bank of his own money and all the cash that everyone in town has on deposit there and take off for Denver or Chicago. He'd do it, bankrupt all the stores and half the miners in the process."

"Good thing to know. I'll have to have a talk with the banker before he can do that."

Morgan stood and paced the six feet across the small room and back. He did that a half dozen times, then sat down again.

"I guess the only way to get Kincaid is the direct approach. Can you get us in the back door, past the guard?"

"I can get in." She grinned. "I could always distract the guard by opening my blouse, let him peek at my breasts."

"Would you? That might be the only way we can catch him off guard. I'll be right behind you."

Star put down the charcoal, wiped her hands, stepped over to Morgan and put her arms around him.

"I just hope this is going to be all over today. I'm getting so tired of putting up with that . . . that animal. And I'm looking forward so much to learn how to paint. It just gives me goose bumps. You're the one I have to thank."

She reached up and kissed him softly, a gentle lover's kiss. He responded and hugged her to him. They clung together for a moment, then she pushed away.

"Is today when we take down Kincaid? I would like nothing better than to get started. How about right now?"

Chapter Fifteen

Morgan hid behind some boxes in the alley as Star knocked on the rear door that led into the Lash Kincaid building. A voice asked who it was and Star answered. A bolt slid open inside and a face peered out. The man saw Star and recognized her.

He smiled. "Yes, miss, I remember you. More than happy to let you in."

He looked around to see if anyone was with her, then opened the door the rest of the way. When he looked back at Star she had pulled apart the sides of her blouse showing both her breasts.

"Figured you deserve a little bonus for being so dedicated a guard," Star said. "Hey, you want to feel them?"

The man stared, his mouth dropped open. He grinned.

Star moved forward a step and he took a half step out the door.

"I can't let you play with me inside, Lash might see. But out here . . . go ahead."

As she said it Morgan eased away from the boxes and came up behind the guard. The sentry had both hands on Star's breasts.

"You must be hard up, Missy. Letting me—"

That was as far as he got. Morgan bounced the butt of his Colt off the guard's head and caught him as he fell backwards. Star closed her blouse and buttoned it, stepping into the small room. Morgan dragged the guard inside and bolted the door. He tied the man's hands behind him with his own neckerchief, and tied his feet together with boot laces.

Then Morgan carried him down the hallway to the first door and pushed him into the holding cell which he recognized as the room where he had been held. He closed the door, put the hasp on and shoved a stick through the hoop.

They ran quickly to the stairs and went up without a sound.

"There must be another man inside his office," Star said. "There was one there this morning. These guys are jumpy so be careful."

At the top of the stairs they went cautiously into the small room and found no one there.

"Right in there," Star whispered pointing to the next door.

Morgan motioned for her to get to the far side of the door and stay there. He had carried his Colt cocked since they started up the stairs. Now he tried the door knob, turning it slowly. It was not locked. He nodded at Star then pushed open the door and jumped into the room, his six-gun in front.

Again his glance evaluated and cataloged the room in one sweeping look: gunman at the far door turning toward him in surprise, Kincaid open mouthed at his desk hands in sight, nobody else in the room.

"Hold it!" Morgan barked. "Freeze, both of you. Not a muscle moves or you get it shot full of holes."

The guard at the far door spun and tried to get a shot off. Morgan's Colt roared and his slug drilled through the man's chest and dumped him against the wall where he slid to the floor. His weapon dropped from his hand and his eyes glazed.

As soon as he fired, Morgan darted his glance at Kincaid.

"I hope like hell you try for that derringer in your desk, Kincaid. That's all the excuse I'll need to blast you four times."

Kincaid overcame his initial surprise. He'd been in a lot of tight spots before. He always won. He stared at Morgan.

"You've been giving me trouble, Morgan. I should have killed you that first day I saw you."

"True, now you're the one almost ready for the undertaker. I've come to settle a few scores. First the widow Vanderstone. You had her husband killed."

Morgan went on talking. He had seen the knob on the door across the room turning slowly. Somebody out there. They had heard the gunshot and come up. The one or two men would be listening.

"What she wants is a cash payoff, a wrongful death fee, if you're legally minded. She told me ten thousand dollars."

Kincaid laughed. "You're crazy if you think I'm going to pay her anything. I've never met the man. You can't prove a thing or you'd have the marshal up here."

"And let you buy off another jury."

The door banged open and two shots fired as it swung to the wall. They had been blind shots, unaimed, for effect. Morgan let the lead whistle six-feet from him, tracked the moving target and fired twice. The lone gunman bursting through the door didn't have a chance to get off another round. He took two rounds in the chest and doubled over, jolting back into the hallway and slamming to the floor.

"Any more distractions around here, Kincaid?"

"Fast, Morgan, damn fast. You should have worked for me, not against me. Now you could ruin everything."

"What's the matter, out of hidden gunmen?"

"Precisely what does it take for a settlement with you?" Kincaid kept his hands in plain sight on top of the desk. His eyes didn't give away anything. He'd be tough in a game of poker, Morgan decided.

Morgan quickly pushed out the brass from his Colt and filled the chambers with four new rounds so he had all six cylinders loaded. He cocked the weapon.

"Settle? First for Vanderstone, then for his friend you had Whitey Odell kill, Ray Eastin, that's another ten thousand. My own fee is ten thousand, which makes a total of thirty thousand."

"Ridiculous, there isn't that much money in town." Kincaid scowled and toyed with a paperweight on his desk. "Hell, I'll give you five thousand to get rid of you. That's your fee, don't worry about the widows."

"Five thousand?" Morgan thought it over. "Why not? Get it!"

"What happened to Odell?"

"Lead poisoning."

"Figured. He was fast, but not that fast."

"How many jurors did you bribe to get that innocent verdict for Jack McCall?"

"McCall was an idiot. Shoot a man with 40 witnesses? Ridiculous. Had to get him cleared. We talked to three, that was plenty. Can I get up and go to the safe to get your money?"

"If that's where the cash is. Paper. Gold is too heavy."

Morgan watched Kincaid closely as he pushed back from the desk and stood. He waddled past one body on the floor to a picture of a dance hall girl on the wall. He swung it outward and turned the knob of a combination lock. He hit the numbers and opened the wall safe door.

Morgan was beside him in an instant and reached into the safe box and took out a derringer.

"Interesting little gun, Kincaid. You weren't going to try to double-cross me, were you?"

"Certainly not. I'm getting the funds. Five thousand in paper money."

Morgan pushed him aside so hard, Kincaid nearly fell. He staggered against the wall.

"Star," Morgan called. She came into the room quickly and went to the safe. She had a cloth bag she had brought from her art studio.

"All of it," Morgan said. He watched Kincaid who stood leaning against the wall, his face beet red with fury.

"Bastard! You're nothing but a common robber."

"Well now, look who is calling me a robber. I'm just finding out about all of the rackets and conspiracies and ways you have in this town to get the gold dust from the miners. You're getting off easy, Kincaid. I could charge you your worthless life. Instead, we'll just relieve you of your petty cash and tie you up. Oh, what about your desk safe?"

Morgan went to the desk and opened the drawer where he had seen the small safe before. It was unlocked. He found another stack of bills, mostly twenties. He shoved them into his pocket.

Star had cleaned out the wall safe. The last was a sack of gold coins, probably double eagles.

"You can't do this, Morgan!"

"Why not? Today I'm a collection agency, satisfying debts owed by you to three women. I collect, pay it to them, take a small fee, and everyone but you is happy. I really don't care if you are pleased or not."

Morgan found some tough cord in the desk and took it. He approached Kincaid who was seething. His face was still flushed red.

"You want to get on the floor, Kincaid, or do you want me to knock you down like I did the first time we met?"

Kincaid leaned against the wall and slid down to the floor. Morgan tied him, hand and foot, but not too tightly. He counted on the big man getting away and making a try for the bank. At least that's what Morgan would do if he was in the fat man's big shoes.

"There, that should hold you until one of your flunkies finds you." He looked at Kincaid. "You're just a beginner at this sort of thing, Kincaid. You'll either get better or die young, I haven't figured out which one yet for you. Enjoy the rest of your morning."

Morgan touched the brim of his hat, took the heavy

sack of money from Star and they walked out the door and quickly down the back steps. The lock was still on the cell door. They hurried out the rear and into the alley, then rapidly down the street to the gunsmith and into her room. Morgan took out $500 in paper currency from the safe loot, rolled it up and put it in his pocket.

"Now, we leave the rest of the money here and go see my new friend Spencer Paulson, Deadwood's friendly bank manager. I might just promote him today."

They walked into the bank and the manager stiffened when he saw Star. She stared back at him and Morgan motioned him to one side.

"Mr. Paulson, your bank has problems. Mr. Kincaid, the owner, is about ready to come charging over here and rob his own bank. My guess is that he's going to take out all of his own money, and then steal every dime your depositors have left with you for safekeeping."

"I don't understand," Paulson said. "Why would Mr. Kincaid steal from his own bank?"

"Because Kincaid is a liar and a cheat, a robber, a killer, a man who swindles the gold from the miners and sends them back to the creeks. Forget the innocent act, Paulson. I know and you know that Kincaid owns the bank. We also both know that he's robbing everyone blind in this town. If you don't want to get painted by the same brush, I'd suggest you listen to my solution."

Paulson motioned them into his small office.

He touched his moustache, wiped at his hair, touched a handkerchief to sweat that had beaded quickly on his forehead. "You mentioned a solution, Mr. Morgan."

"Yes. Take most of your cash from the safe and put

it in cardboard boxes in the storeroom, hide it under trash, under forms and equipment, anything so Kincaid can't find it. Leave maybe twenty thousand in cash in the teller's cages and in the safe. Is that about what his share of the deposits would be?"

"Maybe twenty-five thousand. I keep good track of his worth."

"You won't be risking a thing. I figure Kincaid will come in here with three men, well masked, and take out every penny he can find. Or he'll invent some excuse but he'll take all the money in the bank. Then my bet is that Mr. Kincaid will attempt to flee the county and probably the territory. Now wouldn't it be much better if he took only his own money and didn't plunge every store and depositor in the area, including you, into bankruptcy?"

Paulson thought about it a moment, nodded and excused himself.

When Morgan and Star left the office and went into the bank, they found all but one of the employees quickly taking closed boxes into a storeroom at the side of the bank. Morgan went to the teller still working and deposited $500 to the Martha Vanderstone account. The clerk looked it up, nodded, took the money and gave Morgan a receipt.

By the time the transaction was completed, Paulson came up to them. Now sweat ran down the side of his face.

"We've done it. As you say, if nothing happens, we can move all of the money back into the safe anytime in the next week." He frowned. "How do you know about this sudden turn of events?"

"I have inside information. We just left Mr. Kincaid,

and he was upset about the state of his business ventures here in town. My guess is that he'll be here just after you close. It might be good to get your workers out of the bank as early today as possible."

Morgan nodded, took Star's arm and they walked out the front door.

"Will it work?" she asked.

"If it doesn't, no loss. If it does, the good people in town will be protected." Morgan snorted. "Damn but I am starting to feel righteous. What a strange feeling! I'll have to do something about that."

Morgan took Star back to the alley door of the gunshop.

"You stay inside. I'm going to be watching Kincaid, or maybe watching his bank. I don't trust that big lard ball."

She reached up and kissed him. "Things are moving quickly now. You really get things done. Promise you'll come back here when it's all over?"

"Promise, now get in there and stay safe. Kincaid isn't going to be nice to you if he spots you."

Star grinned. "I won't be nice to him, either." She laughed and closed the alley door.

Morgan went to the livery and saddled the same horse he'd been using. He hitched the bay mare to a rail across the street from the bank in front of the hardware. It was slightly after noon time when he got situated. He told the hardware man he was waiting for someone, and settled down against a display of horse collars and stared out the window.

Nothing happened for two hours. Morgan went across to the Delmonico's restaurant two doors down from the bank and had a quick meal while he watched out the front window. Nothing seemed unusual at the bank.

By four that afternoon Morgan was starting to get worried. What was Kincaid doing? Surely he must know that his days in this town were about over. Maybe he was cleaning out the tills of all of his stores and saloons and whorehouses. Might be it.

At five, Morgan spotted a covered buggy coming up the street. It was not really a buggy but a canopy-top surrey with a fancy fringed top and side curtains covering the rear seat. Morgan didn't know the man driving, but in the other side of the front seat sat the big frame of Lash Kincaid.

Morgan grinned and checked his six-gun.

Kincaid got down from the buggy with help from his driver. The rig parked directly in front of the bank's door. Kincaid went inside and Morgan wished he could be there to see what happened.

Kincaid stepped inside the bank after he had pounded on the front door. Paulson came and unlocked it. He seemed to be the only one there.

"Good, Paulson, you got my note I'd be here. I have a great fear that someone is going to rob our bank. What I'm going to do is ask you to gather up all our assets, all except the small change. Put it in boxes and I'll haul it to my other safe down in my office. If nothing happens tonight, I'll bring the cash back in time for you to get opened in the morning."

Kincaid looked up at Paulson. "Any objections to that, Paulson?"

"Not at all, Mr. Kincaid. I think it's tremendously fortunate that you understand these things and actually heard of some low life who wanted to rob the bank. I'll get started right away. We are a little short on cash now after some of our transfers of money to Chicago.

That one big depositor sold his claim and left town."

"Yes, yes. Let's get busy. My man here can help you."

A half hour later there were four boxes of gold and paper money lined up by the door.

"Now, Paulson, do you have a weapon?"

"Yes, sir. A six-gun. I'll get it."

"I want you to stand guard just inside the door as my man carries the currency to the surrey. Then I want you to lock up the bank and go home as if nothing has happened."

"Yes, sir."

Across the street, Morgan watched the little drama with increasing interest. His evaluation had been right. The big man was moving out . . . again. This time with all the money he thought was in the bank.

When the rig rattled off down Main, Morgan moved out on his horse following Kincaid by half a block. The surrey stopped at the alley door to Kincaid's place and the driver ran inside and came back soon with two big boxes. Might be clothes, food, weapons. Depended where the man went next.

It was dusk when the driver came back for the last time and took the reins. The rig moved out heading south, it soon passed the last houses and tents of Deadwood and kept moving south. Morgan followed.

He had no supplies because he didn't figure on a long trip. When the surrey had turned the last bend leaving Deadwood, Morgan moved up closer. He didn't want to lose the rig in the dark.

He galloped the bay and soon caught Kincaid. Morgan had not planned out for sure what to do once Kincaid wanted to run. He wasn't sure the man was scared enough, but it had worked. Now he had to improvise the capture.

Morgan grinned and pulled out his six-gun. He fed one more round into the chamber so that it held six, then rode hard toward the surrey. When he was 30-feet behind, he fired a shot into the air and then another one over the top of the rig. The driver evidently laid leather on the backs of the horses.

The surrey jolted from a contented walk to a run in a few yards. Morgan stayed with it but kept 20 yards behind. He fired all six shots, reloaded and sent two more over the rig. The surrey was going too fast. This was a strange road for the driver and the darkness was complete now. Morgan couldn't see 20 feet ahead of him.

There was no moon and the two horses charged forward dragging the heavy rig behind them. Morgan felt it before he saw it, they had come to a down slope. His mount angled downward and ahead he heard a bleating cry from one of the surrey horses.

The rig charged down the slope. It was steeper than Morgan remembered coming up here on the stage. The surrey whipped from one side to the other. Then the driver skidded it around a turn. Morgan slowed his mount to get its footing, then dropped her to a walk as the surrey charged down the black slope.

Morgan slowed again and stopped. There was no way the surrey team could be slowed with that heavy rig pushing it. He moved ahead again at a walk down the steep slope, and then he heard a grinding sound and a man's shout of alarm. There was a ripping and tearing and then splintering sounds followed by the screams of a horse far below. Then there were no more sounds.

Chapter Sixteen

Morgan rode forward with care, watching for the turn, for what must be the crash scene of the rig and the two horses. It sounded somewhere ahead and to his left. He edged the bay forward, straining his eyes through the darkness.

He could see 20 feet ahead but no more. The trail kept descending sharply. Here and there he could see skid marks of the steel rimmed wheels. The trail turned to the right slightly, then to the right again in nearly a right angle.

He got off his mount and checked the edge of the stage road. Deep tracks showed where the surrey had plunged straight ahead off the side of the road into the void. He couldn't see the bottom. He rode along the road for a hundred-yards but found no easy place where he could descend.

Back near the point where the rig fell, Morgan tied his horse and worked with caution down the incline. He found boulders that had been pushed off the road, and trees and shrubs to hold on to as he inched his way downward.

By the time he got to the bottom he figured it was about a hundred-foot drop. Just ahead he heard a noise, then the bleating scream of a horse in agony.

Just as Morgan reached the flat bottom of the canyon he saw the surrey. Evidently it had sailed through the air and crashed on the bottom of the ravine with great force. The mass of the rig covered the horses. He didn't see the men anywhere.

Morgan approached the wreckage watching for the driver or Kincaid. He stumbled over a box and figured it must be from the rig. Another step and he saw a man lying face down on the rocky ground.

The driver. Morgan touched his hand. It didn't move. He rolled the man over. His head was a mass of pulpy, bloody flesh. He must have died instantly.

The horse screamed again as only a horse can do when it is in pain and in a deadly situation. Morgan saw it struggling at the side of the mass of wreckage. He ran there. The animal was on its side, both front legs were broken, yet it pawed the ground.

Morgan's shot blasted into the silence of the night and the horse stopped its struggling.

"So you finally came," a voice sounded from the other side of the crash. "You have to be Morgan. Only a bastard like you could figure out my next move. Get over here, Morgan, and help me. I'll make you a rich man."

"Kincaid. I'm surprised you're still alive. I kind of hoped that you'd bought yourself a one-way stagecoach ticket to hell."

"Not a chance, Morgan."

He went to the other side of the smashed surrey and pushed back the top that had ripped loose. Below it on the ground lay Kincaid. His right leg had twisted under his big body and one of the surrey wheel's hub pinned him to the ground. A slash across his cheek seeped blood that ran down his chin and down his neck. One of his arms showed under the wheel but he couldn't move it.

"How do you feel, Kincaid?"

"I've been better. Broken leg for sure. Get this damn wheel off me and I'll be fine."

"Can you reach your derringer?"

"Hell no."

"Don't touch it or I'll walk away and let you die here alone in the dark."

"Yes, yes. Whatever you say. Get this thing off me."

Morgan checked the wheel. It was holding Kincaid to the ground and part of the frame of the surrey pressed down on the wheel.

"Not sure I can move it, Kincaid. Maybe with a pry bar I can lift the wheel and surrey and you can crawl out."

"I'm not much good at crawling, but give it a try."

Morgan found the surrey tongue where it had splintered in the crash. He got a piece ten feet long and about as thick as a two-by-four. It looked like stout hickory. He found the right spot for the pry under the wheel and moved to the far end and lifted.

"Move!" Morgan directed.

Kincaid slid out about six inches and gave up.

"I can't lift it any higher," Morgan said.

He rolled a foot-high rock to the edge of the wheel.

then inserted the thickest part of the board in front of the rock and under the wheel.

"A lever. I can multiply my effort that way. I'll pull down on this end and yell and you crawl out of there or die where you lay."

On the second hoist, the wheel lifted free of the gambler and he slid forward three feet. He was free of the wheel. Morgan let down the lever and checked the big man.

His breathing was fast and light as if he couldn't get enough air in his lungs. A large bloody smear showed through his shirt where the wheel had rested on his chest.

Morgan patted Kincaid's jacket pockets and found his derringer. He took it and stared at the big man.

"Now, Kincaid. How is it going?"

"Better. Can't get enough air into my lungs. Damn wheel hit me hard in the chest. Want you to get back to town and bring out a light wagon so you can take me to the doctor."

Morgan ignored the order. "You cold?"

"Yes."

Morgan gathered up pine branches and downed limbs and some splinters of the surrey body and soon had a small warming fire going. He tugged Kincaid closer so he could hold out one of his hands to it.

"I can't move, Kincaid. There's a hundred-foot bank you went over. Take six men to get you up the hill, that is if I wanted to do that."

Kincaid looked up quickly, staring at Morgan in the firelight.

"Morgan, you get me to the doctor so he can patch me up and I'll make you a rich man. Twenty thousand dollars! All yours, no questions asked."

Morgan took out his pocket knife and began whittling.

"Damn you Morgan, answer me!" Kincaid bellowed. Then he whined in pain and coughed. He touched his lips and found some spatters of blood.

"What the hell, blood? I'm hurt bad, Morgan. You've got to get me to a doctor. No, no, ride back to town and bring Doctor Rodarte out here. Yeah, that's it. Go right now and you've got your twenty thousand!"

"Would that bring Vanderstone and Ray Eastin back to life? And the dozen more men you've had killed?"

"No, 'course not. Nothing can. But you can help save my life right now. You've got to do it, Morgan."

Morgan laughed. "Wrong argument to use, Kincaid. You don't ever tell me what I must do."

"Yeah, old habits. Sorry. I'm asking, Morgan. I'm having more trouble breathing. I got two broken legs and one mashed up arm and a chest that hurts like hell."

Morgan ignored him, looked through the rubble until he found one of the cardboard boxes. He carried it over near the fire and opened it where it had been tied with twine. Inside he found stacks of greenbacks.

"Well, look what I found," Morgan said. "Looks like stolen money to me."

"My money, from my bank. All legitimate. I took out my capital."

"Damn thoughtful of you, Kincaid. The two widows are going to appreciate it. A humane thoughtful gesture of a man on his deathbed."

"What the hell. . . ."

"Now you're getting the idea, Kincaid. I've seen men with crushed chests before. Takes a while, but they say the blood starts to build up in the lungs, and pretty soon there's less and less room for air and oxygen and before you know it, poof, you suffocate on your own blood."

"Morgan, damnit! You ride for that doctor and you can have all the money I have. Must be close to thirty thousand here. All yours. Go get the doctor!"

"Oh, a question. The young boy, Dale Johnson. He got kidnapped from Rapid City and used to tunnel in one of your claims. You send that man up there to get a kid?"

Kincaid looked away. "He had no cause to kill the woman. I told him to find a twelve year old and bring him back. Rest of it was his doing. I hear he's dead now."

"True, you'll be meeting him in hell before morning."

Morgan looked for more boxes, found two held together by the twine. A third one with gold coins broke open. The coins were all in heavy canvas bank bags. Morgan pawed through the wreckage and found all of them so they filled the box.

"Your driver is dead. Must have been thrown out in the fall."

"I figured." Kincaid looked up. "Morgan, maybe I ain't been the best of men in the past. I can change. Had a shitty start in life and I figured to pay back a few people. Only the same ones weren't around so I paid back everybody. You bring the doctor and I'll swear to go straight, never to cheat another living soul. That good enough for you?"

"Kincaid, I'd go, but it won't make any difference. Doc Rodarte is probably in Deadwood because he got run out of a real town. He's most likely some half-trained, country sawbones who doesn't know much more about medicine than you do. He couldn't drain your lungs. He'd kill you quicker than the blood will.

Nothing can save your life. Didn't want to tell you, but there it is."

Morgan put some more wood on the small fire to keep it going. Kincaid's face went white as he thought about what Morgan told him.

Kincaid slammed his fist into the ground and wailed a high keening of frustration and fury and desperation. He felt his chest. His fingers came away bloody. The big man coughed and spit up blood. He looked at Morgan.

"That's bad?"

"Maybe an hour, two at the most."

Morgan added some more branches to the fire, building it higher. "You have any secrets you want to tell me. Like hidden barrels of gold dust, boxes of double eagles?"

Kincaid started to laugh, then stopped. "None. Everything I have is right here." He coughed again and a gout of blood exploded from his mouth spattering in the fire.

Kincaid bellowed in rage. "Life can't do this to me! I plan things too well. How could things have gone so wrong?"

"Like any good poker player you know the odds catch up with you when you've been on a winning streak. I'd say your streak is broken."

Kincaid screamed in pain as one surge after another drilled through him. Tears streamed down his cheeks. "Morgan, you got to give me back my derringer. One round and the pain stops. Please!"

"Can't do that, Kincaid. I don't think you deserve it. You've given a lot of men too much pain over the last few years. You've killed what, ten or fifteen good men, some not so good. You deserve to suffer."

Kinciad screamed at him, but ended in a coughing fit that splattered more blood in the fire.

"Anything, Morgan. Anything. You do it yourself. Execute me, I don't care."

His voice was lower now, softer, so he wouldn't use so much breath. He gasped from time to time as his breath came in short pants, but there was never enough.

"Do it, Morgan. I'll look away and you blow my head off. Anything is better than this."

Morgan nodded. "Seems fair and right. A little of the mercy you never showed to anyone."

Kincaid looked at the fire as Morgan stood and went behind him. Morgan lifted the Colt and put it near the side of Kincaid's head so there would be powder burns.

Kincaid began talking about his childhood. "It was bad. They pushed and used me. Shoved me around, made me work sixteen hours a day. I decided when I grew up I'd do the pushing. That's what I've—"

Morgan pulled the trigger.

Five minutes later Morgan had the scene set. He pressed the derringer into Kincaid's cooling right hand after he fired one round from it into the air. Then he hurried back up the slope to his horse. He had a lot of work to do before daylight.

Dawn was just breaking as Morgan rode into Deadwood with two pack horses and tied them up in back of the gunsmith's shop. On the pack animals were the four boxes of currency and gold from the wrecked surrey. He banged on the back door until Star came out looking sleepy and beautiful in a tousled kind of way.

Morgan kissed her and slipped into the room. He told her what had happened.

"So it's over at last," Star said. She wiped a tear from her eyes and sighed. "Now it's on to a new life. I . . . I can hardly believe this is happening." She kissed his cheek and nestled against him.

"I need a little sleep," Morgan said. "You watch those two pack horses in back. They are richer than a dozen claims. Wake me up at nine o'clock. We've got some more work to do."

At nine-thirty that morning, Morgan walked in to the general store and talked to Mrs. Eastin.

He had sorted through the boxes of money and decided to use up the gold coins because they were so heavy. He and Star checked the bank bags and found that they each contained 100 gold double eagles, that was $2,000 worth.

Morgan set the three bags on a counter in the back room and told Mrs. Eastin to look in them. She did and her eyes went wide in amazement.

"What on earth. . . ."

"This is yours, Mrs. Eastin. It's a settlement from Mr. Kincaid for the death of your husband. He told me that he ordered a man to shoot him, and now he's contrite and wants to do this to help make it up to you."

Morgan left the woman gushing tears and thanks, and hurried with Star to the bank. There they turned in four sacks of the gold coins and received from a grateful Mr. Paulson hundred dollar bills in exchange, $8,000 worth.

Paulson counted out the bills in his private office. Then he gripped Morgan's hand. "I can't express my thanks for your saving the bank. He would have taken everything here if it hadn't been for you. The whole town of Deadwood is in debt to you, Mr. Morgan."

"Remember that, Paulson, and be good to these

people. Don't foreclose and lower your interest rate. Oh, I'd say that you own the Deadwood bank now. Mr. Kincaid had an accident last night. His rig went over that deadman's corner south of town. From what I hear he was smashed up so bad he ended it all with his derringer.

"Oh, my!"

Morgan and Star walked out with the eight bundles of $100 bills safely stowed in her reticule.

"I feel like everyone is watching me," Star said. "I've never carried eight thousand dollars around before."

"Good," Morgan said. "Now you need to get your traveling clothes ready. We'll be riding to Rapid City. Then maybe take a stage on to points south and Denver before we go to Chicago. You get your horseback clothes, and I'll pick up some cooking gear, some blankets, and some food. Forty miles, about three or four days. I'm in no rush."

Morgan carried the last two boxes of greenbacks into the room Star used behind the gunsmith's and checked the denominations. He kept the 20's, 50's and 100's, then took one full box of smaller bills back to the bank and had them count and turn them into larger bills.

By the time it was all sorted out, Morgan had large enough bills that he could pack them all in a small carpetbag that he strapped behind his saddle.

He did some quick figuring. They still had nearly $24,000 left. He had figured $10,000 for the widow Vanderstone, and then split what was left with Star, $7,000 each. He would send most of Star's money to a bank in Chicago from a Denver bank so it would be safe and she would have it when she needed it.

Maybe with his part he could think about buying back

the Spade Bit Ranch. He thought about it a minute, then shook his head. Not until that sheriff was gone from Boise. There would be no point in trying to fight a man with that kind of legal power behind him. Then too, there was always that outstanding wanted poster on him.

He and Star rode out of Deadwood about noon. A misty rain fell and they grinned under their slickers.

"Good old Deadwood," Star said. "I think it rains eight out of ten days here, and the other two it's snowing."

They laughed and rode down the trail. When they went by the spot where Kincaid had crashed, they saw the marshal down there and two other men. A fourth man was digging a grave. They must have decided it was better to bury Kincaid there than try to hoist him up the cliff.

It stopped raining in the afternoon, and they rode another two hours, then stopped in a small mountain valley near the trail beside a bouncing creek and didn't see a gold miner within sight. No claims had been filed here.

The sun came out and dried off the grass and they spread their blankets. Morgan started a small fire and they sat and listened to the wind in the tall ponderosa pines.

"I'm going to miss the sound of the wind in the trees," Star said. She turned and kissed him. "I'm also going to miss you." She unbuttoned the small sized man's shirt she had bought for the trip and Morgan was delighted to see that she wore nothing under it. She slipped off the shirt and leaned toward him.

"For the next few days, Lee Morgan, I want you to teach me how it is to be a good lover, the way it was that first time with us. I want it to be tender and honest and with all the feeling in the world. It will be a kind of healing process for me. Does that make sense?''

''It does. I'll do my best. We have all the time you need.'' Morgan kissed her soft lips so lightly she barely felt it.

''Yes, Lee Morgan, oh, yes that's a fine start.'' She lay down on the blanket and stared up at the clouds drifting by far above the ponderosa tops. ''Yes, Lee, you're making me feel loved already. I can't wait to get back to my brushes and finish that painting of you I started. I think it's going to be the best work that I've done yet.''

He bent and kissed her waiting lips, then her breasts. They did excellent work together the rest of the way to Denver.

BUCKSKIN
RIMFIRE REVENGE

Chapter One

The three of them sat in the dining car of the Oakland Racer. The train was on the regular run from Chicago all the way to Oakland, California, on the main line of the Union Pacific on the transcontinental railroad. They had boarded in Chicago and were half a day out, and it was not quite starting to get dark yet.

Lee Morgan sat on the aisle side of the table and beside him, next to the window, was Claresta Devlin. She was 18 years old, softly redheaded, but the freckles had faded. Across from her at the other window seat sat her mother, Mrs. Amos (Martha) Devlin.

Mrs. Devlin was chattering away about how terrible it was going to be to leave civilization.

"We did have to leave Philadelphia and move to Chicago, of all places. I accepted that quietly. At last we found suitable accommodations, but we were only there for a year and then Amos left for this godforsaken place they call Colorado. I don't know how we will survive." She sniffed and touched a linen handkerchief to her forehead. A pale D monogram showed in the corner.

The way the tables were crowded into the rail car, there was little spare space, and Morgan had to be careful not to move his feet and legs too much or he would kick the woman across from him or touch the leg of the girl beside him.

"Mother, I think we'll find a way to get along. Don't you think we will, Mr. Morgan?" Claresta asked him. As she said it she put her hand on his knee well out of sight under the table and moved her fingers upward.

He looked at her at once and she smiled.

"Oh, I believe the ranch house there will be quite comfortable," Morgan said. "From what Mr. Devlin told me he's spared no expense to fix it up properly."

Claresta turned to her mother, and as she did her hand slipped over the side of his leg to his inner thigh and squeezed it and massaged him gently.

"See, Mother? I told you it would be all right. Daddy won't ask us to come somewhere that is too outlandish. Although he did say the nearest village was Loveland, about twenty miles away. Now isn't that an interesting name for a town, Loveland?"

Claresta's hand moved again, heading toward his crotch.

Morgan coughed and eased his left hand under the table, and caught her hand just before it found the mark. He held her hand.

"I quite agree with Claresta, Mrs. Devlin. From what your husband told me in the letter, he has set up a beautiful ranch house and there will be servants to take care of the cooking and housekeeping."

"But where will I go *shopping* for new clothes and trinkets?" Mrs. Devlin looked out the window at the passing views of the endless plains. There was only the gently swaying ocean of grass for as far as they could see.

Claresta frowned at Morgan a moment, and broke her hand free and rubbed his crotch before he caught her hand again.

"Oh, dear," Mrs. Devilin said with a small groan. "I don't think I'm up to having any supper after all. You two stay and eat. I'll see you soon, Claresta, back in our compartment."

The matron stood, and stared hard at her daughter for a moment. "I'll see you promptly after your supper, young lady," she said again, then turned and, holding to the chair tops and tables and shoulders of the diners, she made her way slowly through the swinging dining car to the compartment car just forward of it.

"Claresta, are you trying to get me fired by your mother, thrown in jail by the authorities, and then shot to death if your father ever finds out?"

Now he had both hands under the table holding her darting fingers.

She smiled and leaned toward him. He relaxed a moment, and she pulled his hand away from his crotch and brought it instead over to her legs, which were parted.

"Claresta!" he said, his voice not in its normal range.

"Just relax, Lee Morgan, and see what you can find. Nobody can see a thing, and you might even enjoy it. You're not one of those men who like other men, are you?"

"Not a chance, but isn't this a little public?"

"Kind of gives it a sense of danger."

She had pulled his hand under her long skirt

now, up her sleek legs, and pushed his hand hard against her crotch. He had turned slightly toward her.

"Your pa told me you were a handful. He said to keep a tight rein on you."

Claresta laughed softly. "How do you like the handful of me that you have right now?" She humped her crotch against his hand. She was still covered down there by soft cotton and something else.

She leaned close to him and whispered. "Lee, you could at least rub me a little where your fingers are to make it all worthwhile."

His fingers began to massage the soft place, and quickly it developed a damp spot.

"Yes, I think you're getting the idea," she said with a catch in her voice. She began to grind her hips against his touch and she moaned softly. Her hand darted back to his crotch, and she found where he had a growing erection.

"My, my, I think you do like girls after all," she whispered. That was when the waiter brought their supper, roast beef with mushrooms and horseradish sauce, steamed carrots and parsnips and side dishes of boiled potatoes and brown gravy.

Morgan quickly lifted his hand away from her when the waiter arrived.

"Mrs. Devlin is indisposed and won't have supper tonight," Claresta said smoothly to the waiter. "We'll pay for it, of course. Why don't you consider her serving your supper for tonight."

The waiter nodded, served them, and retreated with the third tray.

Lee Morgan turned to Claresta in surprise. "You are a handful, aren't you, Claresta? I'm really glad that we'll be on this train only two days at the most."

"Oh, don't be silly. You love it. You didn't really have a handful of me, Lee Morgan. My real handfuls are up here on top." She sat up straighter, pushed out her breasts, and moved her shoulders so her bodice rolled and bounced.

Claresta sent him a secretive look. "Now hurry and eat your supper. Then I have a surprise for you."

Lee Morgan eyed her suspiciously. "Now whatever in the world could that be?"

"You'll see."

The roast beef was delicious and Lee enjoyed himself. Then the dessert was gone and Claresta signed the bill, giving the waiter a generous tip.

He helped her to rise, and she led the way to the railroad car that was made up entirely of compartments, small rooms built along one side of the train with a narrow passage along the other side. Claresta stopped at the first door and took out a key.

"But your room is at the other end of the car," Morgan said softly.

"True, but that one is Mother's and mine." She turned the key, stepped into the small room, and pulled him in after her. "This is a second compartment I engaged just before we left. I had a feeling that I would need a little privacy."

Claresta locked the door behind her and reached up and kissed Lee Morgan's surprised mouth. It was a sexy kiss, with her tongue working at his lips until he opened them, then darting inside and exploring.

As they kissed she pulled him down and they sat on the bed, which was already made up and turned down. By the time they came up for a long breath after the kiss, Claresta had unbuttoned the fasteners on the top of her dress all the way to her waist.

"You are trying to get me shot, aren't you, young lady?"

She grinned, her pale green eyes flashing. "Of course not, I'd much rather you shoot *me.* You know, with your big shooter down there in your pants." She caught one of his hands and pushed it on her bare breasts under her chemise.

"Now, Lee Morgan, you look me right in the eye and tell me that having your hand there on my breasts does not feel good. Can you say that?"

He shook his head.

"And can you tell me that you don't want to spread me back on this bed and help me take my clothes off and then made soft and gentle love to me three or four times?"

Again he shook his head. He began to say something, but she shushed him with a kiss and pulled the top of her dress down off her shoulders. When the kiss ended she lifted her chemise up and off over her head, leaving her two firm, young, and large breasts bouncing.

The steward had lit two lamps in the compartment and Morgan stared at her breasts, ripe and ready, her nipples standing tall, surging with eager and hot blood, her areolas blushing prettily pink.

"You want to, don't you, Lee Morgan?"

"Damnit, yes, and you know it. A woman's breasts are the most beautiful picture in the world, do you know that? Absolute perfection in construction, so marvelously made."

"Then why don't you let them know and touch them or kiss them or something?"

Morgan bent and kissed each throbbing nipple, then sent a ring of kisses around the swell of one breast, then the other. He returned to her nipples and gently bit them until she moaned in total delight.

"Oh, wonderful!" Claresta said, sighing softly. "I figured you were a man who would know his way around a girl's bare tit. Chew them right off if you want to!"

He felt her hands at his fly. He'd let her do the work getting inside. Twice more he circled her breasts with kisses. Then he pushed her gently back on the bed and lay fully on top of her.

"Oh, yes! I love it when a man crushes me into the bed this way. Just so delightful." He felt when she worked inside his pants and her hand closed around his erection.

"My God, he must be huge. I want to see him. Off, off, I want to see your big prick!"

She pushed him away and bent to pull his hard-on from his pants. When it at last broke through she sat wide-eyed for a minute, then giggled with nervousness. She stroked him and petted him, reaching down to play with his scrotum.

"Claresta, for all your bravado, you're not really a virgin, are you?"

"Heavens, no! One boy shot into me five times one afternoon. I've had lots of men."

"More than two?"

"Well, no, but seven times altogether."

"Then you're almost a virgin. Not until after at least twenty five times can you say that you're experienced at all."

Claresta grinned and pulled his hands to her crotch. "We better hurry then if we want to fuck eighteen times tonight."

Morgan laughed. "We better hurry anyway. In another half hour your mother is going to be searching the train for you."

She stood and pulled the dress off over her head, then stepped out of three petticoats and showed him her bloomers.

"They're the latest fashion," she said. He reached to take them off, but she shook her head and stretched out on the bed. "You have to seduce them off me. Let's see you do it."

He began with a long kiss that left her sighing, then petted her breasts and kissed them, and slowly began kissing down from her mounds over her ribs and then down her flat little belly, past her navel. She began to shiver then. He got to the top of her bloomers and he inched them down, kissing his way toward the treasure. When he got to the first pubic hair she moaned in rapture, and then he worked his way on down pushing the bloomers ahead of him. A moment later she powered into a climax.

It was short and sharp, wringing a moan and a long low cry from her as she spasmed again and again. Then she finished and kissed him hotly before lying back down. Slowly her legs began to spread apart.

Morgan planted one quick kiss on her soft pink nether lips and she climaxed again, rumbling and rocking this time twice as long as before.

He pushed the silk bloomers down and off her feet, then rolled her over toward him. She kissed him deliciously, then slid away and turned on her back, her legs parted, her arms held out to him.

"Please, Morgan, fuck me right now before I

explode! Don't even take off your clothes. Right now!"

He kissed her once more, then moved over her and between her silken thighs. He probed once. Her hand helped him find the slot and he worked inside gently. She was so tight he sucked in a breath, waited for more of her juices to lubricate him, then eased it until their pelvic bones touched.

"Oh, yes!" Claresta crooned. Then she surged into another series of climaxes that came so fast one after another that he lost track. Sweat broke out on her forehead and she gasped again and again for more air as she strummed and shivered and vibrated through still more orgasms. At last she quieted.

"Good Lord! I've never been so fast, never so many at a time. This is pure heaven. How can you set me off that way?"

"Magic," he said softly, his hips beginning to rotate and to come in and out with soft, short strokes. "I used magic on you and you were a ready victim."

"Not victim, a partner, Lee Morgan. Oh, glory. If this is what Father meant by your keeping a short rein on me, I'm more than willing to let you rein me in every night."

"You know that can't happen. This is the one and only time. Your mother would have me arrested."

"Yes, and Father would shoot you. So unless you want me to tell them both, you'll be inside me this way whenever we can be together."

"You're blackmailing me?"

"Absolutely. A girl has to use anything that works to get her lover."

Morgan had beaten threats like this before. The secret was simply never to be alone with the young lady. In four days at the most they would be at the Colorado ranch and he'd take the other half of his escort pay and ride off down the trail. But right now . . .

He stroked into her sharply and she looked up surprised, then delighted.

"Marvelous!" she whispered.

He thrust in as far as he could and saw a touch of pain in her face. "Sorry, I won't go in so far. I touched a part of you in there that's extremely sensitive." She nodded.

Morgan teased her. He made his climax wait and wait, and only when she was getting impatient did he reach down and kiss her and then pound another ten times to surge into his own orgasm. It was one powerful explosion, with six more mighty thrusts to eject the last of his fluids. Only when he finished did he realize that his climax had set her off again. She lasted longer than he did. At last they both were done again.

She stared at him with wide eyes. "Damn, nobody's ever been that great! I don't see how you kept me excited for so long." Then they both nestled down on one another and rested.

Soon he lifted away from her.

"Young lady, get up and get dressed before your mother searches every compartment on his train. I don't plan on being hung for rape. Now move!"

She did as he ordered, teasing him as she dressed. When she was proper, she reached up and kissed him.

"I'll go and sit with Mother and make sure she has a sleeping pill. Then I'll be back here before midnight. You be here, Morgan, or you're in big trouble. You hear me?" She slipped a key to the compartment to him, then eased into the hallway and walked down to her mother's compartment.

Chapter Two

Lee Morgan went back to his berth in the car beyond the diner and pushed all of his belongings into the small carpetbag. Soon most of the berths were occupied. He watched for some that weren't, and found two near the middle of the car.

By eleven o'clock no one had used either one. He checked them and found no personal belongings there. He moved from his Berth 14 Upper, to the other upper, which was 28. Shortly after midnight he saw a figure moving down the center aisle. It was a woman in a robe.

She checked the numbers on the berths. When she came to 14 she stepped up on the bottom berth and looked inside the top one. He heard her making some whispered comments, and then she stepped down. She looooked in the berth below, which was occupied. She got only a growl in response.

Now, as Morgan watched her through a crack in the curtain of his berth, he saw that the woman was Claresta Devlin. She was furious. She must have found out his berth number from the porter. He grinned, closed the drape, and waited a moment. She moved down the aisle whispering softly at one after another of the berths.

At one she reacted angrily, stamped her foot, and hurried out of the car toward the compartments. At least now he could get a good night's sleep. He might take a few chances at times, but he wasn't that crazy. That sleek, sexy girl could cost him a lot more than his wages on his assignment.

The next day he made a point of not being alone with Claresta. He took the ladies to breakfast and back to their compartment.

"Yes, I'll be here at eleven-thirty to take you to dinner," he said as Mrs. Devlin asked.

"I do hope they'll have something that I can eat. The food on this train is just terrible."

Behind her mother Claresta was mouthing some words to him. He indicated he didn't understand. She pretended to unbutton the bodice of her dress.

Morgan looked quickly back to the mother. "Mrs. Devlin, if there's anything else I can do for you, have the porter call me."

"Why don't you sit in our compartment for a while and tell us about Colorada," Claresta said. It was not a question.

"Yes, that's a good idea, Claresta," her mother said. "Perhaps that way I can steel myself for the terrible shock of Colorado."

The women sat down on the made-up bed and left the one chair for him. He sat and told them about Colorado.

"It's high country. The state is crossed by the Rocky Mountains, the highest mountain range in the whole country. I'm not sure, but I'd guess the valley you'll be living in is about five thousand feet altitude. That means it will be cooler in the summer than Chicago, but probably much colder in the winter with a lot of snow."

"Young man, you're supposed to be making me feel better," Martha Devlin said crossly. "What is good about the area?"

"The mountains are snow-capped and the prettiest pictures you'll ever see. Great green sweeps of conifer trees that will take your breath away. The wide-open spaces will amaze you. The grandeur of the whole area is remarkable."

"Yes, yes, I suppose. But, dear boy, what is there to do in this area? Is there an opera, or an orchestra, or even a music hall?"

"No, Mrs. Devlin, I'm afraid not. Even the stores will seem primitive by your standards."

"Oh, dear. I know already that I'm going to hate it there in Colorado."

"You hated it in Chicago, Mother. You hated it in New York. You even hated it in Boston."

"Child, that's enough of that. I think I'm going to lie down. I'm feeling the least bit faint."

"I'll be leaving, Mrs. Devlin. Remember, if you need me, just call."

Morgan slipped out of the compartment, but not before getting an angry look from Claresta. He was sticking to his first principle . . . not to be alone with the sexy lady.

He escaped Claresta at the next two meals, but she found him in his Number 14 seat before it was made into a berth. She sat beside him.

"Mother is having a nap."

"Her beauty rest."

"I know, but I don't need any. One man I know told me I was beautiful, especially when I was naked," she said softly, and reached for his leg. He caught her hand.

"You are trying to get me killed, aren't you? Your father would blaze away at me with his shotgun if he knew."

"That's what makes it so perfect. We have another night coming up before we get to Cheyenne. If you don't spend it with me I'm going to tell Father that you raped me. Then you'll really be in trouble. If he doesn't kill you, the local lawman will. So you have no choice. I'll expect you in my compartment tonight, or I'll be going to your funeral in two days. Take your choice. You still have my key?"

"I do."

She reached over and kissed his cheek. "Don't be late. Mother will be dead to the world in her room by nine o'clock. I'll expect you in my compartment by that time."

Morgan nodded. "You're a tough woman, Claresta. I'll be there."

That night Morgan got to the compartment on time, and at last got to sleep somewhere around three in the morning. He was exhausted but smiling. So was Claresta when she slipped down the hall and back into her mother's compartment.

The next morning they rolled into Cheyenne and left the train. The branch line train to Denver would leave in half an hour. Mrs. Devlin now showed a permanent frown. She was a pretty lady, even with the scowl, maybe 40 years old, no more. She had worked at keeping her girlish figure and was trim and shapely. She dressed as if she were still in Boston, her dress around her throat and wrists and brushing the ground.

"Mr. Morgan, is this what it will be like in Colorado?" she asked, her chin quivering a little, eyes wide and unhappy.

"No, Mrs. Devlin. This is the edge of the Great Plains on a high plateau in Wyoming as the land slopes up to the Rockies. We're almost six thousand feet here. When we get to Loveland we'll be more than a thousand feet below that and in the mountains. The valley where your ranch is is a little higher than Loveland, but not much. You'll see a lot more trees around your ranch than there are here. Lots of pines, and firs and blue spruce."

"Oh, dear. I've never liked trees very much."

"Mother, you'll be fine. The air will be pure and clean with none of that Chicago smoke or soot. You'll love it."

The train left on time. It was a 40-mile trip through the rugged mountains and down to Loveland. Morgan had been there before. When they arrived, he tried to look at Loveland as Mrs. Devil might, and saw a one-street town near the tracks. Ten or twelve businesses in mostly unpainted wooden buildings, half a dozen buggies and wagons parked along the street, and a few men wandering about as if they had nothing to do.

"This is our closest city!" Mrs. Devlin spat as Morgan hustled their eight suitcases off the train. The porters levered a steamer trunk off and dropped it on the platform.

"I'm afraid this is the best that Loveland can do," Morgan said. "I'll get a light rig and some directions. Your husband said to inquire at the general store."

"You expect me to stand here in this . . . this mud and dirt of the street?" Mrs. Devil said.

"No, ma'am, you can sit on the steamer trunk

until I bring up the rig." Morgan hurried away, leaving Claresta to console her mother.

Two hours later they had driven six miles to the west from Loveland and Mrs. Devlin demanded a rest stop. For a moment she looked around in panic.

"Where am I to . . ." She stopped and looked at her daughter.

"Mother, haven't you ever been on a picnic? Come over this way behind the trees."

Morgan grinned and checked the harness on the two-horse rig. They had about ten miles more to go, but most of it was along a recently cut wagon road that had been traveled little in the past few weeks. He had the right directions. The store owner had said that Mr. Devlin was indeed out this way, the only ranch in the area, so he couldn't miss it.

Almost three hours later, they came out of a thick growth of juniper and piñon pine and saw the ranch half a mile away at the head of a five-mile-long valley filled with grass and the brown backs of cows, steers and calves.

"There it is, Mrs. Devlin. Your husband calls it the Lucky Mountain Ranch. That's the ranch house there to the right, and to the left is a barn and the corrals and a bunkhouse, I'd guess."

Mrs. Devlin stood to get a better look. "You mean that little one-story building is the house? That's where I'm expected to live?"

"Mother, it will be fine. Just look at this scenery! I've never seen anything like it before!"

Mrs. Devlin sat down and began to cry. Great sobs came and tears flowed like a mountain stream. "Oh, dear. Whatever will become of us? Marooned out here in the wilderness? What if we're attacked by Indians, or rustlers, or bandits? Morgan, I demand that you stay near me every waking minute. I don't want you out of the sound of my voice."

"Wait until you see the place, Mrs. Devlin. I'm sure your husband will take care of any fears that you might have."

Claresta, riding in the rear seat, grinned as she looked at Morgan, who was on the front sprung seat with Mrs. Devlin. Claresta shook her head as if to say that she didn't agree with Morgan.

They rolled toward the ranch buildings, and Morgan was surprised not to see smoke coming from the chimneys. Supper should be in the works by now.

Then he noticed that he had seen no riders. Usually there were men on horseback all over a ranch like this, moving cattle or coming back from working the animals.

A chill hit him as he came close enough to check the corral. The gate was open and there wasn't a horse in the round-pole enclosure.

Then he frowned as he saw what looked like the body of a man near the wall. Morgan grabbed the Spencer rifle from the rig, stopped the horses and tied the reins, and looked for the two women.

"Stay here. Something is wrong. Stay here and don't move and don't make any noise. You both understand?"

Mrs. Devlin began to sag to one side. Claresta moved quickly to the front seat, exposing her legs to mid-thigh, and sat beside her mother and put her arm around her. Mrs. Devlin was breathing heavily, and Morgan guessed she was about to faint.

He dropped off the rig and ran to the well. The

cowboy who lay there had lost his hat for good reason. A battle ax had split his head in half.

Morgan looked at the ranch house. Now he could see a body half in the back door. He ran to the barn. One man lay in hay with a pitchfork rammed through his chest. No one else was there. He touched the body. It was cold and stiff. Dead more than ten or twelve hours. Maybe for two or three days.

He ran for the house, not expecting to find the attackers still there, but there was a chance. The body at the door had two Indian arrows in the chest. He was an older man, in his late forties, and wore a black suit and vest, white tie and shirt. He was almost bald. That had to be Mr. Devlin.

There goes the rest of my pay, Morgan figured. Inside the ranch house he first entered a big kitchen. A small Chinese man lay on the floor, his throat slit, his long pigtail and his scalp both missing.

Morgan found seven bodies—five ranch hands, the cook, and Mr. Devlin. Four of them had been scalped. The other bodies had been slashed and broken and disfigured. It was the Indian way of making sure that if the Indian ever met his enemy in the spirit world, that enemy would be handicapped by his wounds from this world.

Nothing had been taken from the house. It had not been looted as rawhiders would do. But why hadn't the Indians burned down the buildings, if it was Indians who had killed them? Who else would do such a complete job? Since all of the horses were gone it probably was Indians.

He did not find any rifles or pistols, another indication that it had been Indians. If so, the men had been killed silently, one by one as they made themselves available. Then the Indians had come to the house for the last two.

Morgan picked up the Chinese man and carried his stiff body out the back door and out of sight around the side of the house, where he threw a blanket over him. He moved Mr. Devlin to the same spot and covered him. Next he wiped up the blood on the kitchen floor and washed away every trace. There was little blood on the rear steps.

Twice he had checked the women. Mrs. Devlin had fainted, he was sure. She lay slumped in her daughter's lap.

When he had the kitchen and steps ready, Morgan ran back to the light wagon and caught Claresta's hand.

"Your mother fainted?"

"Yes. She's never seen a dead body before."

"I'm afraid it's bad news. Everyone here is dead."

Claresta's eyes brimmed with tears and she sucked in a quick pair of breaths. She shook her head and blinked away the tears. "Father too?"

"I would think so. You'll have to identify him. Let's get your mother into the house and onto the sofa. Nothing else has been taken except the horses. Now our job is to find out who did this and why."

"Then you'll be staying on?"

"Until I can take you two back to Loveland."

"Oh, no. We'll stay here. It's all we have. Mother brought a considerable amount of money with her. We can pay you. You must find out what happened, get these men buried, and hire new ones to run the ranch. It's all we have left."

Chapter Three

It took Morgan a half hour to get Mrs. Devlin into the ranch house. They tried to wake her, but couldn't, and at last he picked her up and carried her from the rig into the house.

Claresta took over at once. She settled her mother on the couch in the big room with a fireplace at one end and the kitchen door at the other. She built a fire to take the chill off the rooms, then watched her mother until she came to.

Morgan carried the suitcases and bags and boxes inside and set them near the woman. He found a wheelbarrow, a sturdy one, and hoisted the heavy steamer trunk onto the barrow and got it to the kitchen door. Then he tipped it up on end, pushed it over to the side, and gently rolled it into the end of the big room, where he got it righted around.

"Mr. Morgan, you've probably ruined half of the things in my trunk. A steamer trunk is *never, never to be tipped upside down.*"

"Next time I'll know, Mrs. Devlin." He paused and pointed around the room. "Well, this is the inside of the ranch house. It's really been built with a woman in mind. Did you see the large kitchen?"

"Mother isn't given much to cooking," Claresta said quickly. The girl looked at her only parent. "The two of us have something important to talk about, Mother. I don't want you fainting again on me. That's one thing you are going to have to stop doing."

"Whatever do you mean, child?"

Morgan walked to the kitchen door, saw Claresta look up at him, and nodded and slipped on outside.

First he had to bury the bodies. He went to each and checked for any identification, but found it on only one of the cowboys. The older man was Mr. Devlin—not much doubt about that after Morgan found a purse and two letters in his jacket pocket.

He buried the six men in a common grave 50 yards from the house, digging deep and wrapping each in a sheet or a blanket. He had just started to throw dirt into the grave when Claresta came out.

"I . . . I looked behind the house. You were right. That was my father. I told Mother he's dead and she broke down and is in hysterics, I'm afraid."

Claresta took a round pointed shovel and began throwing dirt into the hole. Morgan was surprised at the young woman's action, but pleased too.

"We'll have to bury your father today," he said. "You pick out the spot, maybe up on the little rise, and I'll do the dig."

"I can help, I want to help. Mother's the problem now. She's only thirty-eight and she's acting like she's ninety."

"She's had a serious shock."

"About Father, yes. But the rest of it is ridiculous. Usually a child is the spoiled one in a family. In our family it is my mother who is the spoiled one. She used to be practical and reasonable. It's going to be a hard adjustment for her. But she'll survive."

They both worked side by side for half an hour until the dirt was all back in the hole. Morgan tramped it down and they mounded up the extra dirt and he stomped it again. It would settle more until it was level eventually.

Morgan walked with Claresta back to the kitchen. She went at once to the cupboards and the pantry.

"Good, there's enough food here to last for a month or two, maybe more. Even quite a bit of tinned goods. You should be able to shoot a deer for us, and if not, we can butcher a steer. Have you ever butchered a steer, Morgan?"

"More than once."

"Good. I'm afraid I might botch the job, but I could get it done if I had to."

Morgan laughed softly. "I bet you could. I see that I didn't know you at all. You're much more practical than you seem."

"Somebody in the family had to be. Father was a dreamer. Mother had money, and then Father lost most of it for her. Now there's me."

"Claresta!" The demanding call had come from the main parlor. The girl turned and hurried in to her mother.

Morgan went out to the ranch yard and put the two horses in the corral and threw some hay in for them. There were oats in a bin in the near barn. He fed the horses, then pushed the wagon back beside the barn.

He made a complete inspection of the area. Morgan found where the ranch horses had been herded out to the north, toward the end of the valley. Alongside the shod hooves of maybe 25 horses, he found unshod prints. Could have been Indian ponies. Who else in the end of nowhere would want 25 horses and would take them north? There was a lake up there somewhere and tens of millions of acres of ponderosa pine and Douglas fir forest with some blue spruce and Engleman spruce thrown in. But absolutely nothing else for 60 miles.

Around the well and near the back door he found moccasin prints. He checked everything again, and in two places he also found boot prints, some of them on top of the moccasin marks. The boots were at least two sizes larger than his own number 12's. None of the men he had buried wore shoes that size.

Near the back of the barn he picked up two empty cartridges of .45 rounds. Also nearby were the large boot prints again, and shod hoofprints of a horse. The prints were deep in the hard ground as if the animal were ridden double—or carried an extremely large man. Maybe one with size-14 boots.

After nearly an hour of checking the whole area around the ranch buildings, he could find no other clues to the murder of the seven men.

He went back to the kitchen, and found Claresta had started a fire in a small cast-iron cook stove and boiled a pot of coffee. She poured him a cup and watched him as she sipped hers.

"What happens now, Mr. Morgan? Did you find out who did all this?"

"Not for sure. Indians, but why? The tribes in

this general area aren't that savage anymore."

"They stole the horses and probably some of the cows," Claresta said.

"True, but that may have been an afterthought. No firearms were used. They were quiet, struck during the day when the men were working. I don't know why."

"Find out. I talked to Mother. She finally calmed down. I took her to the far bedroom. It's the one that didn't have Father's things in it. She's having a nap. I told her she had to snap out of this great-lady pose of hers and get practical. We agreed that we want to hire you to find out who did this, and why, bring them to justice if possible, and help us get the ranch working again."

"You want me to go to town to bring back some ranch hands?"

"That's about the only way. But you can't be gone at night. Mother is terrified. I'm a little concerned myself. The killers could always come back."

"We'll talk more about that tonight. Right now I better saddle one of those horses and see what I can find out a ways before dark. This far north that won't be until nearly nine o'clock."

"I'll get some supper. You be back at six. Oh, you have a timepiece?"

Morgan showed her his trusty Waterbury pocket watch. She had found a wind-up alarm clock that had run down. She set it by Morgan's watch and grinned.

"About last night. When I don't have anything else to do, I get worked up and all sexy-feeling and restless. Now I have lots to do. I won't be so . . . demanding. But I'm certainly not going to lock my bedroom door."

She reached in and kissed his lips gently, smiled, and moved to the cupboard. "Now, what's for supper?"

Morgan saddled one of the horses he had used on the wagon. He'd drive the rig back when he went to town. Now he could make better time just riding one of the horses. He had found eight saddles in the barn, and picked out the best-looking of the two wagon horses.

The one he saddled had known the leather before. Morgan mounted and followed the track of the stolen horses for a while, but soon saw that they turned from their north route, circled around to the Big Thompson River, and moved upstream almost due west. The route led into an even wilder and more primitive section than the one they were in. After two miles he turned back. He'd have to check out the trail in a few days. With that many horses it would be easy to follow for a week or more.

He rode through the cattle in the valley. It looked like a starter herd. He counted 40 cows and six range bulls. About half the cows seemed to have calves not more than a month or two old. There were fewer than a dozen steers maybe two years old and not ready for market.

There must be more stock here, if the man had had five ranch hands. That many hands could handle 400 head easily.

He found a milk cow and drove her back to the barn, where he put her in a stanchion and went to the house for a clean milk bucket. He found it in the pantry.

"Fresh milk for supper," he told Claresta.

She blew a strand of red hair out of her eyes, grinned, and went back to peeling potatoes.

The cow wasn't used to milking. He swatted her

a couple of times and she steadied down. He got about a gallon of milk from her. The next day's milk flow should be greater. They could use the milk and cream.

Now Morgan took time to look through the bunkhouse with more care. He had looked in before to see if there were any more bodies there, and left it. Now a careful examination turned up nothing unusual. Personal goods, blankets, extra boots, a box of cards and poker chips, a set of dominoes and a checkerboard all set up to play.

He moved on to the shed next to the barn that looked like a machine storage area. A farm would more likely have such a spot. He opened a six-foot-wide door and stepped inside.

For a moment he couldn't believe what he saw. A cross had been dug into the ground, and on it hung the mutilated body of an Indian woman. She hung upside down, her head tied to the bottom of the post, her legs spread wide and her ankles tied with rope to the thick arm of the cross.

She was naked and her whole body covered with slashes. None of the slashes themselves would kill her, but the total would finally cause her to bleed to death. It was a slow and painful way to die.

Around the bottom of the cross he found all sorts of devil-worship artifacts. He had seen some of them before. Black candles, the skull of a goat, the skin and hooves of a goat. Lying in neat order were blood-stained knives made with bone handles, six of them, undoubtedly honed to terrible sharpness.

A crude pentagram had been drawn in the dirt of the floor and outlined with lime. In the pentagram were an Indian medicine bag, the dried scalp of a blond woman, and an Indian arrow broken three times.

The Indian woman had been dead for a week at least. The smell was so strong that Morgan backed out and closed the door. He tried to come up with some explanations.

Perhaps the Indians had been attacking the ranch's cattle, using them instead of hunting for deer, and the owner had captured this woman to make an example of her to the tribe. But how would the tribe know? Would the owner send for a subchief and show him her body and the mysterious superstitious elements surrounding her? In the hope that the evil spirits would keep the Indians away?

If that was the scenario, it hadn't worked. The Indians must have come back and silently wiped out every person on the ranch.

Why hadn't they taken the body away with them? The superstitions and "magic" were tremendously powerful elements in most Indian tribes. Perhaps this woman had been so imbued with the foreign evil spirits that her soul was lost forever and there was no need to take her for proper Cheyenne burial.

Cheyenne. Yes, they would be from the Cheyenne people in this corner of Colorado.

What now?

Bury her.

Morgan went back into the shed and cut the woman's feet where they had been tied. Her body slumped forward, and as it did an Indian tomahawk slashed forward, barely missing Morgan's head. He saw where a thick willow had been bent behind the tomahawk and adjusted so when the body came free it would release the pressure on the split and bent willow spring and project the weapon forward.

No spirits or superstitions here. The Indians had

set up the booby trap to punish whoever removed the woman. It must have been done after they killed everyone at the ranch.

Morgan worked with more care as he finished removing the body. It was stiff in places but starting to decompose in others. At last he found a tarp, and pushed her on it and carried it around the barn. He buried her in back of the barn out of sight of the house.

He heard the clanging of a dinner bell as he finished filling in the shallow grave.

Morgan walked around the side of the barn and looked up in surprise at a man walking a large white horse toward the house. Morgan drew and sent a .45 round into the ground in front of the horse. The man pulled the horse to a stop and looked Morgan's way.

"Mister, just who the hell are you and what are you doing here on the Lucky Mountain Ranch?" Morgan bellowed, centering his .45's sights on the chest of the large man who forked the horse.

Chapter Four

The man on the white horse in the ranch yard lifted his hands slowly.

"Easy there, stranger. Just saw smoke here and figured I might get a hot meal."

"You're no grub-line rider. Ease down off the mount gentle-like on my side of the critter. You've got a lot of questions to answer."

The big man came down. Morgan figured he was at least six inches over six feet tall, maybe eight inches, and could weigh a rock-hard 300 pounds.

"Name?" Morgan demanded.

"Ezra Plainsman."

"Where you from?"

"Denver. I was supposed to come to the Lucky Mountain spread. Is this it?"

"What's your business here?"

"That's confidential, between me and one Amos Devlin. Who are you?"

"You have any identification?"

"A letter from Devlin."

"Anybody could have taken that off the real Plainsman. Drop your six-gun gently to the ground."

"Now see here, there's no need—"

Morgan cocked his six-gun, and the click had a chilling effect on the big man. He took out his revolver with his thumb and one finger, bent, and laid it on the ground.

"Now, let's see the letter from Devlin. Put it beside the weapon and back up six feet."

The man did so, and Morgan grabbed the gun and the letter. He checked it quickly. The letter looked genuine enough. The man supposed to come was an assayer.

"You an assayer, Plainsman?"

"Yes."

"You want to see Devlin, walk around the side of the house to the back."

They walked past the kitchen door and Claresta came out. She held a shotgun over one arm as if she knew how to use it.

"Any trouble?" she asked.

"Not sure. Hold supper for a minute."

Morgan walked the stranger to the back of the house and lifted the blanket off Amos Devlin.

"Be damned!" Plainsman said. "When did it happen?"

"Figured you might be able to help me out on that. What size are your boots?"

"Boots? A man I'm supposed to come see is dead and you ask me about my boot size?"

"What size?"

"Twelve Double E. Is that important?"

"When did you leave Denver?"

"Yesterday, by train. Got off at Loveland and came on out. I didn't figure on anything like this."

"What did you figure?"

"That I'd have some gold ore samples to assay."
"Gold ore? Here at the ranch?" Morgan asked.
"Yes, gold ore. That's my specialty."
"You bring your tools with you?"
"All in my saddlebags."
Morgan snorted. "Gold. Nobody said anything to me about any damn gold mine, or placer on the river. What did Devlin tell you?"
"Simply to report here within a week to do some assay work. He didn't say on what. I'm here."
"Devlin wasn't the only one killed here, Plainsman. The other five men, ranch hands, and the cook were also killed by knife, battle ax, or arrow. Could be Indians. Could be someone who wants us to think it was Indians. You know anything about the behavior of the Cheyenne in this area?"
"Not coming from Denver, I don't. Haven't seen anything about any massacres up this way in the Denver papers."
Morgan caved in. He holstered his six-gun. "Come into the kitchen and meet the rest of the team. Mrs. Devlin is here and her daughter Claresta. We arrived from Chicago about six hours ago."
Then went in the kitchen, and Claresta wiped her hands on her apron.
"I heard most of what you two said. I'm Claresta Devlin. I've put on another plate. Set down and let's eat before things get cold . . . again."
Mrs. Devlin came out. She had changed into a less formal dress and introduced herself to the agent. She said nothing more, ate, and then nodded to them and went back to her bedroom.
The supper was canned stew with added potatoes, fresh-made biscuits, lots of coffee, and a jar of homemade blackberry jam that had been sealed with paraffin.

After the food was gone and they were sipping their second cup of coffee, Plainsman looked up. "Then I'd guess you don't have any gold ore samples for me to assay?"

"Good guess," Morgan said. "If he had some, I wouldn't know where he hid them. Maybe the Indians took the samples, if they were Indians. What happens now?"

"I stay the night, if I may, in the house or the barn, and ride back to Loveland in the morning and go back to Denver."

"Maybe not," Claresta said. "When I heard you talking about gold, I did some looking around. Trying to figure out where Father would hide ore samples. We used to play hide the thimble. I could find it almost every time."

She stood and motioned for them to follow her. In the pantry, a small room with a door, she showed them the footstuffs, then pulled on a handle. It came forward to reveal a bin. That one would hold a 50-pound sack of sugar. The next one had flour, and the third one dry beans.

"I decided to start some beans to soak. Beans are good for a person. Just for fun I pushed my hand deep into the loose beans. Must be fifty pounds of them in here."

She pushed her hand down and when it came up, she had a leather pouch about a foot square. She gave it to Morgan, who untied the leather thongs binding it together.

Morgan spread it out on the counter and shook out a dozen chunks of white quartz rock that was flaked with heavy streaks and veins of gold.

"Gold quartz," Plainsman said. "That's hard-rock mining. I didn't know there was anything like that going on up here."

Morgan stared at the gold ore. It looked better

than average, but it was the kind of ore that took a stamping mill and a processing plant to get at the gold.

"Let me go get my equipment," the assayist said, and hurried out to where his white stallion had been tied to a short hitching rail.

Claresta stared at the gold. "What in the world can we do now, Mr. Morgan? I've been trying to think it through ever since I found it. I knew it was gold ore. Why didn't Father tell us? Where is the mine? Why all the secrecy? And most important, did the Indians kill everyone because they didn't want miners to come into these hills where the tribe lives?"

"I don't know any answers, small one, but I'm damned sure going to find out what's going on."

Plainsman came back in, and set up his gear on the table to weigh out a specific amount of the quartz ore. He broke some of the pieces until he had a precise amount of 29.167 grams.

He looked up. "Do you have a forge here?"

Morgan shook his head. "Haven't seen one. Perhaps you can use the fireplace or the kitchen stove."

"The stove will work. This is going to smell a bit. You might want to wait outside."

"No, I want to see exactly what you do," Claresta said.

They watched as the assayist put a heavy iron pot on the stove and built up a hot fire. He melted the ore sample with some fluxes until it reduced in size to a bunch of worthless slag and a button of ore.

"Usually there is silver mixed in with gold," Plainsman said. "What we do next is called cupellation. This button of metal is now melted in an oxidizing atmosphere to burn off the impurities, and that leaves us with a doré button of pure gold and silver alloy."

When the button cooled he took out a delicate scale and weighed it.

"Now we have the total weight, and we use hot diluted nitric acid to dissolve out the silver. What's left is pure gold. This is subtracted from the gold and silver weight to determine the exact amount of gold and in what proportion the gold is to a ton of gold ore like the sample.

"By multiplying it out we report the value per ton the gold ore is worth, with the gold valued at twenty dollars the sixty-seven cents per ounce."

"Sounds simple enough," Claresta said. "How much is our gold sample worth?"

Plainsman chuckled. "It's going to take me an hour or two to complete the assay. If there's anything unusual, I do the whole thing again with a new sample. I must be absolutely accurate on the assay or I could bring about a disaster for some mine owner who thought he had a good mine but it really wasn't."

"Let's take a walk," Morgan said, touching Claresta's shoulder.

Outside they looked at the surrounding fir and pine-covered hills.

"Where on earth could Daddy have found a mine around here?"

"Usually mines aren't where you think they might be. The best way to discover a mine is to find an outcropping of rock that was pushed up a million years ago by some volcanic action. Now it's an upthrust of different kind of rock than the rest of the mountain, and hopefully it's loaded with gold and silver, platinum, copper, or lead."

"So where do we start?"

"Good question. Tomorrow I'll make a circle

around the ranch buildings and go over it like a Crow Indian watching for a Cheyenne war party. Somewhere I should find a trail of sorts that leads away from the ranch. Your father must have done some work on a cave or at an upthrust and been up and back several times. If so, there should be a noticeable trail I can discover and follow."

"I'll help you. I'm quick picking up new ideas."

"You certainly are."

"Not that. You're thinking evil thoughts."

"Not evil, pleasurable. Oh, you said your mother brought money with her? We'll need to pay the assayist for his two days of travel and the assay. But we can also hire him to engage two cowboys in Loveland, and have them come out here to work the ranch. Two men can do it for now. Then I won't have to ride back to town."

"I'll get money from Mother. How much?"

"I have no idea." He looked at the surrounding hills again, and to the north less than half a mile he could see some rocky ledges where no trees grew. If the scouting circle showed up no trail, the ledges would be a spot to begin the search. Somewhere around here there was the start of a gold mine, and the men who knew where it was were in their graves.

Except Amos Devlin.

He caught her hand. "Let's pick out a spot for your father's grave and start digging."

Well before they had the grave finished, Ezra Plainsman came out the kitchen door and stretched. He saw them and walked up the slope.

"Fine place for a grave," Plainsman said. "It's just high enough so the gentleman's spirit can take flight to the higher life."

"You sound part Indian," Morgan said.

"Not really. That ore is good. Some of the best

I've seen. I checked another sample and it came out about the same. Less than two percent silver. The gold should run about four hundred dollars to the ton."

"We're rich!" Claresta shouted.

Morgan laughed. "Not by any stretch. First we have to find the spot, then we have to dig out that ore, then it has to be put through a stamping mill and then processed and refined, and at last we'd have the gold. It's a long, expensive process."

"Quite right, Mr. Morgan. It would take a good-sized investment to put such a mine into production. Of course, after that investment, there *could* be a fortune there. Unless the vein petered out after twenty feet."

"That happens?" Claresta asked.

"More than not. Mining is an extremely risky business. I've been in and out of gold mines most of my life. If you find the mother lode this came from, I'll be glad to help you evaluate it. Just send a letter to me on the train from Loveland. I'll be here in two days. Oh, my card."

Morgan took the card. It had his name, an address, the title of Mining Engineer, and the words "confidential assayist."

"And all of this is confidential?"

"Absolutely. Not even a court of law can force me to reveal the results of a professional, confidential assay. Public or government assays are another matter. With me it's like a lawyer having privileged information."

"Mr. Plainsman, would a potential mine such as this be enough to make someone kill seven men?"

"Miss Devlin. I've seen men killed for two hundred dollars of gold dust. Yes indeed, an ore sample like this and the knowing where it came from certainly is enough motive to kill a dozen men, if it would guarantee one man the mine."

"I was afraid that might be the case," Claresta said.

"You think that's why the men were killed, Mr. Morgan? I thought you said Indians."

"Could have been Indians. Now that doesn't seem so realistic. Indians have no use for squaw's clay. Gold is too soft to be any use to the Cheyenne."

They finished the grave a half hour later, and just before dusk Morgan brought up Amos Devlin's body, wrapped in a sheet, and lowered him into the hole. Mrs. Devlin came out of the house and halfway to the grave, then sank to the ground on her knees.

Claresta said a few words over the grave, as much as she could remember from a funeral she had been to a year ago. Then she took her mother back into the house and the two men shoveled the dirt into the final resting place for Amos Devlin.

An hour later the men went down the dark path to the ranch house and into the kitchen. Claresta sat at the table drinking coffee. She poured cups full for the men without saying a word.

"Claresta, would your mother sleep out in the woods tonight?" Morgan asked.

"I was thinking about that. The woods would be less specific and much safer than the house in case we had angry visitors. No, I'm sure she wouldn't. The woods would scare her more."

"Then you stay in the room with her tonight. Lock your door and bar the windows. There are wooden shutters inside. I'll be standing guard tonight outside. I'm a light sleeper. If any foot hits the ground within a hundred yards, I'll know about it. Such skills help a man stay alive in Indian country."

Ezra Plainsman shifted uneasily in his chair. "I think I'll take to the woods with you, Mr. Morgan. I don't plan on getting my hair lifted tonight."

It was almost midnight when Morgan heard what could only be a horse walking up the lane. He lifted from his blanket, grabbed the Spencer rifle and pushed off the safety, and stood behind a foot-thick pine. There was almost no moon.

Suddenly a rifle slammed three shots at the ranch house, and a window broke. Morgan quickly fired four shots around the muzzle flash from below the house and heard a screech of pain. Then a horse pounded down the lane away from the house and to the south.

Chapter Five

Lee Morgan fired one more shot at the retreating sniper, then turned to where the assayist had been.

"Plainsman, stay here, I'm going for a short run." Morgan brought the Spencer up to port arms and ran forward, down past the ranch house and along the lane that led south. He sprinted for a hundred yards, then eased off to a trot before he stopped. He listened.

He could hear hoofbeats on the hard lane ahead of him. The rider was moving far away. Morgan settled into an Indian trot. He had learned it early in life, and could still cover six miles an hour for six hours without stopping.

The Spencer carbine slowed him a little, but he watched the terrain, and when he was two miles from the ranch house he stopped and listened again.

Far south he heard a horse neighing to a friend. He didn't know if the animal was one from the sniper or his party, but there had to be more than one horse to make such a greeting. The sound had come from due south toward the river.

Morgan moved out again, a little slower this time, and after another mile he stopped, rested, and listened. He heard no more sounds.

Another half mile and he smelled smoke. Damn thoughtful of the sniper and party to light a fire to lead him directly to them. He moved ahead slower now, homing in on the drift of smoke that came to the north.

It took him a half hour to walk without a sound through the valley, and then through the edge of the brush and scattering of oak and juniper near the tributary to the Big Thompson River.

He had heard some talk, and then all was quiet. Two horses made noises to each other.

Twenty yards ahead he saw the faint glow of a fire. Morgan moved around it like an Apache scout, never brushing a twig or leaf, not breaking a dry branch, staying downwind so the horses would not sense him.

The voices came through faintly.

"The son of a bitch shot me!"

"Told you, dumbbell, fire and move. Always move after you fire at night or when the other guy can see your smoke. That's the way to stay alive. Fire and move. You'll remember next time."

Morgan needed them alive, at least one of them alive.

"Somebody's out there!" the first voice said.

"Hell, yes. You had six drinks of whiskey and now you can see in the dark. You said nobody followed you on horseback. We're four miles from the ranch. Now settle down."

The younger man sat bolt upright in his blankets.

"I can smell somebody out there."

Morgan aimed at the kid who sat up with the Spencer, then bellowed from ten yards away.

"Freeze, I've got a shotgun with double-ought buck. Move and you're both dead."

Even as he barked at them the older-sounding man rolled out of the firelight. The other one dropped down and Morgan fired. The kid screeched in pain.

Morgan could hear the second man tearing through the brush, then the sound of leather creaking and a horse slamming past the willow and mountain mahogany as he fled.

"You still alive?" Morgan asked.

"Damned right and I got twenty rounds. You try to come in and you're the one dead."

"So I just shoot you from here and go back home," Morgan said, his voice flat, disinterested.

"Wait a minute. What do you want?"

"Why did you fire at the ranch house back there?"

"Orders."

"Who hired you?"

"Not a chance. I'll die first."

"Big words, son. How old are you?"

"Nearly nineteen."

"Just a babe in the woods. You saw what your buddy did. He cut and run leaving you to face me alone."

"He warn't shot."

"He abandoned you. Did he tell you to shoot out the windows?"

"No, the boss did."

"Who's the boss?"

"Can't tell you."

"So you think you're being a hero by dying right here, alone, hurting, giving up another fifty years of sweet life. Think about it, son."

"I'm not your son!"

"Hate your father a lot, I'd guess."

"Shut up!"

"So get even with your old man. Die an outlaw and let him sweat. That will really fix him!"

"Stop it!"

"Who's your boss? Who paid you to come out here?"

"Oh, hell. You're right. Not worth getting killed over. Only paid us twenty-five dollars for the two of us. We come out of Loveland. Told us some folks moved in to this place and he didn't want you there, so we should shoot out the windows. That's all the hell we was supposed to do. Then we ride for Denver."

"What was his name?"

"Hey, he never told me. Just gave us the cash and a box of shells and said he trusted us to do the job. Damn but he was a big bastard. Must have been seven feet tall and weighed way over three hundred pounds."

"But he had small feet," Morgan probed.

"Hail no! Biggest damn feet I ever seen. Special-made boots, I'd wager. Had to be fourteens at least."

Morgan chewed on it a minute. Made sense. Big man, Loveland. Anybody in town would know when the Devlins arrived, where they were headed.

"Okay, put down the six-gun. How bad you shot?"

"Shoulder and just a graze on my arm."

"You want me to patch you up?"

"No. You done me enough. Bullet went out my upper arm, I guess it is. I got it stopped bleeding. Thanks for not killing me. I can get back to town by myself."

"You sure?"
"Yeah."
"Get patched up and ride for Denver, be safer for you that way."
There was a long pause. "Why . . . why you letting me go?"
"You told me all you know. I believe you, 'cause I figure you're a lousy liar. Now I got to piece together the rest of it. You know what happened at that ranch?"
"Hell no."
"Seven men and a woman were killed there last week sometime."
"Holy shit!"
"True. Have a nice ride."
Morgan pulled back as silently as he had arrived. The kid went on talking never knowing Morgan had left.

Back at the ranch an hour and a half later, Plainsman came out of the shadows near the front porch.
"That you, Morgan?"
"If it ain't, you're dead, Plainsman."
"Yeah, I'm not good at this shooting stuff. You find him?"
Inside he told Plainsman and Claresta about it. She sat at the kitchen table sipping coffee and wearing a warm robe over her nightdress.
"So I let him go. We're talking about a big man in Loveland. That big man wasn't you, was it, Plainsman?"
"No, but I can understand the question."
"Kid said his boss was seven feet tall and well over three hundred pounds. I found a boot print over some of the Indian moccasins that was at least a fourteen-wide size."

"So he must have been here during or after the Indian raid."

"If it was Indians," Claresta said.

"How is your mother doing?"

"She fainted when the shot ripped through the window in our room. She's getting more angry now than afraid."

"Good way to stay alive," Morgan said. "Now it's time for everyone to get back to sleep. Morning gonna be here in about three hours."

When morning came, Morgan and Plainsman ate breakfast and talked. They devoured plates of hotcakes Claresta furnished and re-filled their coffee cups.

"Settled," Morgan said. "We pay your rail fare, ten dollars a day for the two days, and twelve-fifty for the assay, and we get complete secrecy."

Plainsman handed Morgan the two gold buttons, about the size of shirt buttons, and Morgan gave the assayer $37.

"Now about the two ranch hands. You can do that?"

"Don't see why not. I'll give each one a three-dollar advance on his first week's pay and tell them to bring two horses each. No problem. I'll have to kill a few hours waiting for the afternoon train anyway."

Morgan gave the man a ten-dollar gold piece and they shook hands.

"Oh, and don't say anything about the deaths here or the shooting last night. I want the Big Man to be wondering what happened."

Plainsman had fed his big white stallion and groomed her, and now stepped into the saddle.

"Good luck finding your mine." He touched his

hat in salute, waved at Claresta, and rode down the faint trail to the south.

Morgan turned at once to his work at hand. He waved at Claresta, then paced out from the barn 200 yards and began making his circle around the ranch buildings. It was slow work. He scanned the general area ten yards in front of him, then turned his gaze to the ground looking for any sign of a trail that had been worn through the grass and weeds of the mountain meadow.

If anyone had walked or ridden a horse along the same path even three or four times, it would show up across the grassy valley like a wagon road. The foot-high grass made that a certainty.

He made two circles around the buildings, and when he looked backwards and then forward, the only thing he could spot was his own circular trail.

Morgan went to the kitchen, and found Claresta boiling beans and baking bread in the small oven.

"The heat goes up and then down," she wailed. "How can I ever know if the bread is done?"

"Stick a toothpick in it. If it comes out dry, the bread is done. If it's wet, give the loaves another five minutes."

She frowned. "Where did you learn that?"

"At my mother's knee. How is your mother?"

"I'm just fine, Mr. Morgan," Martha Devlin said. She sat by the window looking at the valley, and he hadn't seen her when he came in. She wore an even more practical gingham dress now, and had evidently combed out her long dark hair and wound it in a bun at the nape of her neck.

"Claresta and I have had a good long talk. I've decided I have a practical and wonderful daughter, and that it's high time I take a little responsibility. Mr. Morgan, you need to know that we do have some money.

"I brought with me from Chicago a total of twelve thousand, two hundred, and sixty-five dollars. That's our total resources. I don't know if this ranch is paid for or not. I would think it is not. Claresta found a legal file and a box of other important papers. I'm going to go through them right now with this fresh cup of coffee."

Mrs. Devlin rose and walked out of the kitchen. Claresta smiled at Morgan.

"Told you she would come around. She's tougher than she seemed coming out here." Claresta moved over to Morgan, and when he put down his cup of coffee, she bent and kissed his lips.

"Mmmmmmm, that tastes good," she said. "I want to order some more of those."

"What would your mother say?"

"Oh, I told her I like you and I think you're sexy and beautiful and kind. She told me to trap you into marriage, *any way that I could.*"

"Meaning she wants you to get pregnant."

"Something like that. We both know even that won't work, but we can at least enjoy each other now and then."

"Now and then is a good plan." He finished the coffee and she checked the bread. It was done. She took it from the oven and, with a sharp knife, cut off a slab an inch thick and buttered it with fresh creamery butter she had found in the coolness of the well house. She gave it to Morgan.

"My mother used to do that," Morgan said. He bent and kissed her lips, took the hot bread with the butter starting to melt into it, and went outside.

He saddled the same bay horse he had used before, and sat there a minute thinking how he would hide the trail to the mine if he had found one close by. Maybe it wasn't close by.

"No trail," he said out loud. How could a horse travel the same route ten times and not leave a trail? Two obvious answers. Follow a current trail, or wallk up the creek.

A tributary to the Big Thompson wound to the north past the ranch buildings 25 yards to the east near the east side of the finger valley where the ranch sat.

The trail south toward the Big Thompson and on east to Loveland wound through the edge of the valley. There were no ridges and no high mountains anywhere near it.

He rode to the creek and looked back the way he had come. There were dozens of tracks from the ranch yard to the creek. A small dam had been made of rocks and dirt to form a pool so six or eight horses could drink at once.

There was no water in the corral, so the horses must have been led over once or twice a day to drink. No help there.

He walked across the hock-deep water to the far side. Here there were a few tracks, but none that went anywhere. Loose horses grazing a moment perhaps.

Morgan looked upstream. The small creek was fairly brush-free. It was eight to ten feet wide in most places and no more than a foot or eighteen inches deep.

A highway. Morgan turned and began walking upstream. When the brush at the sides thinned, he looked farther ahead. Perhaps two miles he could see the rocky cliffs rising from the fir, pine, and spruce that covered green hills. It was a chance.

He worked up through the stream for a half mile, then came out on the west side and rode along watching for any semblance of a trail. He spotted one, but he soon discovered three-toed deer tracks at the edge of the water. A deer trail.

Another half mile upstream the waterway divided into three branches. He took the center one, which seemed to point closest to the rocky ridge, and rode again beside the stream. Another half mile and he found what he had been looking for. A well-worn trail came out of the stream and turned to the north on the west side of the water, which was now a tenth the size it had been at the ranch.

The trail had been made by shod horses. It was not a wagon road, but worn with many trips by horses. The middle of it was almost bare from the cutting effect of the hooves. Morgan nodded grimly as he worked upward along the trail.

It was just past noon. He had nine hours of daylight left to explore this area and see where the hidden trail led.

Morgan came around a small bend in the stream and looked up at the towering rock cliff 50 yards away. Near the base of the cliff he saw three Indians drawing back their bows, each with an arrow tipped with a man-killing, inch-wide, steel point.

Chapter Six

Morgan kicked his horse and it surged back into the brush at the side of the stream. The animal stopped behind two thick fir trees before the arrows could land. Lee Morgan dropped off the mount at once and lifted the Spencer repeating rifle from the boot. He leaned around the tree and saw the Indians firing more arrows, so he put a shot over their heads. They ducked behind big trees and he waited.

The wind whispered through the tops of the tall trees. A crow lifted from a ponderosa pine and sailed away north cawing his displeasure at the intrusion. Somewhere a day-feeding owl hooted. All else was quiet.

For a moment Morgan wondered if the three savages were working around him with one man on each side. No, they had warned him away, but that only made him more curious. Was there a gold mine into a mother lode up there below that cliff? Where else would that gold ore come from that Plainsman had assayed? Had to be.

The tall man moved as silently as any Indian as he began to use the cover of the stream's brush and trees and crept forward. He went 50 feet, peered around a fir at the base, and watched where the redskins had vanished. For just a second he saw an Indian's black hair rise over a log. Then it was lowered. At least one of them was still there.

He changed his angle and went across the small stream and worked up the far side. Now he had the chattering of the creek to cover his movement noise. Morgan checked his flanks at every move. He didn't want to slip up on these three and have ten more watching him from the other side. But he could find no more savages or any evidence that there was a large group here.

After 20 minutes he was where he wanted to be, at the side about 20 yards from the redskins and slightly to the back of them. He fired one round from the Spencer between two of the braves who lay behind a large log.

Morgan stood in plain sight before he fired. He gave the hand signal for friend and watched the Indians. They were duty-bound to reply.

The tallest of the three held his bow ready but without an arrow in it. Morgan knew he could draw an arrow and fire it in less than a second. The man signed with one hand.

"You are not friend."

"Stranger in this land," Morgan signed.

The Indians talked together for a moment.

"You did not kill us when you could have. You move like one of the People. You should understand that this is sacred land. White eyes not allowed here. You must go."

"Did the other white eyes take a woman's clay from this mountain?"

"We don't know. This is sacred land of Cheyenne. You must go."

Morgan lowered his rifle. The three red men lowered their bows down to their sides.

"I will go," Morgan signed. When he had said it, the three Indians nodded at him, turned, exposing their backs to him in a show of trust, and walked away to the north into the trees.

Morgan watched them a moment, then turned his back on them to show his bravery, and walked into cover of his own. He stopped and watched. The Indians did not return to the open, but he knew they must be close and observing what he did.

He jogged back to his horse, and rode toward the ranch house. He could understand a sacred mountain. The Cheyenne were one of the most superstitious, of any of the plains tribes, believers in spirit, ghosts, and helpful gods. But why would they kill the men at a ranch almost four miles away?

They would kill them on the sacred mountain, but not in the valley. All of the men at the Lucky Mountain Ranch had been killed on the spread. If the Indians did it, why?

He rode back to the ranch house with the problem still bothering him. They were Cheyenne and they claimed the "sacred mountain" explained their actions with Morgan. But what else had they done?

He couldn't be sure.

At the ranch house he found Claresta with strands of red hair in her face as she worked on dinner.

"I found a chicken coop out in back. It had ten

laying hens and half a dozen roosters and maybe twenty young ones that will be good for fried chicken." She laughed. "Yes, I will learn how to kill a chicken and dress it and then cook it. But for dinner today we're having omelets, and toast and coffee. These are three egg omelets."

Morgan grinned watching her. She was like a kid with a new toy. A whole kitchen to play with and act like a grown-up. Even so, sometimes she was more grown-up than her mother.

Martha trailed out when Claresta called.

"I'm not feeling well today," Martha announced.

Claresta laughed. "Forget it, Mother. That old story won't work anymore. You're on your last jug of whiskey and when that's gone, there won't be any more. You're going to take over the house and cooking, so you better learn where things are. Tomorrow I'm off to be a cowboy. Somebody has to take care of those critters out there. I've got those riding breeches. I'll have to learn how to throw a rope. Morgan can teach me."

"Can't be done in a day, young lady," Morgan said.

"We've got time. What did you find upstream?"

He told them.

"So there really is a gold mine up there?"

"Looks like it from all the traffic up and down that trail. Of course, the way they tried to hide the trail makes me think there is a mine."

"But the Indians. Will they kill anyone who goes up there?"

"I'd say that's their job right now. Maybe we can do some big talk with their chief and grant him some benefits, maybe beef now that the buffalo are getting scarce in this area. Never were a lot over in these mountains. They feel more at home on the plains and stay there."

"So what's the next step?" Claresta asked.

Morgan finished the omelet and laughed. "I've been trying to figure out the same thing. First I think we better have a look at the cattle and see what they need. Then we'll worry about the mine."

"Good. I'll have my riding pants on in ten minutes. Can I ride that other horse we have?"

"We'll see."

"Mother, I'm leaving the dishes to you. And we're going to expect to have a good dinner tonight when we come back."

"What's to cook?" Martha asked, suddenly jolted out of her daze.

"I don't know. That's your job and I wouldn't think of stepping on your toes." She winked at Morgan and stood. "I'll be right back. Meet you at the barn."

Morgan saddled the second wagon horse. Neither one would be much good as a cow pony, but they were basic transport. When Claresta came into the barn she had her long red hair braided down each side and a perky little bill cap on to shield her green eyes. The riding breeches were tight and showed off her slender figure well.

She looked at the horse. "I'm going to have to learn how to saddle my own horse. Show me how to unsaddle it, then I'll learn how to saddle the critter."

Morgan had time. He still hadn't figured out what to do next about the mine. He showed the girl/woman how to un-cinch the saddle and what else had to be done before the saddle could come off.

"It's heavy."

"I'm not a child."

"Grab it by the horn and the back of the skirt and drag the whole thing toward you off the horse's back. It might be heavier than you expect."

Claresta did, and the 30-pound saddle came off and went straight to the ground. She fell under it trying to catch it.

"Hey, this is heavy!" Claresta said. "You didn't tell me it was so . . ." She stopped and grinned.

"Can you lift it?"

She tried and lifted it up. He pointed to the feed box. "Throw it up on there. Lead your mount over near it and tie her. Then jump up on the feed box and drop the saddle on your horse. I used to do it that way when I was a squirt."

Ten minutes later she had the horse saddled, then struggled to lift up into it after she got her foot into the left-hand stirrup.

After three tries, she made it.

"Always hardest the first time," he said. "Sit tall, back straight." He looked at the stirrups. She could reach only one. "I better shorten those stirrups a little for you." She watched him.

"Take this leather strap right here and move the buckle up and down to adjust it."

They rode out at a walk, and he taught her some of the basics of riding a horse. She picked it up quickly.

They worked down toward the south, checking the cows and calves, counting the range bulls. There were no steers in the herd ready for market.

"Usually takes three to four years for a calf to grow big enough as a steer to go to market," Morgan said. "That's one of the reasons starting a new ranch is so hard. No income for the first four years."

They found one calf stuck in a mud hole, and it took both of them to drag the frightened creature out of the hole. It wasn't quicksand, just a bog near the stream that had a deep bottom of sticky mud.

Claresta sat on the bank holding on to the calf's tail and pulling. Morgan stood in the mire up past his knees, lifting on the calf's chest. Slowly he edged the animal toward the hard shore.

Then one foot came out and the calf surged toward the better footing. Claresta lost her balance and sat down in the mud. She shrieked in surprise and then anger. A minute later she was roaring with laughter.

Morgan finished getting the calf to dry land, then he reached for Claresta. She put her arm around him as he pulled her out, and then kissed him soundly.

"I've missed that," she said when their lips parted.

"Me too," Morgan said. "In fact, that's the muddiest kiss I've ever had."

She stared at him, not knowing whether to scream or laugh. At last both of them hooted with laughter and went to the creek to wash off. Morgan waded in and let the stream help wash away the mud and goo. Claresta sat on the shore using handfuls of water to splash on her bottom until it was somewhat clean. Then she sat in the grass and got the rest of the mud off by rubbing her breeches on the grass. Morgan offered to help, but he was too late. He shrugged.

"Good as new," she said.

Morgan patted her round tight bottom and grinned. "Better than new, it's experienced."

"You want to see just how good it is right here and right now, Lee Morgan?"

"Love to, but a kiss better satisfy us both for the moment. We need to check the rest of the herd before our two cowhands arrive. Are you keeping a count?"

"A count? You didn't tell me to."

"True. We can estimate right now. But soon we'll need a firm count."

They put in another two hours checking three miles down the valley to the end of the spread of the cattle. They drove six of them back north to stay more with the rest of the herd. Just as they turned toward home, they saw two men riding toward them across the green of the valley floor. Both had well-worn cowboy hats and each had a rope on his saddle and trailed a second horse.

"Looks like our two hands," Morgan said. They rode to meet the pair. The four horses pulled up when the people got within talking distance.

"You be Lee Morgan?" the older of the two asked.

"That's right. You the two hands that Mr. Plainsman hired for us in Loveland?"

"About right, Mr. Morgan. He said bring an extra horse, so here we are."

"Just about in time for supper," Morgan said. "This is Claresta Devlin, one of the owners of the spread. Let's ride up to the bunkhouse and I'll show you around the buildings before it gets dark."

Claresta Devlin rode ahead of them. She told Morgan that since they had two more mouths, she'd better help her mother with the cooking.

When Claresta got to the hitching rail ouside the ranch house, she left her horse there and hurried inside. Her mother was in a frenzied state. She had nothing ready and was trying to peel potatoes.

Claresta smiled, told her mother she was doing a good job, and hurried to help. The beans that had been simmering on the back of the stove were done. She cut up some bacon, half fried it, and dropped it into the beans for flavoring, then let it cook some more.

The potatoes would be done in fifteen minutes, and she found a tin of canned green peas. She opened it and added some cream to the peas and heated them. She made two pots of coffee, sliced some of the loaf of bread, put out butter and homemade jam, and by the time supper was due to be on the table, she was ready.

She would need some help to learn how to kill and dress out a chicken. But she'd have Lee Morgan teach her that just as soon as possible.

Supper was a success, mainly because the two hands were average cowboys not used to home cooking, and willing to eat anything that was hot, dead, and not too spoiled. They had even washed their hands and faces and slicked back their hair, for all the good it did.

"Martha Devlin, these are two new hands," Morgan said. "The tall handsome one is Lonnie Seismore, and the shorter, handsome gent is Will Lacey."

After the meal, the hands went out to get settled in the bunkhouse and Claresta helped her mother clean up.

By the time it was dark, Morgan had his horse back at the hitching rail. He met Claresta as she came out to check on him.

"Morgan, you lock your bedroom door tonight and I'll kill you." She kissed him and he enjoyed it.

"Work first," he said. "It's time I find out whether or not there's a gold mine up there. I'm taking a lantern and lots of stinker matches. No, you're not going along. Those three Cheyenne are still up there for sure. I've got to get past them and see if there's a mine or not."

"Be careful," Claresta said.

"Damn right," Morgan said. "With the Cheyenne you're careful or you're dead."

He stepped into the saddle, waved at the young lady in the fading light, and rode north toward the mine and the Cheyenne.

Chapter Seven

Just after dark, Morgan rode the same route north he'd ridden before, working up the other side of the creek to where he knew the trail came out. Then he followed the well-worn track to the place that was this side of the spot where he had been fired at by the three warriors.

There he left his mount and walked forward softly carrying only the unlit coal-oil lantern he had brought from the barn. He stopped often to listen the last 200 yards. When he came around the bend in the trail where the Indians had first seen him, he waited for five minutes. Morgan heard and saw nothing at the base of the cliff.

He moved cautiously again, not making a sound, listening for any talk or movement ahead of him. Nothing.

The trail went past where the Indians had been standing guard. Another 100 yards and the trail turned into a small break in the bluff. The cavity was only 30 yards deep, but here in the dim moonlight he found piles of dirt and two heavy wheelbarrows, as well as several picks and shovels and the long steel star drills for pounding round holes in hard rock.

At the face of the crevice in the cliff he could see in the dim light a natural opening. It had been widened, and there were many tracks where men and wheelbarrows had come out. He moved into it a few feet and lit the lantern that he carried.

There was a natural cavern here that extended back well beyond the feeble light of his lantern. He checked the floor and found the wheelbarrow tracks. He followed them. Another 30 yards back into the mountains, he discovered where the cavern stopped and a tunnel had been cut with pick, hand drill, and hammer.

At the top of the six-foot-high tunnel, he saw where there was an upthrust of the gold-bearing white quartz. It looked exactly like what he had seen in the gold ore pouch Claresta had found in the bean bin.

The tunnel into the hard rock had been cut only a dozen feet, and he saw more of the quartz rock on the sides. Somewhere they must be stacking up the gold-bearing ore, waiting to be able to process it.

At the end of the tunnel, the face of rock showed a two-foot-wide vein of the heavy gold threaded white quartz. If that vein continued for a few hundred feet, this one vein could be worth hundreds of thousands of dollars.

Morgan lifted the lantern higher and examined the face better, then the loose dirt below it. To his surprise and shock he found a large boot print there. It was the same 14 size he had seen twice before. The sole had an X tread pattern he remembered. The big man had been here and knew all about the mine and how rich it could be.

But who the hell was the gent with the big boots?

Morgan retraced his steps out of the mine. He checked carefully with the lantern and made sure there were no offshoot tunnels, no branches of the natural cavern. It was as if in some gigantic upthrusting of the mountain range two big slabs of rock had come together and left this cavern between them.

As he walked toward the entrance to the tunnel, Morgan could see the lighter sky outside and he heard some high-pierced chattering. He blew out the lantern and hurried to the opening of the cavern.

Outside, in the pale moonlight, he could tell that at least three Indians had gathered. Had they seen him go into the cavern, and were they now waiting for him to come out so they could kill him? Or had they found his horse and were they still looking for him?

Morgan edged up to the very lip of the cavern entrance. He could see three Indians in the faint moonlight. They were too close for him to be able to slip out of the cavern without being seen. He didn't want to fight his way out.

He settled down to see what they would do. Morgan had stashed the dark lantern near the entrance where he could find it again. He waited patiently. He had his .45 Colt on his hip and 20 rounds in his belt loops, but that was all. Not enough ammo to fight a war.

The Indians talked rapidly, some pointing at the entrance, some motioning furiously to the north.

Morgan had established one fact. The actual cavern was not an ancient Indian or chiefs' burial ground, so there could be no problem with this being sacred ground. That had been a real worry. With that out of the way, he began to devise some way to escape.

He had to get them away from the front of the mine somehow. At least there was plenty of darkness left. The sky had been clear, so there would be no clouds to cover the moon. He thought of several ways. But the age-old method of leading an enemy away on a false trail seemed best.

He went back into the mine a ways and found six hand-sized rocks and a few smaller ones. He moved to the left side of the cavern opening as he faced it so he could use his right hand more effectively.

He took one of the middle-sized rocks and hefted it, then waited. The indians were quiet for a moment, then began arguing again. As they yelped and talked, Morgan moved a step to the entrance of the cavern and threw one rock over the heads of the Indians and as far as he could into the brush and woods.

The rock hit a tree, bounced off that into some brush, and then struck a boulder as it landed making more noise.

The Cheyenne quieted at once. They looked at each other, then all three began to creep slowly toward the sound. Morgan threw another rock in the same general area.

Again the savages stopped, listened, pointed, and then they split up to surround the hidden man or beast. As they moved 20 feet away from where they had been, Morgan took six of the rocks, crept out of the cave, and threw two more rocks farther to the north. He was in the open now, and if he moved they could see him if they looked behind themselves.

Morgan hoped that they would keep their concentration ahead. He slipped another ten feet south, edging along the side of the cliff itself.

The savages stopped. Morgan froze in place against the wall. He would be hard to see now. He waited until they moved again, then threw his last two rocks toward the chattering of the tiny stream.

Two of the savages charged forward making all sorts of noise. Using the cover of their movement, Morgan slipped farther to the south, stepped into some heavy brush, and let out a long sigh of relief. He fisted his six-gun now, cocked it while muffling the sound, and began working without the hint of a sound down the stream and away from the cave and the Cheyenne.

It took Morgan 20 minutes to travel from the cavern down the 200 yards to where he'd left his horse. By that time he felt fairly sure he had escaped, but he untied the mount and led her another 200 yards along the well-trod path before he mounted up and rode at a walk another half mile. Then he trotted back toward the Lucky Mountain Ranch buildings.

He tried to make some sense out of it as he rode. Six men slaughtered, nothing stolen but the horses. Definitely not any sacred burial ground in the mine. What the hell were the Cheyenne doing?

That damn boot print. It was almost like the guy wanted them to know he'd been there. The two riflemen could have been for the same reason—to scare them and to let them know a big man was after them and the ranch. Nobody was supposed to know about the mine. The big man did.

Morgan knew that he had to go back into town and see what he could dig up. He'd put the two riders to work in the morning counting the herd, to see how many of each category of beef they had out there.

Tomorrow he'd get an early start. He wasn't sure if Loveland or Fort Collins was the seat of the county. He'd find out. Then he could check on the property records. Most of all he wanted to find the big man. Who could it be? There couldn't be more than one or two men that big in that small a town. If there was a cobbler or a shoe-repair shop, that would be his first stop. Big man were hard on boots.

He stabled the horse in the barn, then changed his mind and put her out in the corral with the other five. It was starting almost to look like a ranch again. When he was in town he'd pick up about six horses. If they did any ranch work they'd need a remuda. Couldn't use a horse every day for cutting and branding and driving cattle around. That would be his reason for going to town.

He'd check with Claresta about some food staples she would want.

He walked slowly from the barn toward the house, detoured to the bunkhouse across the yard, and went inside. The two hands were working a game of poker on a spare bunk. There were places for 12 riders with bunks and mattresses. Better than most bunkhouses he'd seen.

"Getting settled in?" Morgan asked.

"Right we are, Mr. Morgan. Are you our manager or our foreman?"

Morgan pushed his hat back. "Well, for right now both, I guess. We'll get this spread set up proper again before long. I'm a friend of the family and I'll be moving on soon. But for now, we'll work together.

"After breakfast tomorrow, I want you men to do a cattle count. Take a pad of paper and some stub pencils and count every cow, every cow with calf, and all the steers and range bulls we got out there. Most of them are pretty well bunched. After you get those, take a circuit of six or seven miles each way and see if you can find any strays.

"Everything in the valley is ours, with the LM brand. That should make it easier. Let me know if you see any animal down or sick. We've got to start ranching here again."

They waved and he went out the door.

Claresta sat in the kitchen working on a cup of coffee.

"About time . . . worried about you."

"I'm still all in one chunk. I found the mine." He told her about it and the Indians.

"I can't figure out why they're there. Sacred mountains, they said. Never heard of that before."

"What can we do about them?"

"Nothing right now. You find any legal papers, anything that tells us about this place?"

"I found some envelopes. In one of them was a title deed. Far as I can tell Father bought this place and it's free and clear. Some other papers I don't understand and some stock certificates that mean nothing to me. At least I didn't find any mortgage."

"That's pleasing. How's your mother?"

"Adapting slowly. You seen enough of Mother to know. Now and then she's a pioneer woman, and the next minute she wants to be pampered and have six servants." Claresta watched him a moment. "Coffee?"

He nodded and she went to the stove and poured him a cup. He took it black and hot.

This time she sat down beside him, her leg pushed tightly against his from the next kitchen chair beside the long plank table.

"Time to get to bed?" she asked matter-of-factly. Only her hand rubbing gently along his inner thigh revealed any secondary motive.

"Soon. I'm going to town tomorrow to try to find out who this big man is. I want to pick up four or six horses if I can find some. While I'm in town I can get some supplies at the same time. What should we get for the pantry?"

She was up in a second to grab a list already made, and brought it to him. "This and two loaves of bakery bread and a magazine if you can find one, and the Denver newspaper. Oh, yes, I want you to find two pairs of pants for a fourteen-year-old boy and two shirts. I'll cut them down and wear them."

"Easy."

"Now, are we ready to go to bed?"

Morgan nodded. It had been a full day.

She gave him a small leather pouch. Inside were ten gold double eagles.

"That should cover the horses and the grub. Now I'm ready for bed."

They went along the hall to the second bedroom. Martha had moved into the master bedroom. She'd cleaned out everything that her husband had owned and dumped it in a pile in the third room. Claresta had unpacked in the one remaining room, second from the end, and she had brought in Morgan's carpetbag and unpacked it for him.

"You could use a new shirt while you're in town," she said.

He nodded and started to undress. She did that for him. When he was naked and lying on the bed, she stared down at him.

"Why are men so damned beautiful?" she asked. "You don't even have an erection yet and I want you so bad I could scream."

"Way nature intended it, I reckon," Morgan said. "It's worked out pretty well so far. Mankind keeps making love and reproducing, so looks like we're on this old globe to stay for a while."

"You trying to get me pregnant?"

"An Indian girl is twice as attractive for marriage if she's already pregnant, did you know that?"

"I'm not an Indian maid."

"You're not a white maiden either. Now come here and let me rip those clothes off you."

He got as far as her blouse, and when her surging breasts fell out he caught one in his mouth, and that was the last undressing of her he did.

Morgan admitted that he was a tit man. There was no chance he enjoyed looking at a woman's legs more than her breasts. Her breasts were hidden, special, amazing, like nothing a man had. They fascinated him. A quick glance down a blouse was a thing of pure joy to Morgan, and he knew some woman teased men that way, but he didn't mind.

Of course after ten minutes with a warm breast, other needs came to mind, but he always would be a tit man.

She stripped off the last of her clothes and lay down closely to him. Her hand caught his erection and she crooned to it. Then she looked at Morgan and kissed him.

"Now, you promised me that you were going to

show me something strange and new and different."

"How strange?" he asked, tweaking her hanging nipples until she shivered.

"Just different enough, maybe not strange."

"Get on your hands and knees," he said.

She grinned. "Hey, already that sounds strange."

She got into the position and looked at him. "What happens next?"

He moved up behind her and spread her knees a little. She looked over her shoulder.

"The usual place?" she asked softly.

Morgan shrugged. "Either one."

"Let's make it the regular one. I'm not ready for anything else yet. Maybe soon."

Morgan moved forward and entered her, grabbed her upper thighs from behind with his hands, and settled into a lovemaking that she would never forget.

Chapter Eight

Morgan used a spare horse one of the range hands had brought with him to ride to Loveland. The Devlins had bought the light wagon and two horses when they drove out the first day, so they didn't have to return them. The cow pony was much easier riding than the wagon horse.

Morgan got an early start, and figured that he could make the trip in just a little over four hours. He pushed the young roan mare and arrived in Loveland just after ten A.M. He checked with the livery stable first. The owner had four horses that were cattle-trained, and three more that could be brought around with a little experience.

The two horse traders dickered for half an hour. When both felt satisfied to move the other man off his stated price, Morgan got a bill of sale and description of the seven horses for $35 each. He knew he'd gained such a good price because there was almost no market for cattle ponies anywhere in that part of Colorado.

Next he went to Major's General Store and gave the owner the list Claresta made out. Bill Major looked over the handwritten group of needed items and nodded.

"Yep, got most of the goods. Take me an hour or so to get it put up, if you've got other business."

Morgan said he did, and checked in at a small shop next to the leather goods store that had a sign in the window that said "Boots and Shoes Repaired."

The small shop was actually part of the leather store where a young man worked on a saddle and a pair of women's fancy high-topped boots at the same time. He grinned and came over to the small counter.

"Got some boot trouble?" he inquired.

"Not that I know of. Actually I have a question to ask you. Can you keep a secret?"

"Long as it don't get me hung."

"Shouldn't. I'm looking for a gent in this area who wears a size-fourteen boot."

The young man held out his hand. "First my name's Hirum Allspauch, and I can make you a dandy saddle."

Morgan took the hand and shook. "Lee Morgan, traveling man."

"Good enough. Now that I've done my advertising, I can tell you there's only one man in town who wears a boot that big. I've done him a half sole twice now. Seems he does a lot of walking in his business."

Morgan drew an X pattern of markings inside an outline of a boot print on a pad of paper on the small counter. "The tread on the new half sole look something like that?"

Hirum reached under the counter and brought up a half sole with a pattern stamped into the hard leather that matched almost exactly what Morgan had drawn.

"Seems as how it fits," Morgan said. "Who is this big man?"

"You're right, he is big. Must go near three hundred pounds and stands about six-seven, maybe six-eight. Biggest man I've ever seen. His name is Josiah Stormer. He's a deputy sheriff sergeant in town, head of our one-man office here for the sheriff over at the county seat in Fort Collins."

"Well, I guess that's the man I need to talk to. Thanks. Next time I need my sole tended to, I'll stop by."

"If I can't help you, maybe the Methodist preacher can," Hirum said with a grin, and waved Morgan out the door.

Morgan pondered as he retraced his steps to Major's General Store and looked at the clothes. He told the owner what he needed.

"Two pair of denim pants, eh? Fourteen-year-old. I reckon we can find a couple. How big his waist?"

"No idea. We can do some cutting and trimming if need be. Put two of those plaid cotton shirts in as well, a red one and a blue one. That'll do it."

Morgan had an urge to ask what the store owner knew about the deputy sheriff, but held his tongue. Talk would get around this town faster than he could walk. He left the store and turned toward a sign that said, "Larimer County Sheriff's Office, Loveland Office."

There were two windows in front and the door was open. Inside was a swivel chair ready to tilt back and be sat upon. Morgan walked in and found himself looking at a huge bear of a man who seemed to fill half of the office even though he was sitting at a battered desk. The man looked up.

Deputy Sheriff Josiah Stormer had a pleasant, open face, and he nodded at Morgan, his expression neutral.

"Sheriff Stormer?" Morgan asked.

"Deputy Sheriff Stormer. What can I do for you?" He remained seated.

Morgan had the immediate sense that the man was hostile and he didn't know why.

"Name's Morgan and I work for Mrs. Devlin out at the Lucky Mountain Ranch north of the Big Thompson."

"Yeah, heard the womenfolk came into town few days ago."

"Want to report six murders, Sergeant. The victims were all at the ranch and dead a day by the time we got there. Included Mr. Devlin, the cook, and five ranch hands."

"Murdered? How do you know?"

"One had two arrows in him, another had a war ax through his skull, the rest were knifed to death silent as spring rain."

"Indians?"

"Could be. Looked like it." Morgan waited, but the deputy didn't comment.

"Wanted to report it. We buried them all, no time to get to town for death certificates or such. Not even sure who some of the men were."

"Band of Cheyenne do some summer camps up in there. Never had any trouble with them before."

"Had considerable trouble this time from somebody."

"I'll make out a report and send it to the sheriff. He'll probably want to come out and talk to you. You got other witnesses to these killings?"

"The victim's wife and daughter."

"Any more details? I'll need a whole report."

"What more is there? We came in and found them all dead and nothing stolen but the thirty or forty ranch horses. Then night before last somebody took three shots at the lighted windows of the ranch house. I caught one of them."

The sheriff's deputy looked more interested. "Yeah, what'd he say?"

"That he was hired by a man here in Loveland to do the job. Supposed to shoot out the windows, then ride on for Denver."

"And you just let him go?" the deputy demanded.

"Last I knew shooting out a window was not a hanging offense. Unless it's different here in Colorado?"

"No, not different. But I'd liked to have talked to him. He say who hired him?"

"Claimed he didn't know. Said somebody talked to him in a saloon and he was a little drunk at the time." Morgan stood. "Just thought you should know, case we have any more trouble out that way."

Morgan walked to the door. "Oh, in case anyone asks, the widow and her daughter have decided to stay on and run the ranch. They figure somebody is trying to scare them off, but they told me they aren't afraid. They said to tell you they have plenty of guns and ammunition and can defend themselves. I better be getting back with the supplies."

He waved at the lawman and stepped out on the boardwalk. The deputy hadn't stood. Strange, unless he didn't want Morgan to see how tall he was. Stormer had almost dropped his teeth when Morgan told about catching the sniper. Twice

Morgan had found the sheriff staring at Morgan's tied-down six-gun. Most men didn't tie them down that way.

Any gunman worth his name did. It could make a hundredth of a second difference in a fast draw. Tying down the bottom of the holster meant it didn't move up hardly at all when the weapon was pulled out. Without being tied down the holster would ride up a half inch or more, and could make the difference between living and dying.

Morgan lifted his brows. He would be especially careful and watchful the next hour or so before he left town, and on the way back. He was sure that someone would be out gunning for him. Did that make the deputy sheriff the big man from the boot prints at the ranch and in the mine? It might, but he didn't have enough evidence to hang the man.

He went back to the general store and looked at the goods he had to take back. The store owner had packed the food and supplies into four gunny sacks and tied the tops of them. With some short lengths of rope Morgan could tie the sacks on the backs of four of his horses.

He picked up the horses at the livery, put them on lead lines from their halters, and then went up the alley to the back of the general store. He had the horses tied when two men came out of the back door of the store next door and advanced on him.

Morgan saw that they had planned it. He was beween the dock of the general store and the long brick side of the bank. The only way out was past the two men. Both were medium-sized, but one held a sawed-off shotgun aimed at Morgan. The other had a eight-inch-long fighting knife, with sharpened steel on both sides of the point for slashing either way.

"You gents looking for some exercise?" Morgan asked.

"Take out your six-gun and drop it on the ground," the smaller of the two said. The shotgunner waved the muzzle at Morgan from ten feet away. Morgan's Colt .45 kissed the dirt of the alley.

"Kick it away."

Morgan did so.

The taller man lowered the shotgun and lifted a baseball bat. He put down the scatter gun now and lunged toward Morgan swinging the bat and laughing.

The bat could break an arm with one connection, Morgan knew. He jumped back out of range looking for a weapon. The four-inch knife in his boot wouldn't help against the club. As he backed one way, the smaller man moved toward him from that side, the sun glinting off the polished steel blade.

"You got a big mouth, mister," the baseball bat man said. "Just don't know when to shut up. That's our job."

Morgan saw a three-foot-long piece of two-by-four against the side of the building. He stopped retreating. Suddenly he charged the man with the bat, timing it so the man's swing had just reached the end of its arc. Morgan dove to the ground under the bat and to the left of the knife-wielder.

He hit with his right hand slapping the dirt, ducked his head and hit on his right shoulder in a front roll, came to his feet, and ran ten feet to get the two-by-four. He was still pinned in the alley, but now he could defend himself.

The man with the bat growled and stalked him, trying to force him to back up toward the smaller knife man. Morgan paid the blade no attention at all for two or three minutes, feinting and swinging the two-by-four at the bigger man.

Then in a surprise reversal, Morgan spun and charged the smaller man, swinging the two-by-four at his arm. The club hit the man's forearm and Morgan heard the crack as both arm bones broke.

The attacker wailed in pain and anger, staring at Morgan. Before the wounded man could move, Morgan leaped ahead and kicked him sharply in the crotch, slamming him to the ground as he wailed and screamed in new pain.

Morgan grabbed the fighting knife where it had fallen. He held it in his left hand and the two-by-four in his right as he raced toward the man with the baseball bat. The bat was swung at Morgan viciously. It missed. Then Morgan jammed his own club in the way of the next swing so the bat hit the two-by-four high on the handle, not six inches from the end.

The bat snapped in half like a toothpick. Morgan swung the two-by-four with both hands now, holding the knife along the wood. He swiped at the big man's legs, then his chest, and connected just over his belt on the side of his back by his kidney, and doubled the man over. The man fell to his knees, then vomited on the ground, the fight gone out of him.

Morgan wanted to kill them both. Instead he took the fighting knife, held his foot on the big man's throat, and sliced an M three inches high in his forehead. Blood surged into the man's eyes and down his face.

Morgan did the same thing to the crotch-kicked man, who could only scream in more pain.

"Tell your boss I don't die that easy," Morgan

bellowed at them. He picked up the sawed-off shotgun, went on up the alley to where his string of mounts waited, and loaded his gear on the horses.

When he rode out of town ten minutes later, he had a dozen rounds of double-ought buck for the ten-gauge shotgun. He moved out of town as quickly as he could.

Once on the main trail south to Denver he relaxed a little, but he kept close track of every rig and every rider who met or passed him. A short way down the south trail he turned west on the Big Thompson River trail. He pushed the horses to a five-mile-an-hour walk. He had almost 20 miles to ride and he had to be alert every step of the way.

Morgan thought about the attack. Only three or four people knew he was in town, including the deputy sheriff. It certainly put another vote for the sheriff as the man behind the attack on the ranch.

Now that Morgan had time to think it through, it was obvious that the same man who'd had the seven men killed on the LM Ranch knew about the gold mine. The boot print proved that. The sniper and now this attack in town could point to the same big man. The Indian connection was what had Morgan stumped.

If the Indians thought the cave was a sacred place, why had they let the men of the LM dig so far into the mountain? It must have taken weeks of backbreaking work to drill through that hard rock and quartz. Where were the Cheyenne all this time? Why a sudden sacred-mountain story and guards at the cavern and the slaughter at the ranch?

In the past he had known of Indian bands that had been easy for some unscrupulous white man to trick into making raids and killing whites. It had been done through the perversion and use of the Indian's natural fears and their superstitious beliefs in many good and bad spirits. Was that what had happened here?

What he needed was one ally in the Cheyenne camp. He kept thinking about the *o-kee-pa* ritual he had suffered through in the Arizona mountains. By showing his scars he might be able to find one Cheyenne he could talk to. It would be a gamble. At last he decided that must be the final alternative.

There had to be a safer way. By the time he made the last turn toward the ranch and saw the buildings less than a half mile away, he still hadn't come up with a better plan.

Chapter Nine

"Anything happen here while I was gone?" Morgan asked as he walked into the kitchen with a sack of supplies. He laid the gunny sack on the table and Claresta investigated it like Santa's sack at Christmas time, exclaiming over each new package of food or staples.

"Happen? No, nothing unusual. The two hands got the animals counted. We have less than I figured. I'll show you the totals later."

"No Indians or snipers running around?"

"Not a one. What did you find out in town?"

He told her about the deputy sheriff.

"You think he's the one who's behind all of this?"

"Could be, but we can't be sure. What I need is a contact inside that Indian tribe. Somebody who will trust me and who I can talk to."

Her clear green eyes were cautious, showing anger and fright. "But if it does't work won't they boil you in oil or something?"

"Something. I need to put away those new horses and talk to the hands."

Outside, he led the horses into the corral and took off their bridles. They weren't the best mounts in captivity, but would be good back-up horses if the ranch ever had much real cattle work to do.

Before he had the animals all in the corral, the hands came up.

"New mounts," Morgan said.

"Seen worse," Seismore said.

"You see anything unusual when you worked the north range?"

"No Indians, no smoke. Nice and quiet," Will Lacey replied.

"Good. Things will settle down around here soon. If you see anything out of the normal, ride back from wherever you are and report it." The men nodded, and Morgan left and let them fork some hay into the corral for the new mounts.

When Morgan walked into the ranch house kitchen, Claresta looked up and grinned. "Hey, I like the pants and shirts. The pants will fit and I'll cut off the shirtsleeves some. Thanks."

"No problem."

"Oh, Mother wants you to have an audience with her. She's in her Queen Bee phase so treat her gently. She's in the living room."

Morgan walked in with his hat in his hand and brushed back his blondish brown hair. He was six feet tall, 185 pounds of hard muscled body, and had one of those faces that looks almost square with a wide, strong chin and strong features. He moved like a mountain lion, smoothly, gracefully, with the threat of strength.

Martha Devlin sat on the couch that faced the window. She wore some kind of robe over another garment. Her hair was fixed on top of her head showing off a long, graceful neck. In front of her, she held a sheaf of papers.

"Mr. Morgan, so good of you to come in. Sit down and relax. Just a little business to do. I see by a letter that my late husband promised to pay you three hundred dollars and your expenses to bring us here from Chicago. An outrageous sum, but I'll pay it. I still owe you a hundred and fifty dollars, is that right?"

"Yes."

She handed him a stack of gold coins. He put them in his pants pocket.

"Aren't you going to count the money?"

"No. Would you cheat me?"

"Of course not."

"So why should I count it?"

She smiled. "Morgan, you can be infuriating, but also terribly nice. About you and my daughter. I know you're a handsome young man, and I don't want you to start anything with Claresta that you can't finish." Martha stopped and looked up at him with clear brown eyes.

"I know that you are not the marrying kind of man. I also am aware that Claresta is eighteen now and getting all sorts of urges. I went through the same stage." She smiled. "You may not understand, but even an older woman of thirty-eight has certain sexual desires now and then."

"Yes, ma'am."

"Just be careful with Claresta. Don't break her heart. Since you're a roaming man, be sure that she understands that."

"I certainly will, Mrs. Devlin."

She smiled at him and nodded. "Yes, I think you will. Those were the two things I wanted to talk about. I won't keep you any longer."

Morgan rose, nodded at her, and walked back to the kitchen. Mrs. Devlin watched him go. One of her hands slid inside her robe and gently caressed one of her breasts.

She smiled. She did fully understand how Claresta felt about such a handsome man. He ignited all of the old desires inside her, and for a moment she hated him for it. Then her hand caressed her breast and her other hand slid down to her crotch and under the robe, and her legs parted just a little.

One more time won't hurt a thing, she told herself. What was it hurting? Her hand rubbed down there, and soon she was panting and knew that she wouldn't stop until it happened.

Morgan walked into the kitchen and found Claresta making a new pot of coffee. She went up to him, pushed her soft willing body hard against him, and kissed his ready lips.

"Mother warned you not to break my heart. I was listening. I think she's getting herself all sexed up again." Claresta laughed softly. "Must be where I get the urges." She slid down her arms, which were around him, until she knelt. Then she kissed the fly of his pants. "Damn, I want to eat you up right now. You have time?"

"What about supper for the crew?"

"Not a chance. Let them find their own girl to chew on." She giggled. "Oh, you meant food on the table. It's cooking. Last of the bacon and beans, mashed potatoes and bacon gravy and fried chicken. The smaller of the hands, Lacey, killed the chicken for me this morning and cleaned it for me. Then he told me how to scald the bird in boiling water before I picked the feathers off it.

The whole thing worked. So we have fried chicken tonight."

He lifted her up from his crotch. "That's no place for a nice girl to be kissing," he said.

She quickly kissed his mouth and spun away. "Want to chase me?"

"Not a chance, you'd get away. How long to supper?"

"Five minutes. You want to ring the triangle?"

Morgan went out and rang the iron triangle with the iron bar, and the two hands came running to the wash basins outside the well house.

After supper, Morgan sat in the kitchen and watched as Claresta put things away and washed the dishes.

"You'll make some lucky man a good ranch wife," Morgan said. "You're young and strong, and don't seem afraid to work. Frankly, I'm surprised."

"I'm not all that much like my mother," Claresta said, flashing him a smile. She walked over to him bumping and grinding her hips at him. "As soon as it gets dark, let's take a walk down by the creek. I've never been done before in the grass out in the open that way and under the beautiful stars. They look so close here, like I could reach up and gather in a few dozen and hold them in my hand."

He kissed her gently and shook his head. "An hour before dark I have to start moving north. I want to see where this band of Cheyenne is camped and what I can find out about them. Cheyenne usually don't stay put in one place very long. They run out of graze for the horses."

"You be careful."

"Never did hanker to toast myself over an Indian fire. Don't figure on starting now." He brought out the Spencer repeating rifle and cleaned it and oiled the barrel, then tore down his six-gun and cleaned and oiled it.

"Tools of the trade," he told her. She had turned a chair around, and sat astride of it and watched him, resting her arms on the back of the chair.

"Can you shoot?"

"Never tried it," she said.

"Tomorrow you get shooting lessons. No ranch wife should be in this country long without knowing how to use a six-gun and a rifle and hit what she aims at."

Morgan left a half hour before dark, making sure the Cheyenne wouldn't see him coming in the daylight. He got to the spot near the mine, and could hear guards talking and whispering. He left his horse well below, and moved halfway up on the wooded slope across the 50-yard-wide valley, edging around the lookouts cautiously.

Why did they put so much importance on this part of the mountain? It was not a burial cave, that was for sure. After 100 yards in the woods, he came back down toward the creek. The valley had narrowed to little more than a gully here, with the stream only an enlarged spring. Still, there was a well-worn path along the water to the north. He walked the trail for 20 minutes. Then it climbed to a low notch in the hills. Beyond that, he looked down on the start of a new stream.

Morgan sniffed and could smell smoke. The Cheyenne camp must be nearby. He found a new trail that headed down the ravine, which widened into a canyon and then a small valley. The smell of smoke was stronger, and a half mile more and he could see fires through the trees ahead.

He left the trail and went across the small creek and into deeper woods as he moved north along the stream that quickly curved to the east. He spent an hour working up slowly on the camp of Cheyenne. He had done it before. Slow and easy, no noise, no sudden movements.

In the dark the could get within 50 feet of the Plains-type tipis. As he moved in, he could see the men of the tribe walking to an open area where a large fire burned. A council.

The warriors gathered around the far side of the fire, and one of the men rose and began to talk. Morgan didn't know enough of the Plains Indian dialects to understand any of it. Some of the voices came loudly, forcefully. Others were more measured and cautious.

At last one of the younger men with one feather in a headband stood and shouted something, pointing to the hill on the far side of the camp from Morgan and behind the council.

The warriors all stood and stared at the hill, but nothing unusual happened. Some of the men grumbled. The young warrior shouted the same words again, and this time the sky lighted up with a blue burst of flame. Then small balls of fire shot into the air one after another. Sometimes there were two or three in the air at the same time.

The warriors shrank back. One ran away in panic. More shouted, and two or three wailed and began chants, perhaps to appease the spirits dancing on the mountain.

When the balls of fire stopped, two large rockets lanced in the air and burst high over the camp with a brillaint white light. When that faded, a loud explosion thundered far up on the hill.

Morgan scowled. Someone was playing tricks on the Indians. A confederate on the hill had come in almost on cue, lighting the roman candles and the flash powder, then setting off the rockets, and following that with a stick or two of an exploding dynamite bomb.

The young warrior now talked again to the council. Each man could have his say, and most of them stood and spoke. At last the pipe was passed and the young warrior came out victorious.

Morgan wished he knew what the discussion had been all about. Perhaps he could: If there had been a setup here, a confidence game of some sort to swindle or use the Indians, then someone from the tribe might be contacting the confederate on the hill tonight.

Morgan worked to the near end of the village and crossed the creek, then went up the other side of the forested hill until he was below where the fireworks had been set off. He waited.

It was two hours later after the camp below had quieted and most of the bonfires had gone out, when Morgan heard someone coming up the hill. The Indian was half drunk, making a lot of noise on his way up the hill, not at all like an Indian.

Morgan watched as the savage passed within ten feet of him. In the bright moonlight he could see that the person was a Cheyenne warrior, but he carried a bottle of whiskey in one hand and sang a little song to himself as he walked.

He stopped, looked upward, and kept on going. Morgan snorted at the silent Indian and followed him, staying close enough not to lose him in the dark spots of the timber. They climbed another 50 yards, and Morgan heard a low chuckle from the darkness ahead.

"Well, well, Running Fox," a heavy voice said in the shadows under the tall firs. "You couldn't stay away from the bottle, could you? You did well at the council tonight. How did the council like my little display of the anger of the spirits of the sacred mountain?"

"Plenty scared," a softer voice answered. "Leader still not sure spirits."

"But he can't outvote the council. How many smoked the pipe?"

"Nine smoke, six do not."

"So we win. The council will continue to guard the mountain near the small cave. That will protect the mine until we can take it over."

"Soon?"

"As soon as I can. Now you keep three warriors on that spot by the creek all night and all day. My job is to get rid of the rest of the Devlin family and whoever else they have working for them. The concil liked the horses, didn't they?"

"Yes. Like horses. Running Fox need more whiskey."

"Next trip, Running Fox. You take it easy on the sauce, or I might cut you out of the profits. Remember, lots of gold coins for Running Fox."

They said something else that Morgan couldn't hear, and a moment later the Indian came striding back down the hillside. He slipped and fell and the bottle smashed against a rock, shattering. Running Fox lay where he had fallen, talking rapidly in his native tongue. Then he got up and made his way down the steep hillside more slowly this time, like any drunk trying to get home.

Morgan figured the white man above had a horse. There would be no way he could find and tail him in the darkness. The man must know this area completely to be out here in the middle of the mountains at night. He certainly knew how to get back to where he came from—Loveland probably.

Morgan worked upstream on the small watercourse, making sure he was above the village, and then moved to the ridge and down the other side until he found the stream that ran past the gold mine and into the LM Ranch. He would work around the Cheyenne guards and then find his horse and get back to the ranch house. Now he knew a little more about what he was up against here. But how the hell did he deal with a band of nearly 50 warriors and a murdering white man who wanted to steal the Devlins' mine?

Chapter Ten

When Morgan slipped quietly into the ranch house, he found a note from Claresta.

"Sorry, I couldn't stay up to meet you. I'm dead tired and sleeping on my arms at the table. I'm not used to doing all this work, but I love it! See you in the morning. C."

He crumpled up the note and dropped it in the fire that had been laid in the kitchen stove for the morning. Then he went down the hall to his room. It had been a long day.

When morning came, he was up at six and shaved and ready for breakfast as soon as Claresta had it made. Over a plate of bacon and eggs he told her what he had found on the mountain.

"So there is a white man goading them into action. He should be held responsible for murder too."

"He will if we find out who it is. Hard to get courtroom evidence in a case like this."

"Maybe we could hold our own court. Oh, right

after breakfast I want you to show me how to shoot."

They started with a .38 caliber derringer.

"This is not a long-range weapon," he told her. "It's designed for use from three to six feet. Not much farther than that because you don't know where the round might go. It has a short barrel so the bullet gets little direction."

She fired the first shot at a tin can four feet away on a post. She missed.

"Wow! that's loud!" Claresta said, holding one hand over her ear.

"Not half as loud as it would be in a small room. Now try the other barrel."

She moved a foot closer to the tin can, and this time hit the post under it.

He showed her how to get the empty shell casings out and put in new .38-caliber rounds. He made Claresta fire 20 rounds through the derringer.

"Hey, I can shoot it now without closing my eyes and wanting to cover my ears."

With the last three shots she hit the can from four feet away.

"Now try this one," he said, handing her his .45. She nearly dropped it when she took it in one hand.

"So heavy!" She looked at him in wonder. "You hold it so easy."

"Try it with both hands."

He showed her how.

"First you have to cock the hammer. Pull the hammer right here back until it clicks. Then the trigger will fire it."

"You want me to shoot off this . . . this cannon?"

"If you want to."

She cocked it and aimed at the post and fired.

Both her hands flew into the air over her head and she stomped two steps backwards to keep her balance.

"Well now," she said, handing him the big gun. "I think I'll stick to the derringer. You have one I can buy?"

"That's an extra. Make it a present." He handed her a box half full of .38 rounds. "Don't use it unless you really need to."

"Don't worry. Now what happens next? Somebody going to try to run us off our ranch?"

"Most likely. I'd guess they'll make a move on us tonight. We're the big fly in their jar of honey right now."

"So we put out guards?"

"Half on, half off, all night."

"Count me in."

"You sure?"

"As long as I'm with you, Morgan."

He left her at the kitchen door holding the derringer and went to find the hands. He told them both to go back to the bunkhouse and get some shut-eye.

"You'll be needing it, we're on guard duty tonight."

By ten o'clock, Morgan had taken a ride to the south pasture. He sat under a big pine at the far side of the small valley and watched the trail into town. He saw nothing. Not a thing moved except a doe and her young fawn as they grazed contentedly near the brush ready to leap into cover at he first sign of danger.

Morgan rode back to the ranch house at two that afternoon and ate a sandwich of peanut butter and jam.

Claresta stared at him. "Mother say anything

about hiring you to help us find out what happened here and get it all straightened out?"

"No."

"Figures. We can't go on imposing on your good nature and your sexy ways. We need an understanding about how much we should pay you."

"You're in trouble. I owe it to you to try to get things straightened out."

"Not at the chance of getting your body roasted over one of those Cheyenne fires you always talk about. You name a price to clean this all up and get us ranching or mining, whichever works out. Name a price and I'll talk to Mother. We've got some money as you know."

"Ten percent of the mine or the ranch," Morgan said, not stopping to think it through.

"But the mine might not pay out for two years, and the ranch for at least three or four."

"So it won't cost you anything until then."

"Doesn't seem fair."

"First I have to figure out who is trying to stampede you off the land, and who else knows about the mine."

She watched him, her soft green eyes measuring him, wanting him. At last she grinned slowly. "Guess I'll get a nap before I start supper." She hesitated and grinned. "I'd invite you along, but then neither of us would get any sleep."

"Right you are. Lock your door."

She shook her head. "Lee Buckskin Morgan, as long as you're in the house, my bedroom door will never be locked." Claresta smiled and walked away, making her tight little bottom under the calico wiggle a lot more than was required.

Morgan watched her exit with pleasure. Then he thought about the ranch. He figured if anybody hit the spread they would concentrate on the buildings and it would be after midnight. He put the two hands on duty from dark to midnight. Then he and Claresta would take it to six in the morning. He showed her how to shoot a rifle. It didn't matter if she hit anything or not at night. A second gun firing would give anyone out there pause.

They perched in the second floor of the barn. The hayloft had been put in to hold hay to the roof when they could cut some from low places along the river. Morgan hoisted up the big haymow door three feet and tied off the rope. It gave them a complete view of all the ranch buildings.

"What about the back?" Claresta asked.

They found a small four-pane window there. Morgan pried out the window frame that had been nailed in. Now they had firing points in both directions. Morgan hauled up a barrel to sit up and watched out the back window. He had Claresta watching the front. She lay down on some hay on the floor looking out from the floor level to make a smaller target.

They waited an hour.

About one A.M. Claresta crept over to where Morgan sat and kissed his cheek.

"Do we have time?" she asked.

"No."

"Oh." She caught one of his hands and put it over her bare breast. "I thought we might have time for a fast one."

He squeezed a breast and caressed it gently, then reached down and nibbled on her nipple.

"Now put your blouse back on and keep a lookout. We'll have time. I'll make time, but not while we're on watch."

Her hand rubbed his crotch and she sighed. "All right, but I bet we do have time. We'll see."

She went back to the front of the barn. Morgan had been watching the shadows from the half-moon. It was getting larger and brighter now every night.

Fifty yards out he could still make out the brush and trees along the small creek. At first he had wondered why they hadn't put the buildings closer to the water, but now he was glad that they hadn't. The brush and trees provided perfect cover for an enemy force working up the trail from the south.

A rifle shot slammed from the brush toward the house. Morgan saw no muzzle flash from the rear. He ran to the haymow door and slid to the floor.

"See the flash?" he asked.

She pointed south of the house 50 yards.

Morgan angled and Spencer repeating rifle toward the spot and moved Claresta out of the opening.

Another round jolted into the stillness, and he heard window glass break in the ranch house.

This time he saw the flash, and he pumped three rounds into the area around the flash. There was no sound of pain. Morgan rolled to the far side of the haymow door and behind the shiplap, with just his eyes around the wood watching the creek.

Two shots almost at the same time came from the brush toward him. Both hit the barn, but well below where he and Claresta lay. Morgan rolled over and pounded three more shots into the area where the shooters had moved to. Just as he finished the third round, Claresta fired a shot in the same direction.

They both rolled away from the opening.

In the barn below, Morgan had saddled the best horse, a buckskin, with good speed and lasting power.

Morgan waited ten more seconds, and when no

shots came from the woods, he rolled over to where Claresta lay.

"Did you get a new round in the chamber?" he asked her.

"Yes, it's easy."

"Good. Stay right there and fire toward that spot in the brush every thirty seconds or so. But then duck back to cover behind the wall. Fire ten rounds. Got that?"

"Yes."

"I'm going down and riding out and try to cut them off to the south. They had to leave their horses downstream a ways."

"Be careful," she said, and kissed him.

Morgan went down the ladder to the stable area below, swung out the big door, and mounted the buckskin. He walked her to the door, then outside, and took off at a gallop around the back side of the barn and south angling toward the stream, still 40 yards away.

He heard a shot behind him, and hoped that it was Claresta. Morgan rode what he guessed was a quarter of a mile. Then he stopped near the brush of the small stream and listened. At night a warrior's ears were his best weapons. An Apache Indian scout had taught him that on one of Morgan's few jobs as a scout with the U.S. Cavalry.

Morgan could hear nothing unusual: the soft lowing of a night bird somewhere, the screech of a nighthawk making a dive on an unsuspecting mouse.

He moved into the edge of the brush and waited again. As he sat there he watched the dim outlines of the ranch buildings.

Walk in your enemy's moccasins.

If they were smart they would try to burn down the ranch house. They knew there were two women here. Most women would not live in the open or in a bunkhouse. The ranch house would be the prime target. Fire in any of the buildings would be acceptable. Eight. He counted another shot from the barn. She was firing slower now, but that was fine. Her gun might keep the raiders away from the barn.

A stick snapped along the creek upstream. A branch of an oak or mountain mahogany swished back in place after being bent out of its normal position.

Morgan lifted his Spencer. He had inserted a fresh tube of seven more rounds into place in the long gun as he rode. There was one more tube in the saddle boot, but he had left two full ones in the hayloft.

"Damn!" a voice whispered.

Morgan knew the man was too close now for a dismount. Morgan had to do the job from the saddle.

There was a flash of movement in the half-shadows ahead of him. Then a man ran in a short bust toward a solitary pine tree. Morgan tracked the figure with the Spencer and fired. Morgan watched the runner slam to the side and drop a six-gun he carried.

"Christ!" the wounded man cried out in agony.

"You figured it would be easy?" Morgan asked quietly.

There was no reaction. Morgan stepped down from his mount and with his six-gun covering the silent form, he moved up from directly in front of him. The man lay on his chest. Morgan bent and touched the revolver's muzzle to the man's forehead, then gently rolled him over.

There was the unmistakable smell of human feces. The attacker's eyes stared wide open at the sky. He had ridden the owlhoot trail once too often.

Morgan reacted to the twelfth round from the barn. He knew the sound of her rifle now. Where was the other attacker? Morgan had heard two rifle shots close together. The attackers would have heard him ride south from the barn. This man might have come back to bring their horses forward. If so, one more enemy was between Morgan and the ranch buildings.

Morgan tied his mount where she stood, lifted the rifle and holstered his hog leg, and worked cautiously up the bank of the creek toward the house. Up there somewhere was one more attacker. He might have cut and run when he heard the rifle shot, and he might not have. He could be anywhere.

Twenty yards of slow moving and Morgan stopped to listen.

Nothing.

He walked out to the edge of the brush and jogged without a sound north along the stream. Every 20 yards now he stopped to listen. He saw movement ahead and brought his six-gun to bear, only to see the white tail of a rabbit jump into the brush.

Another 20 yards. Where was the bastard?

By now Morgan was coming closer to the buildings. He could see all plainly. Claresta had stopped firing from the barn. There were no lights on in the house or the other buildings. He figured that the two ranch hands were up and waiting with six-guns. He had to be careful not to get shot at by a friendly.

A shadow moved. He froze. The shadow was near the barn. Morgan waited. The shadow had blended with the side of the barn nearest him, but he wasn't sure where barn shadow stopped and a possible man shadow started. It could be one of the hands.

Morgan heard a noise. A curious crackling sound. Then he heard a scream. It was a woman's scream—Claresta!

As he watched in horror, flames burst out the back door of the barn where he had ridden out a few minutes before.

The barn was on fire and Claresta was trapped up there in the haymow!

Chapter Eleven

The fire in the barn flared again and a burst of flames came out the rear door highlighting the man running away from it. He still carried a torch in his hand, and was too heavy to be either of the ranch hands.

Morgan fired three times with the rifle, the last one as the light died. He heard a scream and the man pitched to the ground.

Then Morgan dropped the rifle and sprinted for the front of the barn. There was no way to stop the fire. The man must have slipped in the back way and torched the hay in the stalls and a pile on the floor.

Morgan ran around the front of the barn and saw the flames hadn't reached there yet. He saw Claresta hovering on the edge of the haymow door ten feet off the ground.

"Claresta," he called. She looked down.

"Hang by your hands on the edge and drop. I'll catch you."

"I don't know if I can, it looks so far down."

"You can. The flames are getting closer."

She tried, but froze on the edge.

Morgan tore into the barn, and held his arm in front of his face to shield it from the heat as he raced past some blazing hay to the ladder. He went up the rungs two at a time and looked in the haymow. The fire hadn't reached there yet.

Quickly he surged over the top of the ladder, stepped to the floor, and ran to where Claresta lay on the haymow floor. She was shivering and shaking. Morgan picked her up and turned toward the ladder down. A gush of flames from below surged upward through the opening as it acted as a chimney for the fire below.

Not a chance to get down there. He put Claresta down and looked for some rope. He could find only the half-inch rope that held up the hawmow door. Furiously he used his boot knife and sawed off the 20-foot end of it.

Near the haymow door he saw a ladder going upward. He tied one end of the rope solidly to the ladder rung, and threw the other end out of the open haymow door.

Morgan picked up Claresta and slapped her gently.

"Honey, can you hear me?"

She nodded.

"This place is buring like a matchbox. We've got to get down. What you must do is lean over on my back, hold on around my neck with your arms and lock your legs around my waist. Can you do that?"

Claresta nodded.

He turned.

The fire broke through a hole in the floor where hay was pitched down to the stock, and suddenly half the hay in the mow burst into flames.

"Quickly!" He turned and she put her arms around his neck and then her legs around his waist. Morgan grabbed the rope and tested it, then held it tight and stepped backwards out the haymow door, his feet solidly against the wall of the barn.

He took a tentative step downward. Then a gust of wind carried some of the burning hay toward them. Morgan ducked and took two more steps down the side of the wall, letting out rope as he went. He could lean outward to give his feet more pressure against the wall.

That kept him from slipping. He took another step downward, then another. Now flames spewed out the haymow door. How long would it take the half-inch rope to burn through? He moved faster, and six more steps and his foot hit the ground. He spun Claresta around so he held her in his arms and ran away from the burning barn.

"I knew I was going to die!" Claresta whispered to him. Then she began to sob and shake. Morgan backed farther away from the fire until he was almost to the bunkhouse. He saw and heard their two hands herding the horses out of the corral, which was too close to the fire. The hands moved the horses behind the bunkhouse and tied them all.

Will Lacey came up shaking his head.

"Sorry, Mr. Morgan. She was too far gone before we saw it burning. Somebody torched her good from the inside. We moved the horses. The bastards still around who burned her?"

"Around but not going anywhere, I'd guess."

Claresta had stopped shaking. He took his arms from around her.

"Lacey, take Miss Devlin up to the house, will you? Then come back and we'll see if there's anything we can get from the barn or the shed."

A half hour later, they realized there was nothing more that could be saved. Lonnie Seismore, the second cowhand on the spread, had seen the fire start and dashed inside the barn and pulled out six saddles and the harness for a two-horse rig. Everything else had burned to a cinder.

Morgan and the two men hunted in the dim light for the fire-starter. Lacey found him about 30 yards from the fire. He had dragged himself the last ten yards. The man wavered between life and death.

Morgan squatted down beside him.

"Can you hear me?" Morgan asked.

The man nodded.

"Who hired you?" Morgan asked.

The man looked angry at first, then he softened. "Denver man," he said.

"Name, what's his name?" Morgan pressed.

"Didn't say—just said burn—didn't say nothing about me getting shot—"

The man's head rolled to the side and he let out the wind of life . . . and he was dead.

"Denver man," Seismore said. "Don't figure. Why would a Denver man hire this saloon-hopper to burn us out?"

"I agree, Seismore. Doesn't make sense. A ranch is just half a loaf with no buildings, especially the barn."

"Maybe they want the timber or to farm the valley," Seismore suggested.

"Maybe. We'll bury this one in the morning. Should be another one down in the brush. At least we'll get their horses and saddles."

"You think it's safe now?" Seismore asked.

"I figure they sent just two men to harass us and burn down something. A barn is easy to set on fire. Always the first target. Yeah, I think we're free of them for the rest of the night, but you guys get to bed. I'll stay up awhile just to be sure."

Morgan patrolled the smoldering ruins of the barn and the rest of the ranch yard for another hour. There was no movement, no noise. When the Big Dipper pointer stars told him it was about three A.M. he went into the ranch house and silently to his room. He didn't light a lamp, just kicked out of his boots and pants, checked the loads in his six-gun, and slid into bed.

Almost at once slender arms went around him and a sleek, naked body pushed up against him.

"I just can't go to sleep alone tonight," Claresta whispered. "Please let me stay."

He turned over and held her in his arms, smoothing her long amber hair, kissing her cheek.

"Hey, you're fine. You did great with that rifle tonight. Everyone is afraid of a fire, especially one exploding like that barn did. Don't think a second about it. We both got out and that's the important thing."

"I guess so." She reached up and kissed his lips. "Damn, I wish you would stay here forever and let me love you. But I know you won't. So I want you to love me now and make me feel needed and wanted and a whole woman again. There for a while tonight I felt like a little girl who had done something terribly wrong. I was so frightened that I couldn't move!"

She put his hand on her breast and crooned softly as he petted her.

"You are such a good lover, Lee Morgan. I hope you never leave my bed." She sighed. "But I know you will, so that way you won't be able to break my heart. You'll only tear it in half and still allow it do its job in my chest."

Gently she pushed him on his back and hung

over him. "Tonight I will make love to you, Lee Buckskin Morgan. I will start every new move, I will seduce you, I will make you beg to use your life-giving weapon inside me, and it will be so delicious that you will never want to leave such wonder."

"Just don't let me go to sleep," Morgan said.

She dropped a breast into his mouth, working on it like a huge lollipop.

Claresta had figured several interesting ways to entertain him in the foreplay, and Morgan lay there amused, amazed, and in no danger whatsoever now of falling asleep.

After teasing, coaxing, and playing with him for nearly a half hour, she at last moved over him and gently lowered herself so his lance plunged delightfully into her anxious scabbard. Claresta shuddered just a moment, beat down her own climax, and began working forward and back, drawing out and dropping hard on him until their pelvic bones scraped.

"Oh, damn, but you are good," Morgan whispered to her. "I might just consider wrapping you up and stowing you in my saddlebags and taking you with me."

She brightened. "Why not on a horse by your side?"

"Too dangerous. I don't allow my lovers to be shot full of holes. It's a quirk of mine. Too many people try to shoot me dead too often to have a ride-along companion. Also, it would put me at a disadvantage. Someone could threaten you or capture you and they would have a 'handle' on me. They would have a tremendous advantage over me in battle or negotiating and in the emotional side of any fight. You see, I'm really thinking of my own welfare as well as yours."

"I hate you, Lee Morgan!"

"Yes, I can feel that hate now encircling me, working me higher and higher."

"It's a strange kind of hate."

Then she proved it by rocking over him like he was a young stallion and she was riding him as hard as he would go. Morgan felt the tension mounting, felt the surging, driving forces unleashed within him, and then he couldn't control it anymore and it spewed out like a volcano, straight upward, and he thrust time and time again until he was drained and he fell back on the bed and a warm blanket or softness and warmth flowed over him, covering him and dropping him into a void so dark and deep he didn't know if he would be able to live or breathe again.

Finally he could gasp in enough air to satisfy his screaming body, and his breathing returned to near normal and his racing heart slowed and slowed to a calmer, natural beat.

The warm blanket over him shifted and moved and lifted up so he could focus on the amazingly pert and pretty face.

"Now, cowboy, was that enough to make you stay home and not go rambling all over the country?"

"That's one hell of a fantastic start to do the job," Morgan said.

"Don't worry, I'm just getting warmed up," Claresta purred. "Wait until I really get moving. You won't remember which steer knocked you down just before the stampede."

Claresta was right. As far as sleep went, they both could have stayed on guard duty all night for all the shut-eye they got. At last, when it was nearly five in the morning, they drifted off to sleep, both too exhausted to stay awake a moment longer.

There was no breakfast for the troops that morning until Morgan eased out of bed about seven o'clock without waking Claresta and went down to the kitchen. He had eggs and bacon and coffee ready by the time Claresta pranced into the kitchen. Morgan was the only one there. She kissed him warmly, patted his flat stomach, and ordered her breakfast.

"Just like in Chicago?" he asked.

"No, better." She looked back at the door then whispered. "In Chicago I didn't sleep with the cook."

Morgan laughed. He shook his head as he served up her eggs, bacon, toast, and coffee. Then he kissed her cheek.

"I'm taking the hands out to dispose of some trash. Be back soon. Don't follow us, please."

"Those two men . . ."

"Yes."

"I wonder if they had families somewhere, a wife . . . a child."

"Maybe. Doesn't matter. When a man takes a gun and shoots at somebody, he's inviting that person to kill me. If he winds up dead in the process it's his fault for giving someone the chance. I'll see if I can find any papers and personal effects to give to the sheriff. Although there's a chance the sheriff already knows these men."

Morgan and the two hands had eaten earlier, and now took shovels and one horse and a rope and walked out behind the barn to the first body. He was chunky, maybe 30, and Morgan found no identification of any kind in his pockets. There were two double eagles, a pocket knife, a single key—perhaps to a house, and that was all.

Lacey tied the lasso to the man's foot and wrapped the other end around the saddle horn and the horse dragged the body over toward the stream. Morgan picked out a spot 30 feet from the water on a little rise, and the hands went to work digging.

Morgan came back ten minutes later with the second body slung over the saddle.

"At least this one has a name. Jonathan Barlow. Sound familiar?" Both ranch hands shook their heads.

Morgan tied up two letters, some pocket change, and another two gold double eagles in a kerchief and set it aside.

"Looks like they got themselves forty dollars each to try to burn us out," Lacey said. "Not a damned lot of cash money to risk getting yourself killed."

"Guess it depends how bad you need forty dollars," Morgan said.

They buried them four feet under the sod and rounded up the top of the grave. They didn't put up a marker. The Cheyenne were notorious for liking to dig up white men's graves.

Seismore took the saddle horse and rode south on the creek looking for the two horses that the dead men must have ridden. He brought them back a half hour later. Neither horse was worth more than ten dollars. The saddles were much worn, cracking and coming apart.

"A pair of drifters," Morgan said. "Somebody picked them out of a saloon and waved gold in front of them."

Neither horse had a brand. The hands stripped

off the saddles and turned them into the corral. They would do for a day or so if the cattle work got going.

The three men were putting up wood over the newly shot-out window in the front of the ranch house when they heard shots down south. Morgan yelled at Seismore, and the two ran for the corral, where the saddles hung on the top rail.

"Lacey, you stay here and guard the place," Morgan said. "Dig out those Spencer rifles from the kitchen cupboard. Bring us two of them and five of the loaded ammo tubes as well."

Three minutes later the two men were mounted up and riding south at what looked like three or four men on horses shooting the cattle.

Chapter Twelve

As Morgan and Seismore rode hard toward the gunmen a mile or so away, they could see one animal down and another go down after the crack of a rifle.

Morgan lofted the barrel of his Spencer and slammed off a shot at the cattle killers, not that he hoped to hit one, but as a warning that they were coming shooting. It might back them off. As Morgan and Seismore rode closer, the four men on horses took one shot at them, then faded into the trees on the trail south along the creek.

Morgan put two more rifle shots into the trees, and the gunmen kept on riding until they were out of sight. Morgan knew it was possible he was heading into an ambush, but at 500 yards, Morgan and Seismore had taken no incoming rounds. They decided not to push their luck, so they rode into the cover of the brush and trees along the creek and worked down the stream that way.

It was slower, but at least the chances of a bushwhacking were much reduced. It took them almost 15 minutes before they found the trail the four horsemen had left in the soft ground along the stream.

It looked as if they didn't care if they were followed or not. Or maybe they wanted to be followed so they could ambush their pursuers later down the trail.

Morgan sat looking at the tracks.

"Looks like they killed two of our cows," Seismore said as he came back from the edge of the brush. "We going after the bastards?"

"At least for a ways. I can't figure out what they hoped to accomplish with a raid like this. They knew we'd hear them and then see them and come boiling down here. Oh, damn!" Morgan whirled his mount around and waved at Seismore. "Come on, it's a trick. We're heading back to the ranch house as fast as we can get there!"

"Why?" Seismore called as he caught up with the galloping mount Morgan pushed.

"This had to be a diversion, nothing but a jab down here to get us away from the ranch. I hope that everyone is all right up there."

As he spoke two rifle shots sounded from the ranch. Both men kicked their mounts to run faster. They were still nearly a mile from the buildings.

A half mile from the house they had to slow their horses to a trot.

"At least I don't see anything burning," Morgan shouted to the other man. As they neared the long one-story ranch house they parted and one went on each side of it. Morgan was on the inside of the yard. The first thing he saw was a man down near the well. He stopped his mount and leaped off and knelt beside the man.

"Lacey! What happened?"

Lacey tried to sit up. He had a bloody wound in his shoulder and a bruise on the side of his forehead.

"Oh, God. I couldn't stop them. They came out of the brush along the trees and hit me with a rifle shot before I knew anyone was there. They got in the house, four of them. The kidnapped Claresta. Left a list of things we have to do if we ever want to see her alive again. All of them wore masks."

Morgan raced into the ranch house. Seismore rode up and began bandaging Lacey's shoulder wound to stop the bleeding.

Morgan slammed through the screen and ran into the living room.

"Too late," Martha Devlin scolded. "They came when you went racing off to the south range. Just the way they planned. They kidnapped Claresta and it's all your fault."

"Where's the list of demands?" Morgan said quietly.

She handed him a paper that had fancy writing all done in a flowing and beautiful hand. There were five points.

"1. Pack up and move everyone off the ranch by noon tomorrow.

"2. Discharge the ranch hands and the bodyguard and see that they get on the train for Denver tomorrow.

"3. Make out a bill of sale for the ranch for $15,000 and sign a receipt for the cash as paid. Sign both and leave them on the kitchen table.

"4. Be on the train for Cheyenne and Chicago by nightfall two days hence.

"5. Do not try to follow us. If you do, Claresta will be killed at once.

"When all of these requirements have been met, the girl will be returned to you at Cheyenne within three days. You have no right to bargain or change any of the conditions. Follow them to the letter or your daughter is dead and buried and you'll never see her again."

Morgan put down the letter and went to the kitchen. He took out five of the empty tubes for his Spencer rifle and began loading them with the .52-caliber cartridges.

"What are you doing, Morgan?" Mrs. Devlin demanded.

"Getting ready to track them, and bring Claresta back. There were four of them?"

"The demands say specifically that—"

"I know what it says. You can't deal with kidnappers by following their instructions. That's giving up. They can't go far. I'll find them, kill some, and run the others off before they can harm Claresta. Do you have a better plan?"

"We should do as the letter tells us."

"You want to give up everything your husband worked for? He at last found a fortune on his own and you want to throw it all away? Claresta has a right to some say in that matter. We'll find out what she wants to do when she's safely back here."

"Or dead."

"She won't be harmed. They have to make sure of that or the deal is off. Now, make me some sandwiches." Martha remained on the sofa dabbing at her eyes.

"Mrs. Devlin!" Morgan barked. "Get on your feet and make me some sandwiches, six or eight. I might be gone two days. Do it now, and none of your hysterics!"

Morgan hurried out to the yard and found that Lacey had been moved into the buckhouse.

"How are you feeling, Lacey?"

"Could be one hell of a lot better. I'm sorry I let you down."

"They fooled us all. Which way did they ride out of here?"

"Went to the west, beyond the stream. Then I saw them turn north."

"Figures. Four of them. Was one a huge man, over six-six and three hundred pounds?"

"No, all smaller than you."

"Figures again. You two stay here. I'm going after them."

"Can I come?" Seismore asked.

"No, you keep guard here. Oh, saddle me a fresh horse. Best one we have left. I won't get to ride far, but every bit helps."

When Morgan got back to the kitchen after checking out the horse and his six-gun and a fresh box of .45 rounds, he found that Mrs. Devlin had made eight sandwiches and wrapped them in white paper. She put them in two sacks.

"One for each saddlebag," she said. She looked up. "Morgan, sorry I yelled at you. I . . . I get emotional at times."

"Don't worry about it. I've got to get moving. Thanks."

The kidnapping attack had come an hour after noon. Now it was about two o'clock as Morgan moved out on a dun, heading across the creek. He found the tracks of the four horses at once. One of the mounts was riding double. That meant they weren't planning on riding far. Where?

The Indians, he decided. They would go through the Indian guard point and make a camp, figuring they were safe. They might even camp in the cavern. It would be an easy place to keep Claresta held prisoner.

Morgan worked the trail north until he figured he was less than 300 yards from where the Indians had posted their lookouts and guards. He'd have to walk from now on. He took the Spencer and two spare tubes of rounds which he had taped to the stock. He ate one of the sandwiches and pushed to more inside his shirt. He didn't know when he might need them.

He worked slowly and quietly north through the brush that crowded in on the smaller and smaller watercourse. When he was 50 yards from the guard spot, he settled down to watch the area.

Less then ten minutes later he saw two Indians change positions behind some brush. Even if he moved cautiously into the woods up the slope of the canyon, they would see him. He had to wait for darkness.

After 15 minutes, Morgan got so jittery he knew he had to do something. The kidnappers could be swinging down the other side of the ridge and back to the Big Thompson River, and be half way back to Loveland by dark.

He checked the side of the ravine again. It was barely 20 yards to the Indians. He could make it at night under cover of darkness, but there were bare spots where he would be easy to spot in the daylight.

Maybe his rock-throwing would be a good way to distract them. No, there were three of them. One would go look to see what made the noise, while the other two would be especially alert. After another 20 minutes he was almost ready to try it. He found three fist-sized rocks that would make lots of noise when they hit.

For a minute he watched the Indians. He'd have

to pick just the right time when the guards were all looking the other way. He'd throw the first rock beyond them. He was almost ready to throw, but realized he didn't have enough overhead open space. He crawled six feet uphill and found a spot.

Now he watched the Indians. Two looked the other way, but the third stared at the creek which was in front of Morgan. Not yet.

The guard looking toward Morgan's position said something to the others, and then turned and looked where they were pointing.

Now! Morgan's arm was back, and he had almost thrown the rock when he saw a black nose of a brown bear push through some brush 20 feet from the Indians.

Morgan grinned. It was a half-grown male. Morgan cocked his arm and threw the rock at the bear. It missed the bear by inches. He threw again quickly, and this time hit the bear. It roared and stood on its hind legs looking around. It spotted the three Cheyenne, who jumped up in surprise. One tried to get his bow ready. One of the guards turned and ran to the north. The third stumbled and the brown bear charged them.

Morgan wasn't sure if the young bear was chasing them for the sport of it or in anger, but in ten seconds the guard post was vacant as the three Cheyenne and the brown were well north on the trail. Morgan ran quickly past the guard area into the deeper brush on the far side and worked slowly north, following along the same way, but well off the trail he had taken to the mine.

He was 50 yards from the cavern where the mine was when he smelled smoke. A good sign. He didn't see anything of the three warriors or the half-grown brown bear. Then, around the bend, he spotted the bear again standing on his hind legs staring up the slope. The bear snorted, dropped down, and moved into the side of the trail where a berry bush grew, and began clawing off the berries and eating them.

Soon the bear had his fill, and wandered back down the trail toward the guard post where he had been interrupted in his afternoon stroll.

Morgan crouched behind a pine without moving as the bear meandered past. Then Morgan crept slowly up the slope toward the cavern entrance.

He slid in back of a giant Douglas fir and peered around the side directly into the cavern from 30 yards away and across the trickle of the stream. A fire burned near the entrance, and he saw two white men sitting beside it. Farther back in the cavern he could see torches burning.

Good, the kidnappers were here. Had to be. Why should they run farther when they had a safe haven. *They thought.*

The first shadows slanted across the small valley, which was no more than 20 yards wide here. It would be dark in two hours. He had to pick them off one at a time.

"Hey, watch things, I'm taking a piss," one of the men said. He went out the cavern entrance and into the brush. A moment later he went back inside. Morgan grinned, moved through the heavy growth to the north out of their sight, crossed the creek, and hurried back into the heavy trees and brush near the far side. Then he worked silently down toward the mouth of the cavern.

Twenty minutes later, well before dark, the other man at the front of the cavern came out and headed the same direction the first had taken. He came just past where Morgan hid behind a tall Ponderosa pine. He was relieving himself when Morgan's big .45 gun butt smashed down on the top of his head. The man crumpled, and Morgan caught him before he hit the ground. He dragged the man 50 feet through the brush north, gagged him, tied him hand and foot, took his six-gun, and then cut some pine boughs and laid them over him hiding him completely.

Down to three.

Morgan waited for the search. Soon two men came out with guns drawn looking for their missing friend. They moved north almost to where Morgan hid beneath some brush, then stopped.

"Hell, Charlie got himself lost. He'll be back," one of the men said.

"Either that or them damn Cheyenne are cooking Charlie right now in a pot for their supper. Aint' this the bunch that are cannibals?"

The two walked back to the cavern entrance and went inside.

A half hour later, it was dark. Morgan slipped down closer to the cavern. He saw that the fire had been built up, but still cast heavy shadows around the cave. Could he fake his way close enough to use his knife? Maybe. There was still only one man at the guard fire.

Morgan thought of something, jogged back to where he had left the gagged kidnapper his friends called Charlie, and took his hat. It was distinctive: floppy, dirty, and a dank brown.

A few minutes later, Morgan came running into the cavern, his head down, his hat showing in the light.

"What the hell?" the kidnapper by the fire growled.

Morgan held his throat as if wounded. "I'm Charlie, idiot," Morgan wheezed. He staggered toward the other man, who hesitated just long enough. Then Morgan charged him with one hand now holding his four-inch bladed boot knife. The steel went into the outlaw's chest and drove deep. Morgan turned it and sliced it out, grated it off a rib, and pulled the knife free.

The man sank to the floor, blood streaming from his mouth. His eyes looked at Morgan a moment, then went blank with death.

"Down to two," Morgan said. He moved cautiously back into the cavern. There were two torches. Near one a second small cooking fire glowed. Two men huddled over it working on something in a fry pan.

Ahead he saw Claresta sitting on a blanket near the second torch. He crept forward in the shadows. When he was 20 feet from the two men he straightened, took off Charlie's hat, and drew his six-gun and cocked it. The click made an ominous, deadly sound in the depths of the cavern.

"Freeze, gents!" Morgan barked. "Move a muscle and you travel directly to Hell!"

Chapter Thirteen

One of the kidnappers grabbed for his gun, and got it out before Morgan shot him. He spun to the ground, brought up the weapon, and snapped a shot at Morgan that missed. The next round from Morgan's .45 drilled through the kidnapper's throat, snapping his neck and splattering his carotid artery open. The man bled to death in a minute and a half.

"You going to be stupid too?" Morgan asked the last of the four men.

"Not a chance. Not for twenty dollars a day."

"Morgan! That's got to be you. I'm back here." The call came from Claresta.

Morgan motioned the kidnapper ahead of him as they went back in the natural cavern to where the last torch burned. The girl sat on a blanket tied hand and foot.

"Get those ropes off her," Morgan ordered. "No, wait. Let me check you out first." Morgan patted the kidnapper's pants legs and chest, found a knife and a derringer, and pushed him toward Claresta. He untied her, Claresta ran into Morgan's arms. He kept his .45 covering the kidnapper.

"I just knew you'd come. I told these guys they wouldn't get away with it." She kissed him.

Morgan held her away and nodded. "I'm here, but we aren't out of here yet." He looked at the kidnapper. "Where are your horses?"

"Just south of the cave."

"Let's go get them."

Claresta stayed close to Morgan and shuddered as they walked past the two dead men. She caught his hand and held it until they got to the front of the cavern.

"Move easy, hardcase, or you're asking for a bullet, you understand?"

"Hey, I'm not anxious to wind up dead. Where's Charlie?"

"Tied up back a ways. He'll get loose tomorrow. Worry about your own skin."

They got to the horses. Morgan lifted Claresta into a saddle. She said she could ride. He tied the kidnapper's hands to his saddle horn, then tied a lead line on the other horse, and they trailed down toward the Indian guards. When they got there, no one was on duty.

Morgan led them on through and down to where he'd left his horse. He picked it up, and then they rode faster for the ranch. When they got to the ranch yard, Claresta dropped off her horse and rushed into the house for a tearful reunion with her mother.

Seismore came out grinning.

"Damn, you nailed them. Is this one of the bastards?"

"Indeed. He's going to talk to us in the bunkhouse."

They pushed the man to the bunkhouse, where two lamps burned brightly. Morgan sat the kidnapper down on a bunk and stared at him.

"What's your name?"

"Fred."

"All right now, Fred. We can make this easy or tough. It's up to you. I'm going to ask some questions and you're going to give me the truthful answers. If you don't there'll be punishment."

"Got nothing to hide."

"Fine. How much you get paid for this kidnapping?"

"A hundred dollars each."

"You were to keep her at the cave how long?"

"Three days. Then someone would pick her up."

"You're doing fine, Fred. Who paid you to do this?"

"It was the man—" Fred stopped.

"What man, Fred?"

He shook his head, and then took a long breath. "You know I can't tell you that. Confidential."

"One way or the other you're going to tell me, Fred."

"Beat me up, I still won't tell. I've got some principles."

"Not a whole lot, Fred. What's it to you to lose one more? You think your boss would take a beating for you?"

"Don't matter."

"You ever been branded, Fred?"

"Hell, no. You wouldn't do that."

"How do you know? You've never seen me before, don't know a thing about me. I might drag guys like you bare-assed through a thorn thicket."

"Only Indians do that."

"I'm half Cheyenne."

Fred stared at him harder. "Don't see it."

Lacey walked up. "This the bastard who shot me?"

"Could be," Morgan said.

"You need him beat up, I've got a good two-by-four I want to use on him. If it breaks, I'll get a new one."

"Might call on you." Morgan looked over at Seismore. "Didn't you say you saw a nest of rattlers down by some rocks?"

"Spotted some yesterday. You said not to kill them."

"Glad I did. Go down there with a forked stick and bring me back a nice big one. He and Fred here are going to get to know one another."

"I ain't afraid of snakes," Fred said.

Morgan laughed softly. "Good, Fred. Because that rattler sure ain't gonna be afraid of you either."

Morgan talked with Seismore a moment before he left, then went back to Fred.

"Plenty of time for you to tell me who hired you. Give me his name and description. That's all I need."

"Then he would gun me down for sure."

"Might not. He'd have to catch you first. You could ride around Loveland and get to Cheyenne and be west on the next train. Besides, by the time he finds out, he'll be in jail or dead."

"I don't want to leave Colorado."

"As the saying goes, Fred. It's your funeral."

Morgan began re-arranging the bunks in the building. He moved two back to give more space on the wooden floor. He got some quarter-inch rope and tied Fred's ankles together.

"You might as well lay down and get comfortable, Fred. Stretch out right here on the floor on your belly."

"Why?"

"Because if you don't I'll throw you down there and stomp you a few times. Good enough reason?"

Fred nodded and lay down. Morgan tied the long end of the rope that bound Fred's ankles to a washstand nailed to the wall. He stretched out Fred until the rope was tight. The second rope went around Fred's chest and cinched up snug, then extended to the front and tied off to one of the heavy wooden bunk legs. The bunk was pushed back until the rope was tight. Now Fred couldn't move either to the front or rear.

"Cozy there in your new home?" Morgan asked.

"What the hell you doing?"

"Encouraging you to tell us who hired you."

"Never do it this way. I can go to sleep this way."

"Not for long, I'll wager," Morgan said.

Seisore came in then holding a three-foot long rattlesnake by the back of the head. He was a man who had handled snakes before.

"This guy is ready and mad as a wet setting hen. He really wants to sink his fangs into somebody." They tied a piece of leather boot lace around the rattler's tail just in front of eight rattles. Then they put him on the floor in front of Fred.

"What the hell you doing?" Fred shouted.

"You and your friend the rattler here are going to play a game. It's called three strikes and you're out, just like baseball.

"The whole game is, we tie the rattler so he can almost reach you. The problem is, friend rattler will be so close that you'll have to lift up your shoulders and your head as far as you can off the floor. That way the snake can't strike you. But if you get tired and let your head drop down, you'll come five inches closer to the snake and he'll nail you with two or three strikes."

Morgan stopped and watched Fred.

"You ever been bitten by a rattler, Fred?"

"No." It was a low, cautious response.

"Well, one or two strikes can kill a man, especially if he does a lot of strenuous activity. Three almost always puts a man down and in Hell before he knows it."

Morgan waited a minute. The rattler was on the floor stretched out toward Fred but still a foot from his head.

"You want to forget all this and tell me who hired you, Fred?"

"No. You won't let him strike me. That's murder."

"No such thing," Seismore said. "Snake's the one striking at you, not us."

Morgan nodded at Seismore, who caught the snake by the neck of the head and stretched him out until he came close to Fred's head. Seismore made a mark on the floor as Fred lifted his head and shoulders, bending his head back as far as he could.

Seismore put the snake's nose tip on the mark on the floor, then stretched the leather thong out behind the snake three feet and wrapped it around Lacey's boot. Then he let go of the snake.

"So, you're on your own, Fred. You could try for the record of six minutes. Much longer than that and your shoulders will cramp and your forehead is going to smash down on the floor. Whichever way you want it."

Fred stared at the ugly head of the rattler. It darted its tongue out testing the air, black slit eyes glowing with fury and the need to kill.

"Get it out of here!" Fred screamed. The snake pulled back six inches and tried to strike Fred, but he was out of reach.

"Christ! Pull him back!"

"So you'll tell me who hired you?"

Fred turned and looked at Morgan, who knelt near him but out of the range of the rattler.

"Hell, no! This is inhuman. You can't do this!"

"But it's fine for you to take a hundred dollars to kidnap an innocent young woman who has never harmed you?"

"Get it away from me."

"Can't do that."

The snake struck again, but Fred's face was still five inches out of danger.

"Fred, you're getting tired. It's been just a minute so far. How long do you think you have to live? That's what it amounts to. I lied to you about the rattlesnake venom. It's the deadliest of all the snakes. Takes about fifteen minutes to kill you. And the pain. Hurts like hell. Course we could lance the puncture wounds and draw out enough of the poison—"

Fred's head sank an inch lower toward the floor, and the snake pulled back and struck again. Barely two inches remained between the snake and Fred's face.

He jerked his head upward in panic, but his back muscles and neck muscles were tiring.

"For God's sakes get it away from me!" Fred bellowed.

"Whenever you give me a name and a description," Morgan said with a calm voice. "It's up to you if you want to go on living, or die right here flat on your belly with a rattlesnake striking you until it runs out of energy or poison."

Fred looked at Morgan. "Soon as I tell you his name, you might kill me. So what am I gaining?"

"Might isn't doing it. You get a chance. That

rattler won't give you any chance. With him it's kill right now."

The snake struck again. The hard, scaly nose of the snake feather-touched Fred's cheek it came so close. Fred screamed. The snake pulled back, curious at the noise. Its tongue darted out checking the smell. Yes, there was still a live victim there.

Fred lifted his head and his jaw tightened as his muscles strained. Slowly his head began descending. The snake pulled back to gain striking power.

Then Fred's head pivoted forward, he screamed, and his head hit the floor boards. The rattle struck, its blunt nose jolting into Fred's head, and he screamed and jerked back up.

"All right! Deputy Sheriff Josiah Stormer hired us."

"Describe him."

"Six-six, six-eight, three hundred pounds."

Morgan nodded and Lacey pulled his boot back, dragging the snake a foot from Fred. Seismore lifted the leather thong and caught the snake by the back of the head again.

They untied the front rope, and Fred sat up. His fingers felt his face. "Where, where did he strike me?"

In answer, Seismore held up the snake with one hand and forced its mouth open.

"He didn't strike you with his fangs, Fred," Morgan said. "Only his nose. Seismore broke off his fangs before he brought him inside. The rattler really wanted to kill you, but he couldn't."

Fred shook his head. "And I fell for it."

"Don't blame yourself. Everyone is afraid of a striking rattler. You couldn't win."

Fred shook his head. "Damn, I never should

have got into this thing. Sheriff said he'd jail me for a year if I didn't help on this kidnapping."

"What else do you know about the deputy's plans?" Morgan asked.

"What good will it do me to tell you?"

"If you know something that will help us, I'll turn you loose. You can still ride for Denver or Cheyenne, or wait around until we get the deputy arrested for murder, conspiracy, and a dozen other crimes."

Fred nodded. "Sounds fair. You know about the fireworks he's using on the mountain?"

"Seen some if it couple of nights ago."

"He's due out there tonight about midnight. The Cheyenne have lots of superstitions about midnight."

"He'll be in the same place?"

"Far as I know. Tonight's supposed to be special. He's going to convince them to kill everyone left here at the ranch and then let his own men live here and work the mine."

Morgan looked at his watch. "You said the big show is on for midnight. It's not quite nine o'clock. We've got lots of time. Fred, I'm tying you up until morning. By then most of this might be resolved. All right with you?"

Fred nodded. "Damn, after that rattlesnake I can stand anything."

"Lacey will provide you with some company and be your guard."

Morgan and Seismore went to the ranch house. On the way Seismore ran north of the bunkhouse and tossed the rattler into the brush. With luck he could survive even without his fangs.

In the ranch house, Morgan looked for a shotgun, and found two in a closet with a box of birdshot shells and one box of double-ought buck. He grinned.

"Seismore, you and I are going hunting. Hunting for a deputy sheriff and a long talk with a band of Cheyenne who are going to be extremely angry. You still want to come?"

Chapter Fourteen

Both men carried shotguns and their revolvers as they worked on foot and in the dark around the Indian lookout post, which was again manned. Morgan and Seismore went past the mine on up and over the ridge and down the other side, where they could see the Cheyenne camp. Then they moved across the small creek, going down that side of the mountain and up the side of the slope while hunting the spot where the deputy sheriff would put on his sky show.

As they came near where it had happened before, Morgan could hear men talking quietly. He and Seismore edged closer, and could see in the modest moonlight three men moving around an area where there were upthrust slabs of rock and few trees. A grand stage for the master showman.

Morgan motioned to Seismore and whispered, "Let's just lay low until we see what happens. What I want to do is discredit whoever is putting on the show. I want to prove that there are only men, white eyes at that, and that it's all a trick."

After another hour of preparations, the three men moved off a ways up the hill. Morgan and Seismore trailed them, keeping them in sight and then settling down in good cover when the others stopped.

Morgan watched the night sky's clock. When the pointer stars on the Big Dipper aiming at the north star showed that it was nearly midnight, he studied the three men closely.

"Let's get it started," one man said. Morgan thought he was larger than the other two, but he couldn't be certain.

Far down the slope of the mountain they heard a high-pitched call followed by several more shouts and pleadings. All was quiet. Then the same series of words and singsong messages came a second time.

Suddenly the mountainside was streaked with light as furiously burning lines of black powder flamed up and sparked in small explosions while the fire lines raced across the landscape.

Calls of wonder and excitement came from the Cheyenne camp below.

Then a rocket fired high in the sky, leaving a trail of fire, and exploded high overhead as a flare burned slowly and fell back to earth on a small parachute.

One of the workers came within half a dozen feet of the two men hiding, and Morgan leaped up and clubbed him over the head with the butt of his six-gun. The man crumpled, and they dragged him back to their cover and quickly bound his hands and feet and gagged him with his own kerchief.

"That might cut down on the show a little," Morgan said. Two more rockets blazed into the night sky. Then what Morgan figured was a stick of dynamite exploded away from them and a large flash blinded them a moment. Two more dynamite blasts went off. Then the Roman candles took over, shooting 30 balls of fire into the sky.

When the fireworks seemed to be over, Morgan and Seismore moved slowly across the area just above the flat rocks searching for the two men. They found one about to mount his horse. Seismore grabbed him and fastened one hand over his mouth before he could cry out. A moment later the man was tied and gagged.

They heard a horse a few yards away and crept that way. The man was already on a big black horse. The man looked huge. Morgan told Seismore to walk up as if he belonged there and then grab the horse's reins.

He did and with the distraction, Morgan charged in from the other side of the horse, grabbed the man's leg, and heaved upward, propelling the man out of the saddle and dropping him to the ground with a startled cry.

Seismore dropped on top of him, and by the time Morgan got there and grabbed another arm, they had him controlled.

"Well, Deputy Sheriff Stormer, what a surprise to find you here trying to confuse and hoodwink the Cheyenne band below. They aren't going to be happy at all knowing a mere mortal did all of this spiritualistic show of fire."

They tied Stormer's hands and feet but put no gag on him.

"No rebuttal, no argument, Stormer? You better have some good explanations when the Cheyenne get up here."

"Don't know what the hell you're talking about. Up here investigating some illegal gun sales to Indians."

"Oh, hell, yes, you were, Stormer." Morgan told Seismore to go release the other two men. "Tell them to get on their horses and ride as fast as they can out of here."

Morgan turned then and jogged down the hill toward the Cheyenne village. When he was 100 feet from the first teepee he shouted some English and the two words of Plains Indian he knew. One was "friend," the other was the word for signing.

Then he held his gun belt in his hand and walked into the silent camp. He shouted again, and a sleepy warrior came out of his tipi. When he saw the white eyes in the pale moonlight, the warrior screamed a warning cry, and soon a dozen warriors stood around Morgan.

He began to sign slowly so they could see him in the moonlight.

"I wish to speak to your chief," he signed.

Someone hurried away.

"The fire on the mountain was not spirits," Morgan signed.

A man close enough to see the signing in the half-light spoke the words aloud for the rest who couldn't see. There was a murmur of disbelief.

"Bad white eyes make fire, make rockets and balls of fire," Morgan signed. Some of the signs were not right for the words, but the idea got across. Again there was cries and disbelief in the group of warriors, which had now grown to 40.

Soon a man came through the crowd. It parted for him, and Morgan greeted the chief with signs.

"Who are you?" the chief signed.

"Friend of the Cheyenne. Enemy of bad whites who made your mountain burn. It was not spirits, only bad white eyes. He is tied up on the mountain. Come, I will show you his tricks."

A young warrior standing near Morgan

screamed and laughed at Morgan with a knife held high. Morgan parried away the arm that held the knife with his left arm. He drove a straight right fist into the attacker's chin and kicked upward between his thighs. The warrior went down in a heap, moaning and screaming.

"Does this warrior speak English?" Morgan signed.

The chief signed that he did.

"He has been riding double on his pony with the white eyes. This one was given firewater and woman's clay for his treachery."

Again his words were spoken by one close enough to see the signing.

Shouts arose from the back.

The chief raised his hand.

"Hold this warrior here," the chief said. "Now, show us the fire magic."

Morgan nodded. He held out his gunbelt and revolver as a gift for the chief. These Cheyenne knew how to use long guns, but they had never trusted the short weapons. The chief took the belt and gun, put them around his shoulder, and pointed up the hill.

Morgan hoped that there was still some of the black powder left in rows that the man they'd knocked unconscious had had no time to light.

Warriors ran and brought back half a dozen torches, and gave one to Morgan who led them. They went directly up the hill to the spot where Morgan and Seismore had grabbed the first of the sheriff's helpers. Morgan examined the ground closely, picked up a handful of the black powder, and set it on a rock. He touched the torch to it and it flashed up with a sudden burst of fast burning. The warriors jumped back.

Morgan showed them the line of powder on the

ground. He waved them all back, and when they were out of the way, he signed to the chief.

"Torch sets fire to black powder. Powder burn. No spirits here, only bad white eyes."

Morgan pushed the burning torch into the start of the line of powder. It whooshed into fire and flame and raced across the land for 20 yards lighting up the whole area.

Six of the warriors screamed in terror and ran for the valley. The rest held their hands in front of their faces, then when the fire went out they chattered and laughed.

Morgan signed again to the chief. "No evil spirits here, only bad white man."

"Where is this white man who would treat us like children and cheat us?" the chief signed. Morgan led the way to the other side of the fireworks display area. Deputy Sheriff Josiah Stormer shouted at the chief, and began to deny everything.

Morgan laughed. "The only one who speaks English is being held in the camp." Morgan shook his head. "Just hope that you've made peace with your maker, Stormer. You'll be on the other side damn soon."

Morgan signed to the chief again. "This is the man who brought firewater to your band, and who tricked your people. He is a man who kills his own kind. The other white eyes give him to you for any punishment you think right."

It took him a long time to sign it, but the chief understood. When he was sure the chief knew what he said, Morgan gave his torch to another warrior and the Cheyenne closed in around Deputy Sheriff Stormer. They cut the bindings on his feet and pushed him down the hill.

As they went down, Morgan faded upward and settled down out of sight. When all had moved to the village again, Morgan whispered Seismore's name. The tall, thin man sat up less than 20 feet away.

"Damn, but you did a job on old Stormer. He's liable to get his feet roasted."

"Roasted is right, but I figure you've got the wrong end. The other two men get off and running?"

"Damn fast. They didn't understand what was happening here."

"I figured. Want to move down to the better seats and get a good view of the ceremony?"

"You mean . . . watch them burn this guy?"

"About the size of it. We need to know what happens so we can report to the sheriff at Fort Collins."

They worked down the hill slowly and without a sound. Already below there was a council fire roaring. It was three feet across and lit up half the camp. Twenty of the elders sat around deliberating. Every one of the council members who wished to could comment. At last it was over, and the 150 people who watched roared with approval.

A small fire already burned 50 feet away under a tall tree. An overhanging branch had been stripped of leaves and a rope thrown over it. Shouts and taunts and jabs of sharp sticks heralded the arrival of the guest of honor.

Josiah Stormer had been stripped naked. Four Cheyenne warriors with knives in each hand led the deputy sheriff through the people to the tree. He saw the fire and the rope, and Morgan figured he would faint. He staggered, but didn't fall.

One of the Indians knocked forward both of Stormer's knees and pushed him to the ground.

A few minutes later Josiah Stormer hung by his ankles from the tree limb, all 300 pounds of him.

The small fire below was directly under his head. He hung five feet over the flames. On a curt order the rope was loosened from the trunk and the big white eyes dropped to within three feet. Then slowly they edged him lower.

A cry went up when the first tendrils of his hair caught fire and flamed up. The rope was tied off, and a moment later his hair caught fire and burned off in fifteen seconds, leaving him bald and his skull a dull black.

Stormer screeched and bellowed in agony and rage as his hair burned off.

Then the crowd of some 150 Cheyenne sat and watched in silence. They were waiting to see what kind of courage this white eyes had. One outburst of pain and fear was allowed. Any more and they would start to throw small rocks and pebbles at him.

The rocks would not be big enough to harm him, only to show their displeasure at such a weak white eyes.

A woman, well qualified for her task, sat near the small fire and fed into it dry sticks and twigs to keep up a constant heat. Gradually she built up the fire.

Stormer screeched with rage as the added heat hit him. It hadn't been enough to kill him before, only make him sweat and fear for his life. Now the heat warped his judgment, began to affect some of his brain functions.

A drop of blood oozed from Stormer's right ear. The Cheyenne who could see it applauded. Then blood dripped from his nose. They were throwing pebbles at him now. Ridiculing him. Stormer bellowed and roared in his agony again, and then the tenseness around his face gave way to slackness.

"My God! The blood in his brain must be boiling!" Seismore whispered.

"He's been dead for about a minute."

"Then what are they waiting for?" Seismore asked.

"You'll see."

The Indian woman built the fire higher by half, then scooted backward away from the figure and the fire.

Three minutes later, Josiah Stormer's head exploded like a ripe mellon hitting a rock from a long fall. Blood, brains, and bits of his skull rained down on the people. They stood, and without a word the people returned to their teepees.

The body would hang from the tree for five days.

Seismore shivered.

"Christ, you've seen this before?"

"A time or two, but not from Stormer's viewpoint."

"Let's get the hell out of here before they decide they want another show, with you or me as the victim."

"No chance, at least right now. They had a man accused of a serious tribal crime. He was given a trial by their band's ruling council. The council sentenced him to death by fire. It was all legal and just according to their standards."

Morgan and Seismore didn't bother to look for Stormer's horse. They faded from the rocks and trees to the dense woods, then hurried away from the village to the low pass, and down the other side. They took no chances with the guards, going well above them on the slope of the mountain.

Then they came back to the creek where they had left their horses.

Seismore had little to say on the ride back to the ranch. As they put their horses in the corral and dropped saddles on one of the poles, Seismore shook his head.

"That's got to be about the worst way to die that there is," the cowboy said.

"There are worse, but not many. I'd say it's past bedtime. I'll see you in the morning and find out if you want to go and play Indian with me."

"You mean you're going back up there?"

"I need to. We haven't straightened out this problem of the cavern yet and the gold mine. I figure that's still part of my job."

"You better plan on going alone. I've seen all the Indians that I want to for a hell of a long time."

Morgan caught the shotgun Seismore tossed him.

"See you in the morning," Morgn said, and walked with weary steps toward the ranch house.

Chapter Fifteen

It was after three in the morning when Morgan stepped into his room in the ranch house. He lit the lamp and pulled off his boots and pants and his shirt. He had just sat down on the edge of the bed before falling into it when his door opened.

A woman in a long robe slipped in and closed the door. When she turned around, he saw that she was Martha Devlin. Her long brown hair was combed out and fell around her face and the robe hung partly open, showing a light pink nightdress with lots of lace on it.

"What happened with the Indians?" she asked. "I couldn't wait until morning to find out. I've been pacing in my room watching for you to come back."

He started to stand but she motioned for him to stay there, and glided over to the bed and sat beside him. As she did her leg brushed his.

"Tell me all about it."

The robe she wore barely covered the lacy nightgown she had on. At her chest the nightdress was cut so low that he could see a deep line of cleavage.

He told her briefly about trapping the deputy sheriff and that the Indians killed him.

"Oh, my!" she said.

"He deserved it. He's the one behind the whole thing. He either killed your husband or ordered him and all the hands killed. With him out of the way, there shouldn't be any more trouble at the ranch."

"Good, I appreciate that. About my husband. Morgan, my husband and I were not exactly an ideal couple. He had several lady friends in Chicago. To get back at him I seduced one of his good friends."

"I'm sorry. I didn't know."

"It doesn't matter. Will we be able to save the ranch and the mine?"

"Now I think that we can."

She let out a big sigh and her robe fell open more, showing firm breasts half hidden under the silky, sheer nightdress. "I'm so pleased. I had to know tonight. Now I think I'm too tired to get back to my own bed."

She looked at him. Morgan kept his hands in his lap and said nothing.

She smiled. "Morgan, you might at least be gentleman enough and be kind enough to offer to share your bed with me for the rest of the night."

"Yes, of course, Mrs. Devlin. You're more than welcome to the bed. I'll sleep on the floor."

She caught his face with both hands and kissed him. Her tongue drove quickly into his mouth. When she broke off the kiss she was breathing faster, the color in her face higher, and her chest rose and fell rapidly.

"Beautiful, handsome man, I have no intentions

of letting you sleep on the floor." She found one of his hands and pushed it down the top of her nightgown. Her breasts were warm already, firm and hot-tipped.

"Can I make my desires any more plain to you, Lee Morgan?" She leaned backwards until she fell on the bed and pulled him on top of her, one of her hands finding his crotch and moving at once to his stiffening penis.

"Yes, yes, that's the way. I've wanted you to make love to me since the first day you came to our rooms in Chicago. Now, at last, I'll find out if you're as good as you look to be." She pulled his head down to her breasts. Her night dress had buttons in front, and by then they were open and her bare flesh delightfully exposed in the lamp-light and waiting for him.

Morgan was tired, but not that tired. He devoured her breasts, sat her up and pulled the nightdress and robe from her, then kicked out of his short underwear and rolled her on top of him.

"Morgan, do you like me?"

"Martha, you are an exciting, beautiful, naked woman who has kept her figure and has an intense desire to be loved. What more could a man ask for?"

She moved off him and kissed down his chest past his crotch hair, and sent a line of hot, wet kisses up his penis. It jerked from the attention and she crooned to it. Then she kissed its very point and licked the entire purple head. She sucked it half into her mouth and hummed softly, then let him free and moved back up so she could hang her big breasts over his face and lower one to his mouth to be chewed.

A minute later she fell on her back and pulled him with her.

"Now, please. God, right now! Come inside me or I'll scream and wake the dead!"

He settled into her saddle and she guided him, and he drove into her in one stroke. She was lubricated and eager to receive him. At once she gripped him with her inner muscles and her bottom began making small circles, and Morgan felt her body heat growing from warm to hot to white hot.

"Yes, dear, yes! Deeper, more, I can never get enough of you."

She humped upward against him until their pelvic bones clashed, then dropped and did it again. This time he met her, and together they pounded against each other until she wailed in ecstasy and trembled and then shook as if she were having a seizure.

She finished her climax almost as quickly as she started, and worked on him, then thundered into a second climax that was stronger than the first. This time she wailed and cried and screeched until Morgan knew for sure the men in the bunkhouse could hear her, not to mention Claresta.

Just as she was finishing the third wild orgasm, Morgan could hold his own no longer, and blasted into her with his load powering ten mighty strokes, and then collapsed heavily on her.

"Oh, yes! I love to have you fall on me and press me into the mattress. There's something so basic, so subservient about it. You are man, you are master, crush me, beat me, scream at me as long as you make love to me."

When their breathing returned to normal he could feel her moving under him.

"Are you sleepy?" she asked.

He laughed softly. "With a beautiful sexy

woman still tightly around my manhood, how could I be sleepy?"

She grinned in the faint light, and began moving her hips and squeezing his fading penis. A moment later new life came and he quickly was rigid again.

"Knew I could do it," she said. "Something unusual, strange, wild this time. I know something I've always wanted to try. Get on your back."

They came apart and he rolled to his back. She went astride of his waist with her feet bent back under his thighs, then lifted so he could enter her again. She moved slowly as she came down fully in place. She sighed a moment, gripped him inside, and then leaned back as far as she could.

"Oh, God, now! Do it now before I break in half," she whispered, and tried to hump herself against him.

He tried, but something wasn't working right. He had her lift up a little, and then straightened and leaned forward and turned to the side until she was half way from him. Morgan stroked, and she yelped and grinned and told him to do it again. She edged back a little and then nodded.

Now they had the angle right and he drilled into her 20 times. Then without any buildup she slammed into a series of five hard climaxes that seemed to keep going and going and going.

Somewhere in the middle he broke over the top as well and his orgasm was more powerful than his first.

She came down slowly, bent forward, and turned around until she was over him, then dropped flat on top of him, her breasts crushing against his chest. Two minutes later she was asleep. Morgan grinned, wondering what the hell he should do now. He moved slightly and she woke up, then came away from him and lay on her stomach and went right back to sleep.

Morgan pulled the sheet over her and then himself and closed his eyes. He was asleep before he could figure out what he had to do the next morning.

When Morgan woke up about seven, he was alone in the bed. He sat up, yawned, and tried to figure out if he had been dreaming last night or if Mrs. Devlin had really been there. At the foot of the bed he saw her silk and lace nightdress with the two snaps in front. She had really been there.

He got up, poured some water in the bowl, and cold-shaved, making only one small cut. He dressed in some fresh clothes—a brown shirt, vest, and pair of denim pants—and went down to the kitchen.

Claresta worked on some fried eggs in a skillet over the hot wood fired kitchen stove.

"The men are at work already. You slept in late."

"True, sorry."

She stared at him, blinking back tears. "Morgan, *how could you? She's my mother!*"

"I figured that out. And you're her daughter."

"But, she's so . . . so old!"

"You told me your mother is thirty-six, twice your age. Much closer to my age than you are. Look, you have no reason to be angry or jealous. I love you both. It just happened. She came to find out about what happened last night."

"I bet!"

"Ask her."

"I damn well will!" She broke four eggs into the big skillet and flipped them expertly. Then she looked up. "How was your work last night?"

He told her quickly. "So I think the ranch is safe now. All we have to do is get back in the good graces of this band of Cheyenne."

"How can we do that?"

"I'll go talk to them, take them some presents, maybe offer them six steers a year in winter when they can't find any game. The chief and I can sign pretty good. He seems to be a smart man. I'll talk about the good of his people. If all else fails I'll convince him that I'm half Indian."

"How will you do that?"

"I'll tell you if it works."

He ate the eggs, and some fried potatoes she had grated into another frying pan. They were delicious. He had seconds, then began to work out his plans for the talk with the Cheyenne.

He would ride right up to the lookout, giving the signing for "peace" and "friend" as he went. No, they might shoot him before they saw his signing. He would leave the horse at the usual spot and slip up and appear in front of them, and then sign. He watched Claresta staring at him over her cup of coffee.

"You through being mad at me?" he asked.

"Almost. How can I be mad when you risk your life to save our little ranch? It's not very nice of me."

"And usually you are extremely nice—all over."

She grinned. "You say the most wonderful things."

He stood. "You are a wonderful lady." He bent and kissed her gently on the lips. "Now, I better go take a walk to the Cheyenne camp and have a chat with their chief. I never did ask him about his name."

"Are you sure you have to go?"

"If we ever want to work that mine, or sell the mine, I have to go get this misunderstanding cleared up with the Cheyenne. Otherwise they'll threaten anyone going to the mine."

"Maybe since the deputy talked them into putting up the guards, they won't have them there anymore."

"Possible. But I still have to check and to make sure that your people, or whoever works the mine, can do so without any raids by the Cheyenne. They are a proud bunch. The chief probably will be expecting me." Morgan sipped his coffee. Horses. The Cheyenne treasured horses. He'd take the chief three horses, the ones they had taken from the sheriff's men at the cavern. Yes.

Outside he told Seismore to put rope halters on the three spare horses he'd brought back from the cavern, and then he went in to see Lacey. The bullet had gone through his shoulder so they wouldn't have to go see the doctor. Morgan checked the bandage, then took Lacey into the kitchen and asked Claresta to put on some salve and some new bandages.

"I don't know how," she wailed.

Morgan laughed gently at her. "You didn't know how to do a lot of things before you did them right here on the ranch. This isn't hard. You'll learn by doing. Fix him up. You need this young man around here to run your ranch, so smile at him, do a good job, and be gentle with him."

Outside, Seismore walked up with the three horses. "Hey, Boss, ain't you forgetting something? You gave away your iron the other night. Don't tell me you going into that Cheyenne camp without a sidearm?"

"You bet I am, Lonnie. What good would five

rounds be against fifty Cheyenne braves with rifles and bows and arrows, war axes, and fighting knives?"

"Oh, damn, I see what you mean." Seismore shuffled his feet and drew a line in the dirt with his boot toe. "Damn, I guess I should be going with you, but blamed if I can talk myself into it."

"Don't worry about it, Seismore. One man is lots less threatening to them than two. I figure this is the best chance I have for doing what I need to do and walking out of there in one piece and with my hair."

Morgan caught the mane of one of the horses and vaulted onto its bare back, took the rope halter, and moved to the north. He saw Claresta come running out of the house. She waved at him, and he thought he saw a tear running down her pretty cheek.

Morgan had a half hour to think about the situation as he rode north on the bareback mount. It had been a long time since he'd ridden this far without a saddle.

He didn't see why they were so concerned down at the ranch. It was as easy as catching a trout in a stream. The Cheyenne were not the bloodthirsty savages they were made out to be. He'd walk in and talk to them, make a deal and walk out.

He hoped.

Chapter Sixteen

Morgan rode up the now-familiar trail from the ranch house to the north along the stream to the spot just below where the Indian lookouts usually were. He rode deeper this time, using the cover of the woods and brush. At last he left the three horses in the woods and ran lightly forward watching for the Indian lookouts.

He didn't see any.

He probed farther, and soon was at the spot where they often had been hiding. No one was there. Good. The chief must have decided that if the evil spirits on the mountain were only the work of the bad white eyes, then there was no need to post guards and lookouts on this side of the mountain.

Morgan ran back, mounted his horse, and led the string of gift horses up the trail. There was no set horse path over the top of the ridge, but they found an easy way up, and for a moment Morgan paused and looked out at the millions and millions of tops of the fir and pine trees in the unending green forest. It was the sort of sight he never failed to appreciate and to admire.

So many trees no one could ever count them. He had seen the cut-out wooded hills of Michigan and Minnesota. He hoped somehow that the people here would be able to cut just enough to leave seed trees for a new crop. Why not farm the forests the way a farmer managed the land? Why not plant a new crop of pine and fir trees every year so that in 35 years there would be a whole series of areas ready to be harvested?

Perhaps some day.

He rode down the slope. Ahead he could smell the smoke of the Cheyenne fires. To the left ahead in the small canyon that would widen into the tiny valley, he could see a pair of Cheyenne with bows and arrows stalking something in a patch of brush.

A moment later a buck deer with a rack of five points on each side burst from the brush, bounded twenty feet in the air, and ran and jumped away spoiling the hunters' aim. The buck got away.

Morgan made no attempt to hide himself or his horses. He rode straight down the valley, close to the stream. The two hunters he had seen hurried out to the trail and stared at him. He signed to them his greetings, and that he was a friend, and continued on his way past them, never once looking back.

Each of them could be nocking an arrow in his bowstring for all Morgan knew. Most Indians appreciated bravery in others. Now was his true testing. Even if he didn't feel brave, he had to put on a strong front or he'd never get to the first teepee alive.

Morgan saw two more Cheyenne warriors. One

was hunting and the other was looking for a certain kind of rock in the edge of the tiny creek. One of them had a front tooth missing. Morgan recognized him from last night. He signed "greetings" and "friend," and the warrior signed back, "welcome."

It was with a small sigh of relief that he reached the first teepee, and wound through the ropes and stakes toward the largest of the teepees. It was the one with a crude drawing of an elk on the brown buffalo hide covering.

He walked his horse slowly, leading the other two horses. He did not make any sudden moves or look behind him. As he wound his way around and between 20 teepees, he knew that several people were following him.

He could hear talking and whispers, the chatter of small girls and the wild screeches of older boys. He never wavered. Near the big teepee stood a mountain mahogany bush 15 feet high with more than a dozen shoots and branches all filled with a white bloom that made them look like giant balls of fluff.

Morgan untied the three bareback horses and secured them to the brush near the chief's teepee. Then he went where he could be seen through the flap of the chief's shelter, and stood silent and patient. If the chief wished to speak with him, he would come out or ask Morgan to come inside.

Morgan stood there without moving for 15 minutes.

Then there was movement at the flap of the chief's teepee and the same broad-shouldered, sturdy man Morgan had seen briefly last night in the darkness came out. He was taller than most of the Warriors, standing about five-ten. His face showed two long scars—from knife wounds, Morgan figured. His eyes were coal black, and now his face settled into a benign smile.

He signed quickly, then slowed as Morgan struggled to read it all.

"You have returned. You are friend. I am White Owl, leader of this band. We thank you for showing us how the white eyes deceived us. You know many of our customs."

Morgan signed back to him. "I respect the ways of the People. I am part Indian and carry the sign of the People. I bring you these three horses as a gift if you will accept them."

White Owl lifted his brows. "I have known few white eyes, but the ones I have seen want something in return for such a valuable gift. What do you want in return?"

"Only the friendship with the White Owl band. I have friends in the land below the next ridge, the ranch where many cattle will be raised. They will not come on this side of the ridge, will not bother the Cheyenne."

"And what of the devil mountain where the other men dug into the cavern?"

"It is true, the cavern is a part of the ranch and the owners want to dig into the mountain. But truly it is not a devil mountain. There are no evil spirits there to be released upon the People. The evil one was the giant white eyes who now hangs from the tree with a shattered head."

Chief White Owl thought on the words for a moment, then nodded.

"It shall be. We shall be friends with the white eyes on the ranch with wooden teepee in the next valley. Their friends shall be our friends."

"No!" screamed a young warrior in English. He had been standing nearby. Morgan saw that this was the same warrior who had attacked him last night. Morgan was surprised that he was still in the band after his teaming up with Deputy Sheriff Stormer and his deception.

The warrior shouted a dozen words and then pointed directly at Morgan.

The chief turned and held up his hand and the young warrior quieted, but his scowl held a deadly hatred.

"Lonesome Bear challenges you, friend. He says you are not part Indian, that you have no rights of the People."

Slowly Morgan took off the vest he had worn that morning and the heavy shirt, and turned his back to the chief so he could see the scars left by the *o-kee-pah.*

There was a shout of recognition of the wounds and the scars from the more than 100 warriors and women and children who had heard the talk and gathered.

The chief looked at Lonesome Bear and then back at Morgan. He signed again.

"What tribe inducted you into the ways of the *o-kee-pah?*"

"The Chiricahua Apache," Morgan said softly.

"Aiiiiiiii," one of the warriors shouted. He had heard the name of the tribe far to the south. Around the circle the warriors nodded and whispered among themselves.

"So it is true you are one of the People, not by blood but by withstanding the bravery ritual of the Chiricahua. Indeed you are a worthy friend of the People."

Lonesome Bear walked up to Morgan and glared at him. Slowly he took out his knife, an eight-inch long blade that was sharp on both sides of the point. He lifted it slowly and tapped the flat of the blade on both sides of Morgan's face, then he stepped back.

"Since the white eyes snake has the bravery of the People, he must follow the customs of the People. I challenge him to a fight with knives as we hold an arm's length of rawhide in our teeth!"

The chief stepped between the combatants as was the custom. He looked at Lonesome Bear.

"Do you truly wish this fight to the death with Speaks the Truth?"

Chief White Owl stared hard at the young warrior, who was no more than 21 winters old.

"How did he gain this lofty name?"

"I gave it to him for his service to the Cheyenne People," Chief White Owl said. "Is it still your wish to fight? You may decide differently now and no one will lose any magic."

"I still wish to fight."

White Owl signed the conversation's essence to Morgan. Then he went on. "You may decline to fight, but if you do so, you must leave the band and will not be allowed to return here. All that we have said about friendship will be forgotten."

"Then I must fight. Our friendship with White Owl's band is important."

"You have the knife?"

"I have used one before, but have none now."

White Owl walked into his teepee, and returned with an eight-inch fighting knife. The tip of the blade was sharpened only on one side. The chief showed it to him and shrugged. "I do not fight anymore."

Morgan hefted the weapon. It was heavier than any knife he had ever used, more like a short sword. He lowered it to his side.

"When?" he signed to Lonesome Bear.

"Now," Lonesome Bear signed back.

Morgan took off his shirt again and dropped it. He took all items from his pocket except two $20 gold pieces, and hefted the heavy blade again. This would not be a finesse fight. He had heard about the rawhide strap fight, but never seen one. It meant both men would be well within killing range at all times.

Such a fight could not last long. It had to be a matter of a dramatic attack and disarming or killing the other fighter. There would be no use for clever tactics or strategy here. Brutal, blunt force was the answer.

Morgan stood four inches taller than the other man and had to be 40 pounds heavier. That would be an advantage.

Someone ran out of a teepee with a strip of rawhide. It was 30 inches long, Morgan estimated, and had a half-inch knot tied in each end. The strip itself was about two inches wide so it would not tear or break.

White Owl took the rawhide strip and held it. The warriors led the two men to the council fire area and stood in a circle about 20 feet across.

"Must stay inside the circle," White Owl signed.

Morgan nodded. He watched Lonesome Bear. The Indian was confident. He had done this before. He figured the white eyes would know nothing of such fights, perhaps could not even handle a knife. He figured on a quick kill, and then he would regain some of the stature he had lost by siding with the giant white eyes who had deceived his tribe.

The chief held out the rawhide, and both men took hold of it.

"Hold the knot behind your teeth, bite it hard," White Owl signed. He said something and signed to Morgan, but already Morgan had the knot fitted behind his teeth. He could bite down hard and breathe fully through his nose.

The chief stepped back. He held a pine cone in his hand. "When I drop the pine cone, the fight begins," White Owl signed. He looked at both men, then into the sky, his lips moving. He held the pine cone high over his head.

A moment later he dropped the pine cone.

Lonesome Bear leaped forward, the knife slicing at Morgan's throat. Morgan dodged sideways, dragged the man with him, and threw up his left arm to take the biting slice of the sharp blade. Morgan had been caught with his knife too low for the opening move. Now he lifted it and pointed it at the Indian.

He shifted to the left, then back to the right. If the Indian charged again . . .

Lonesome Bear feinted one way, then drove forward, his blade held at arm's length like a spear. Morgan ducked down, and swept his thick-soled boot at the Cheyenne's right foot, which was thrust forward. Morgan kicked it to the Indian's right, where he had no lateral support.

Lonesome Bear threw his knife hand into the air to maintain his balance, and Morgan dove at him. Morgan brushed back Lonesome Bear's arm holding the heavy knife, catching it with his left hand and holding his arm skyward as the two men crashed to the ground, Morgan on top of Lonesome Bear, whose knife was pinned skyward in a useless position.

Morgan came down with his left shoulder on the Indian's chest and slammed most of the air from his lungs. Morgan heard the yells of surprise from the whole village as they watched.

Slowly Morgan brought his unfettered knife

down and pressed the point against Lonesome Bear's throat.

He left it there as his strong left arm pressed Lonesome Bear's knife hand downward until it slammed into the ground and the knife fell from his fingers.

There was a shout of surprise.

Morgan picked up Lonesome Bear's knife and half rose, pressing his knee into the grounded warrior's chest as he knelt over him, the point of his heavy blade still poised at the Indian's throat.

Morgan lifted the blade, and then quickly stabbed it deep into the ground near Lonesome Bear's head. There was a shout and wails from the watchers. Morgan took the Indian's blade and rammed it into the ground on the other side of his head.

Then with both hands he signed. "There has been too much killing. This Cheyenne shall live today."

There was a cheer and much clapping and yelping in approval as Morgan stood and stared down at the man he had beaten but let live.

When Morgan looked in the Lonesome Bear's eyes, he knew he had made a mortal enemy. The man was more dangerous now than before. Now he was humiliated. He could not stay in this band. The story of how a white eyes had beat him with a knife would follow him wherever he went.

Morgan turned to sign something to the chief. There was a sound behind him, and Morgan looked over his shoulder in time to see Lonesome Bear jerk his knife from the ground, surge to his feet, and charge.

Morgan timed it perfectly. He spun on his left foot, and shot out his right foot in a spinning back kick. The heel of his boot caught the warrior flush on the side of the head and pounded his head to the left, snapping his neck as neatly as a hangman's noose would. Lonesome Bear's eyes glazed, the knife fell from his hand, and he collapsed to the ground, dead in an instant.

For a moment total silence ruled over the small mountain valley. Not a word was spoken, not a noise made. Then every throat in the camp exploded with cheers and chants and clapping. A dozen warriors rushed up and said words to Morgan he didn't understand. All were smiling and grinning and laughing.

When the frenzy quieted, White Owl motioned Morgan to one side. He signed slowly.

"Friend of the Cheyenne. Lonesome Bear was not one of my best warriors. Twice he violated our trust, but still I let him stay in the band. After you beat him and gave him life, he knew he had to leave. He sought to kill you with trickery, even though we all would know."

"I didn't mean to kill him," Morgan signed.

"My warriors were congratulating you. It is a fighting move they have never seen before. Even now some are trying it against a bit of brush. You were a great teacher for them."

"Will your people camp for the winter here?"

"No. For that we will go deep into the mountains where not even the cowboys can find us."

"Do you have enough jerky prepared for the long snow?"

"No, but we will kill more elk."

"I will bring you six of the white man's elk, the steers, from the ranch. Butcher them as you would an elk. The meat will make some jerky for your winter pemmican. Anytime you are short of food, come to the ranch with one of your wives and talk of white eyes cows to feed your people."

"You will not be there?"

"No, I must ride on soon. Two women own and run the ranch. One's husband was killed."

White Owl looked up quickly. "My people did not kill the six at the wooden teepee. Lonesome Bear and the giant white eyes did it, to blame us. We have no anger with the two white eyes women who run the ranch."

"We found a young woman of the People, no more than twenty winters. She was on the ranch, cut with a thousand slices and with signs of bad spirits around her. What do you know of her?"

The old Indian stared hard at Morgan for a moment, then signed.

"She indeed was an evil spirit, sent here to plague us. Whoever killed this evil one did a great service to our People. She is dead and under the ground?"

"Yes. I put her in the ground and left no marker. Her evil signs have been consumed by fire."

The leader of the band smiled. "It is good. She was an outcast from all the Cheyenne tribes, lived to do evil and hurt our People. We are pleased."

Morgan nodded and the subject was closed. He found his shirt, shook it out, and put it on.

"You must stay a few days, learn more of the People."

"I have many jobs to get done, but I thank you for your kindness. May the three mares breed quickly and strengthen your herd."

Morgan saluted the old chief, and walked slowly through the village and back to the low pass that would lead him to the mine and on to the ranch house below. He only then noticed that the cut on his arm was much deeper than he had thought. He dug out his kerchief and wrapped it around his arm. He wouldn't bleed to death. Not now. Now his only problem was how to tell Claresta and Martha Devlin that his work here was done and that he had to be leaving.

Chapter Seventeen

It was not yet noon when Lee Buckskin Morgan walked into the ranch yard. Both the hands and the two women rushed out to greet him.

"You're still alive, and with your hair!" Claresta called to him with a catch in her voice.

He laughed and stepped down. "Alive and well and only a small cut on my arm."

They hurried him into the kitchen, where Claresta put salve on his cut forearm and bound it together tightly so there would be no room for scar tissue. Then she wrapped it with a second bandage to halt any more bleeding.

"The peace is made with White Owl and his band of Cheyenne. I promised him six steers along toward fall so he can butcher them and make pemmican for the winter months."

"For peace with the tribe we can more than afford six animals," Martha said.

"We're having steak for dinner," Claresta said. "Seismore rode down and butchered out one of the cows the riflemen shot yesterday. We decided it was still good and no sense letting all that meat go to waste."

The hands both told him how glad they were he was back, and then drifted outside. They were repairing the corral and seeing what they could salvage from the burned barn and the shed beside it.

Morgan looked at the two women. Both had combed and brushed their hair, scrubbed their faces and had on fancier dresses than usual.

"Ladies, we've got to talk about the ranch. I can't stay with you forever, you know. Where are those figures the hands counted on the herd?"

Claresta brought the sheet of paper with the figures written down: 40 brood cows, 10 two-year old steers, 15 uncut bull calves, 6 range bulls, 23 young first-year heifers.

"The idea is to keep the heifers to add to your brood stock. Your cows should drop about eighty-five percent calves or up to ninety percent, depending how good your range bulls are. Each year after fifty percent of the calves should be heifers to add to your herd.

"After three to four years the cut steers will be big enough to sell. Then you start getting some income. You should be able to drive them to Loveland and ship them to the stockyards in Denver on the train.

"Tell Seismore what you want done and make him your ranch foreman. He'll take care of all the details. Oh, give him a raise to forty dollars a month. Hands should get twenty-five a month and found . . . that is, board and room."

Claresta wrote on a pad of paper, taking down

what he said. She was going to be running the ranch and the mine soon.

Both women sat on chairs near the kitchen table watching him closely.

"Now, the next small problem you have is the mine. With the assay report you shouldn't have any trouble finding a partner who has development money. It's going to cost maybe fifty thousand dollars to get the mine into production and developing ingot gold you can sell.

"You need a reliable firm that won't cheat you and will develop your mine for the benefit of both of you. What you might consider doing is selling forty-nine percent of your ownership of the mine, in exchange for an investment of, say, fifty to a hundred thousand dollars in the project. All costs after that would be taken from production gold and profits shared at a forty-nine and fifty-one percent ratio."

Morgan stood and walked around the table. "Tell you what. I have a friend in Denver who knows mines forward and backwards and is honest. I'll have him come and visit you. He'll look over the mine, check the ore again, and then recommend exactly what you should do. He should be able to find a buy-in partner if that's what he decides is best for you.

"Right now it's just a worthless hole in the mountain until it gets developed."

He sat down and sipped at a cup of coffee that Martha had set in front of him.

"Don't we have to tell the county sheriff about the death of one of his deputies?" Claresta asked.

"Yes. I can do that when I go into Loveland."

"And wouldn't it be better if you drove six of our

young steers up to the Indians before you left?" Martha asked. "They could let the animals graze up in their valley, and butcher them one at a time and have lots of time to make their jerky."

Morgan nodded. "Yes, that would be fine. I can do that without any problem."

"Good, and I think it would be great if you could bring back this mining expert of yours from Denver," Claresta said. "Then we'd be sure he was the right man and could trust him."

Morgan sat back and laughed. "You two are trying to give me more jobs to keep me here. Come on, admit it. That's what this conspiracy is all about."

"We don't have the faintest idea what you're talking about," Martha said, and touched a linen handkerchief to her forehead. "Mr. Seismore said he thinks he can build a new barn out of logs. Of course he'd need all three of you men to do it. He says with a good block and tackle and a spar pole, and the horses to pull a long rope, he could build a square, serviceable barn in two months with logs from the side of the valley."

"As long as I stay and help?" Morgan asked.

"Yes, two men to build a log barn isn't enough," Claresta said with a grin.

Morgan finished his coffee. "Not a chance, ladies. But I'm in no big rush to leave. Another day or two, then I really do need to get to Denver. That's why I took the job in the first place was to get myself to Denver."

"Dear boy, we knew that," Martha said.

"Oh, one more thing you'll need to do is go to the county clerk at Fort Collins and sign over the property from your husband's name to yours," Morgan said. "That should finish the legal work."

"Lee Morgan, that's enough of this talk," Claresta said. "We have something we want to show you right down there in the other room."

Martha led the way past the parlor and into the hall and down to the big bedroom at the end. She walked in, and then Claresta did. When Morgan entered, Claresta closed the door and threw the bolt.

"Lee Morgan, we have decided it's time to show you our total appreciation for what you've done for the Devlin family and for the Lucky Mountain Ranch and Mine," Martha said, standing near the window. "Without you we both would have gone screaming back to Chicago and forgotten all about this place. We owe you more than we can ever repay."

"We've decided your ten-percent offer for a pig in a poke is not acceptable,." Claresta said. "It's unfair to you. Instead we want to offer you a thousand dollars right now for your work in saving the ranch and the mine for us. As well we'll write up papers making you a five-percent owner of both mine and ranch and responsible only for the profits, but none of the debts that might occur."

As she talked Claresta unbuttoned the fasteners down her bodice, and as she finished the little speech, she pulled the dress off over her head.

Morgan looked at Martha, who had performed a similar exercise. Now both ladies stood in chemises of soft white cotton and petticoats.

"We also want to show you our combined appreciation, Lee Morgan," Martha said.

"We think you're man enough to take on both of us at the same time, Morgan," Claresta added. When Morgan looked back at her she had lifted off her chemise and stood there topless, her breasts gently rolling from the motion. She shook her shoulders and her large, ripe breasts bounced and rolled again.

"You think you can take on a challenge like this, Lee Morgan?" Martha asked. He looked at her, and she smiled and lifted the chemise off, showing him her big breasts with the wide brown areolas and thumb-sized nipples.

"I've died and gone to heaven," Morgan said. The two women laughed gleefully and grabbed him and backed him up to the big bed and eased him down on his back. They took turns dropping their luscious breasts into his mouth for him to minister unto.

Claresta worked hard getting his boots off. Then they both took off his vest and shirt.

"Always loved a hairy chest," Martha said. "Never knew but one man who had any hair on his chest." She twirled it and kissed it, then found his man breast and sucked on it until Morgan pushed her away.

"Stop!" Morgan shouted. Both women sat up startled.

"Whatever is the matter?" Martha asked.

Morgan grinned. "I've never had two such delicious ladies in my bed at the same time, and I want to appreciate this moment to the fullest."

"Oh, you old tease," Claresta said, and went back to unbuttoning his fly. They pulled his pants off and his short underwear.

"Oh, my!" Martha said, one hand to her mouth.

"What a wonderful one. He's so . . . so . . . so big and beautiful and so hot and ready!"

Claresta bent and kissed his erection, giggled, and lay down on top of him. She still had her petticoats on.

Martha wasted no time. She pulled down her three petticoats, wiggled out of some new underwear the ladies were calling bloomers, and stood before him naked and shivering. Her waist was pinched in, her hips woman-broad but her legs slender and lovely. Martha's breasts hadn't sagged a bit and she held them out proudly.

"Me first," Martha said.

"No, Mother, it was my idea. We both agreed that I get to go first."

Morgan shushed both of them. "I'll settle the problem. Both at once," he said.

Martha's brows shot up. "How in the world—"

Morgan laughed and pulled both women down on the bed, one on each side of him. His hands found their breasts and he caressed them, then reached over and kissed each one long and lingering and like a sex-starved wanderer.

"I still don't see how you can . . . both at once," Martha said with a small whine.

"Trust me, we'll figure it out. Right now, Claresta is behind. She has to get rid of some clothes."

Claresta did so. She knelt in front of him and pulled down her petticoats slowly, teasing him. Then she made a production of getting out of her bloomers.

Then she posed over him naked and lovely for a moment, before she lay beside him and grabbed his manhood.

"Now, Lee Buckskin Morgan, show us exactly

how you're going to make love to both of us at the same time. Not that I don't think you can, but I want to feel it to believe it."

Twenty minutes later both ladies lay beside Morgan. And both believed him and kept asking for more.